Accidental Assassin

The Harper Sisters, Book One

Ken Konet

M.Ed., MBA

Accidental Assassin: The Harper Sisters, Book One

Published by Humbolton Press

humbolton.com

First Edition

ISBN (Paperback): 978-1-966703-34-1

Abstract

Lana Harper has built a small, ordered life out of a six-year-old's worth of unanswered questions. Three monitors. Three master locks. A consulting practice with twelve enterprise clients. A Taekwondo academy with her name on the door. A converted industrial loft in Chicago, a deeply opinionated rescue cat, and a mother she only half-remembers from the summer afternoon in 2002 that ended with sirens, the wrong kind of smoke, and a silence that never quite went away. She has, in her careful way, made a peace with that silence.

The peace, it turns out, was on a timer.
When a cream envelope arrives at Lana's apartment with no return address, no logo, and her name printed in clean block letters, the timer runs out. Within forty-eight hours, Lana will meet a man who came to her home to kill her, the older sister she has not seen in fifteen years, a former case officer who appears to know everyone's mother, and a plan, twenty-three years in the making, to finish a piece of work that her own mother began on the morning she died.

The work has a name. The name belongs to a man at 17 Petrograd Embankment in St. Petersburg who has spent two patient decades on the careful, unhurried end of a global criminal financial network and who is, by the time the Harper sisters find him, the most surprised man in his profession.

What follows is a nine-day cascade across three continents, conducted with a laptop, a tactical van, two devastating sisters, one impeccable Mr. Halloran, and the unblinking attention of a cat who is, in his own opinion, in charge of the entire operation.

Accidental Assassin is a fast, sardonic, quietly devastating spy thriller about the long arithmetic of competent women, the patient unfairness of family silences, and the difference, in the end, between revenge and finishing the work.

It is also, in its private way, a love letter to anyone who has ever inherited silence and decided, at long last, to break it.

Table of Contents

Prologue

A summer afternoon. Heat shimmering up off the grass in waves you could see if you squinted. The smell of cut clover, baked earth, and somewhere far off, charcoal smoke from someone's barbecue.

A smaller hand was tucked inside her own. Fingers tangled with hers, sticky from a popsicle that had melted faster than anyone wanted. Skin warm. Dirt under the nails.

Laughter. Bright and high and impossibly carefree. Wind chimes in a breeze.

"Bet you can't catch me, Lana!"

A voice that was hers but wasn't hers. Higher. Lighter. Threaded with the kind of mischief that only existed before you knew what mischief actually was, before you understood that some games had stakes.

Sun through oak leaves. Patterns shifting on the grass like coins at the bottom of a wishing well. Bare feet pounding the earth. Lungs full and laughing.

Then. A phone. Her mother's phone, on the picnic blanket, ringing in that older, warbling way phones used to ring before they decided to be polite.

Her mother answering. The smile sliding out of her voice between one syllable and the next. "Yes. Yes, I understand. I'll be there in twenty."

The blanket gathered up too quickly. The cooler closed with a snap.

"I have to go, sweet pea. I'll be back. Just an hour. Promise."

A kiss on Lana's forehead. A longer one on her sister's, with a hand cupping the back of her sister's head, holding her there for a breath longer than was usual. Always a little longer for her sister. Lana had never been able to figure out why.

Car door. Engine. Gravel under tires, getting smaller.

The afternoon stretching long. The shadows getting taller and meaner. The smaller hand still in hers, the fingers gone cold somewhere along the way.

A siren in the distance, growing closer instead of fading. Then another. Then another.

The smell of smoke on the wind that was the wrong kind of smoke. Not charcoal. Sharper. Chemical. Wrong.

Her sister, twelve years old and already smarter than anyone gave her credit for, going completely still beside her, the way an animal goes still when it knows the thing in the bushes has seen it.

"Lana," her sister whispered, and her voice didn't sound like her voice anymore. It sounded like a grown-up's voice in a child's mouth. "Lana, hold onto my hand. Don't let go."

Lana didn't ask why. She held on.

And then, somewhere on the other end of the smoke and the sirens and the long afternoon shadows, a silence opened up. A cold, hollow silence that was worse than any scream.

She would carry that silence inside her for twenty-three years and never know what it was.

Chapter 1: Normal is a Relative Term

Lana Harper's eyes snapped open.

Her heart was doing something unforgivable inside her ribs, the kind of high, rapid thudding that she usually associated with espresso, deadlines, and the moment in a horror movie right before the cat jumps out of the cabinet. The dream clung to her like wet clothes. She could still smell the wrong kind of smoke. She could still feel a smaller hand inside her own.

She lay very still in the loft bed and stared at the exposed-beam ceiling, waiting for her pulse to remember it was a Tuesday.

"It was a dream," she said out loud, because that was the rule. "It was a dream, you are alive, and Pixel is judging you for not feeding him on time."

A small, judgmental *mrrp* from somewhere below the loft confirmed at least the third part of that statement.

Lana scrubbed her hands over her face. The dream came two or three times a year, always in the warm months, always with the same pieces. A summer afternoon. A smaller hand. The smell of smoke. A silence that felt like a held breath that never let go. Her therapist (the one she had stopped seeing four years ago because he had developed an alarming habit of being right) had called it *somatic memory.* Her father, when she had finally worked up the courage to ask him about it during a long, drunk Christmas, had called it *the brain doing what brains do, kiddo, don't go borrowing trouble.*

Lana mostly called it *the dream* and tried not to think about it.

She swung her legs out of the loft bed and slid down the library-style ladder, her bare feet hitting the cool concrete floor of the apartment. For a moment she stood at the bottom of the ladder, hand still on the rung, and let the morning prove itself to her. Three monitors glowing at her workstation. The smell of yesterday's coffee. A patch of early sun on the brick wall opposite her windows. Pixel, gray and disapproving, perched on the edge of the kitchen counter with the air of a deposed monarch waiting for breakfast.

Real. Awake. Tuesday.

The past was a locked room. No point in rattling the knob.

She rattled the knob anyway, just for half a second, the way you press a bruise to make sure it still hurts. *Bet you can't catch me, Lana.* Then she shook her head hard, like a dog coming out of water, and got on with her life.

The rhythmic *clack-clack-clack* of keys was Lana's preferred meditation. She could not sit cross-legged in a quiet room and breathe through one nostril without immediately thinking about her email. But put her in front of three monitors of green-on-black with a fresh mug of coffee and an active threat trying to wriggle through somebody's firewall, and she could find an inner stillness that would make a Tibetan monk slow-clap.

It was 6:34 in the morning. By 6:35, she had a brute-force SQL injection probing one of her clients' admin portals.

"Seriously?" she muttered, fingers already moving. "A brute-force? Did you find your hacking tutorial in a cereal box? Have some pride."

She watched the attack pattern for another four seconds, just to confirm it was as embarrassing as she thought it was. It was. She rerouted the attempt into a honey-pot server she had built herself, populated with sixteen thousand recursively nested directories, each one containing a single file labeled *important_document.txt*, each of those files containing a single sentence of the entire script of *The Princess Bride*. Whoever was on the other end of this attack would spend the next six hours decrypting their way through Inigo Montoya before they noticed they had been had. Lana had, on a particularly slow afternoon two years ago, animated the rejection screen herself: a tiny, exploding Death Star with the words ACCESS DENIED unfurling out of its expanding fireball like a banner.

The Death Star bloomed across her left monitor. She leaned back in her ergonomic chair, the kind that screamed *I sit for a living and my spine is filing a formal complaint*, and took a long pull of coffee.

The small victory did not chase the dream away.

She turned her head and let her gaze drift to the corner of her desk, where a small, framed photo sat between a soldering iron and a USB hub the size of a deck of cards. Her father, twenty years younger than he was now, grinning hugely at the camera. A streak of black grease across his cheek like war paint. He was holding a wrench in one hand and what appeared to be a small, deeply annoyed Lana in the other, both of them covered in something that was probably motor oil and might also have been pancake syrup. The story behind that photo had been a moving target for three decades. Her dad changed details every time he told it. She had stopped trying to figure out which version was true and just enjoyed the telling.

Love you, old man, she thought.

A faint, judgmental meow pulled her attention away from the photo. Pixel had migrated, as Pixel did, to the edge of her main monitor and was now perched there with his tail twitching like an angry antenna, his green eyes fixed on her with the slow burn of a cat who had not been fed for what was, in his opinion, a geological age.

"What, Cat-thulhu?" Lana said, scratching behind his ears. "Did my emotional dysregulation interrupt your plans for world domination? Fun fact. Mine just involves caffeine and aggressive billing."

Pixel responded with a slow, deliberate blink. The kind that, in cats, qualified as a love letter, but which in Pixel's case was more like a court summons.

"Fine," Lana sighed, getting up. "I am a bad provider and I deserve to be fired. Let me get you your six-dollar-a-can salmon mousse, your highness."

While Pixel ate, she walked her morning loop of the apartment, the way she always did, because she liked the apartment and she liked walking through it and she liked the small, mildly obsessive ritual of it.

The apartment was a converted second-floor of an old industrial building, all exposed brick and original beams and big factory windows that gave her a postcard view of the city skyline if you ignored the dumpster directly below. She had spent four years and most of her savings turning it into something that was less an apartment and more a shrine to her two competing personalities. One wall, the long one, was floor-to-ceiling shelving stuffed with tech books, bound printouts of obscure RFCs, three different oscilloscopes she had bought during a particularly committed manic phase, and enough cabling to gift-wrap a small spaceship. The opposite wall had her Taekwondo belts in a neat vertical column, a row of certificates and tournament photos, and a framed shot of her at sixteen kicking a sparring partner so hard in the chest that the sparring partner's face was, in the photo, in the middle of a fascinating distortion. That photo always made her laugh. She kept it for the days when she felt small.

Day Lana lived in front of the monitors, outsmarting other people's bad password policies and taking calls from CEOs who thought *synergy* was a security control. Night Lana lived on the dojo mat, teaching teenagers how to make bullies regret eye contact. Both Lanas had agreed, sometime in her late twenties, that they would tolerate each other if neither one tried to expand into the other's wall. So far, they had kept the peace.

She drifted past the kitchen counter on her way back to the desk and her eye caught on a small pile of unopened mail. Bills, a flyer for a nail salon, the perpetual reminder from her dentist that she had been overdue for a cleaning since the Bush administration. And, at the top of the pile, a plain, unmarked envelope. Slightly crumpled. Cream colored. No return address. No logo. Just her name, hand-printed in clean block letters.

Lana picked it up, frowned at it, turned it over. The back was blank. The paper was heavier than ordinary mail, the way wedding invitations were heavier than ordinary mail.

"Junk," she said out loud, because saying things out loud made them true, and tossed it back onto the pile. The envelope landed face-down on top of the dentist reminder.

She did not know it yet, but she had just held the only piece of paper in her life that had her real name and her sister's real name written on the same page.

She did not know it because she was going to throw it out, unopened, in two days.

She went back to work.

* * *

The scent of sweat and determination hit Lana the way it always did when she stepped onto the polished wooden mat of the Harper-Kim Taekwondo Academy: full in the chest, a little sour, oddly comforting. The dojo was small. The dojo was hers, more or less, by virtue of teaching the morning and evening adult classes and cleaning the mats on Sundays in exchange for a percentage and a name on the door. The dojo did not, in any direct sense, smell good. But it smelled like work, and Lana approved of work.

A dozen students were going through their warm-ups under the watchful, slightly exasperated eye of her junior instructor, a college sophomore named Han who had the patience of a saint and the resting face of a man trying not to laugh at a funeral.

Lana paced the mat, her gi crisp, her bare feet making soft sounds on the wood. Her eyes settled, as her eyes always did, on Kevin.

Kevin was a broad-shouldered college athlete who had walked into the dojo six months ago with the air of a man doing the dojo a favor by showing up. Kevin had played JV football in high school. Kevin had taken one karate class at summer camp when he was nine. Kevin, in Kevin's mind, was already most of the way to becoming an action hero. Kevin was, in actual fact, currently performing a side kick that looked less like a martial arts technique and more like a man trying to ward off a swarm of bees while wearing socks on a freshly waxed floor.

"Nice try, Kevin," Lana said, her voice cutting through the room. "But you are not auditioning for the Bolshoi Ballet. It is a pivot, not a pirouette. The power comes from your hips, not from flailing your arms in the universal sign for I have made some choices."

Kevin flushed crimson. The rest of the class chuckled. Lana stepped beside him.

"Watch."

She set her stance, dropped her center of gravity an inch, and put a roundhouse kick into the air that snapped at the top with the clean *whip* of a wet towel. Hip first. Knee chamber. Ball of the foot. Body relaxed all the way through the strike, then pulled back into stance with the same fluidity, like nothing had happened. The kind of kick that took eighteen years to make look like nothing.

Kevin watched. The class watched.

"Self-defense," Lana said, "is not about looking cool. It is about being ready for what comes next.

And trust me, Kevin, there is always a next. Even if the next is just your own bad knees in twenty years."

Kevin nodded, looking like a confused giraffe trying to make peace with new information.

"Try again."

He tried again. It was marginally less embarrassing. Lana counted it as a win.

She was watching the rest of the class drift back into their forms when a small voice said, "Sensei?"

Maya was thirteen, weighed approximately as much as a large bag of birdseed, and had the unblinking, ancient stare of a child who read too much. She was currently looking up at Lana with her head tilted.

"What's up, kid?"

Maya hesitated. "You seem distracted today."

Lana blinked.

She thought, briefly, about saying *I'm fine,* which was the answer she had been giving for thirty years. She thought about saying *I had a bad dream,* which was the truth. She thought about saying *Maya, you have the spiritual perception of a forty-seven-year-old midwestern aunt and it is, frankly, a lot to deal with at seven in the morning.*

She forced a smile and patted Maya's shoulder. "Just life being life. Don't worry about it. Nothing a good pivot kick can't fix."

Maya, for the first time Lana could ever remember, did not smile back.

"Okay, Sensei," Maya said, and walked back to her line.

Lana stood there for a beat, watching her go, with the strange, prickling feeling that the dream had not entirely let go of her.

* * *

The boardroom of Beauchamp & Klein Industries reeked of stale ambition and that aerosol air freshener that someone had decided, at some point in the late nineties, was what *clean* smelled like. Lana sat across from Chuck Beauchamp, the company's CEO, with her laptop open on the conference table between them. Chuck was leaning back in his chair with the comfortable confidence of a man who had inherited the family business, the family wealth, and the family inability to ask for directions.

"So, uh," Chuck said, folding his hands behind his head, "how long do you think this audit is gonna take? Because I told the board it would be quick. Can we, like, fast-track it?"

Lana, whose fingers had not paused on her keyboard, smiled the smile she reserved for clients who said the words *fast-track*.

"That depends, Chuck. Do you want it done right, or do you want it done cheap? Because right now you are running a network with the security posture of a Post-it note on a refrigerator."

Chuck blinked. The smile faltered.

"Is that, uh, a metaphor?"

"It's three metaphors, in a trench coat, having a meeting." Lana turned the laptop toward him. "See this? This is your password policy. It currently allows twenty-eight separate variations of the word 'summer' followed by the digits one through nine. One of your senior vice presidents uses 'Summer1' for everything from your client portal to, I assume, his Pinterest board."

Chuck's face did something complicated.

"How serious is this?"

Lana clicked a tab. A red flag bloomed across the screen.

"Serious enough that someone breached your old client files four months ago and you didn't notice. Whoever it was poked around for about six hours, took some files, and left. They were professional. They wiped after themselves. The only reason I caught it is because I was the one you hired to look."

Chuck stared at the screen. His face, behind the spray-tan, had gone a color that Lana would have described as *recently embalmed.*

"Don't worry," she said, gently, because Chuck was, despite everything, a person, and she did not believe in being cruel to people about things they could not undo. "I'm going to fix it. I'm going to set you up with a real password policy, real two-factor, a real intrusion detection system, and a half-day training for your staff that I will personally deliver, in language that will not embarrass them. And next time someone tries to get in, they will get to admire a very nice digital fence."

Chuck exhaled a breath he had probably been holding since *summer.*

"You're a lifesaver, Lana."

"I am an expensive lifesaver," she said, closing the laptop. "I am sending you the new statement of work. Stop using 'password123.' I beg of you."

She gathered her things. As she headed for the door, she passed two young employees huddled by the glass wall of the conference room, voices low, the way people talked when they were sharing the kind of office gossip that wasn't really gossip.

"Stanton has theirs locked down tighter than Fort Knox," one was whispering. "Like, military grade. Heard they hire ex-NSA. They don't have these problems."

The other one nodded. "Must be nice."

Lana's pace did not change. Her face did not change. But somewhere just behind her sternum, a small, fast bell rang once and went still.

Stanton.

The name landed with the weight of something she was supposed to remember and didn't.

She stepped into the elevator, pressed the lobby button, and watched the floor numbers count down. By the time the doors opened, the bell had stopped ringing, and she had filed *Stanton* away in the part of her brain reserved for things that probably didn't matter.

It would, in fact, matter quite a lot. But not until later that night.

* * *

There were two things Lana Harper did when her brain got loud. The first was hack something. The second was take her motorcycle apart and put it back together. The first kept her current. The second kept her sane.

By two in the afternoon, she was on her back on the cool concrete of her parking garage, half under her 2014 Triumph Bonneville, doing absolutely nothing important to its perfectly fine carburetor. The carburetor knew it. The bike knew it. Lana knew it. The point was not the carburetor. The point was the *click* of the wrench, and the smell of the oil, and the way her hands knew exactly what to do without consulting her at all.

Her phone buzzed against the concrete next to her.

She rolled out from under the bike, wiped her hands on a rag, and squinted at the screen.

DAD, the screen said.

Her face, without permission, smiled.

"Hey, old man."

"Hey, kiddo." Her father's voice, warm and gravelly, came through the phone like something cooked slow over a long fire. "Just checking in. Making sure you're still alive and not, you know. Eaten by your cat."

"Pixel respects me too much to eat me. Or fears me. I'm not entirely sure which."

Her father chuckled. The chuckle turned into a cough, the cough turned back into a chuckle. He had been doing the cough-into-chuckle conversion for about three years now, and every time Lana asked him about it, he claimed it was allergies. She had stopped asking.

"You been eating?"

"I have been eating, Dad."

"Real food?"

"I had a kale smoothie this morning."

"Lana."

"...and a poptart."

"That's my girl." He laughed, properly this time. "Listen. Why don't you take that bike out for a real ride this weekend? Get out of the city. Clear your head. You always sound better after a long ride."

Lana looked at the bike, half-disassembled at her feet, the chrome catching afternoon light through the parking garage's dusty windows. Her fingers twitched.

"Maybe. I've got that conference tonight, but. Maybe Sunday."

"Good." A pause. "You sound tired, kiddo."

"I had a weird night. Bad sleep."

"The dream?"

She closed her eyes.

Her father had stopped pretending years ago that he didn't know what *the dream* was. He had never been able to give her details. He had, the first time she had asked, said only that her mother had died when Lana was very small, and that there had been a fire, and that there were things he could not talk about because talking about them did not, in his experience, help anyone, least of all him. And he was the only parent she had, and she had loved him too much to push.

She still loved him too much to push. But this morning, with the smell of clover still somewhere in the back of her sinuses, she heard herself say something she had not planned to say.

"Dad. Do you ever think about her?"

The line went very quiet.

For a second she thought maybe he hadn't heard her.

Then, in a voice that was not quite steady, he said, "Every day, kiddo. Every day. Why do you ask?"

Lana opened her mouth.

She closed it.

She thought about the small hand. The smell of the wrong kind of smoke. The silence at the end of the dream that always felt like it went on for years.

She thought about how her father had raised her on his own and how he had never, ever leaned on her, and how the cough had been getting worse, and how this was not, somehow, the right phone call for this.

"I just had a weird dream," she said, lightly. "That's all. Nothing big."

The pause on the other end was longer than the first one had been.

"...okay, kiddo," her father said. "Okay. You take care of yourself. You hear me?"

"I hear you, old man."

"Love you."

"Love you too, Dad."

She ended the call and sat on the concrete for a while, her wrists draped over her knees, looking at the half-disassembled bike and not really seeing it. There was a small, inconvenient pressure behind her eyes that she ignored on principle.

Then she got up, put the carburetor back together, and went to get ready for the conference.

* * *

The presentation hall of the Drummond Hotel was a long rectangle of beige carpet and beiger ambition, with three hundred folding chairs in neat rows and a digital screen at the front displaying her title slide.

ENCRYPTION AT THE EDGE: PROTECTING DATA YOU CAN'T SEE IN ENVIRONMENTS YOU DON'T CONTROL.

PRESENTED BY LANA HARPER, HARPER CYBER SECURITY.

The room held maybe two hundred people, mostly mid-level corporate IT, a handful of academics, three sales guys from a competing security firm pretending not to take notes, and a sprinkling of executives who had been told this talk was good and were here to look like they cared. Lana liked talks like this. She knew her material cold. The slides were good. The room was warm. The microphone worked.

She was in the middle of a clean, confident explanation of layered encryption, gesturing at a diagram on the screen, when her brain stuttered.

It was a small stutter. The kind nobody else in the room would have noticed.

Her eyes had drifted, the way her eyes drifted during talks, in a slow scan across the audience. Her brain, the back-channel monitoring part of her brain that had never stopped being a security analyst, was running pattern recognition on the room. Posture, attention, hands, exits. The thing she did automatically every time she walked into a space full of strangers.

And in the very back row, on the aisle, at a perfect ninety-degree angle to the seats around him, sat a man who did not match any of the patterns.

He was wearing a sharp black suit, tailored. He was not taking notes. He was not on a phone. He was not fidgeting. He was watching her with the absolute, unwavering focus of a man who had been told to watch her, and who was very good at his job.

Lana's mouth said the next two words of the slide deck on autopilot.

The rest of her brain went *what.*

She kept talking. She gestured at the diagram. She advanced the slide. She did not look at the man again, because her body had already decided, on its own, that looking at him a second time would be a tactical error. But she could feel him there. Forty rows back, dead center of her peripheral vision, a still point in a sea of small movements.

Calm down, she told herself. *He's a corporate security guy. He's a federal something-something. He's a contract recruiter. Half the people in this room are being watched by someone, you just usually don't notice.*

It didn't help.

She finished the slide. She finished the next slide. She got through the Q&A on muscle memory, fielding three questions from the audience and one from a sales guy who was trying to set her up to plug his product. By the time the moderator was thanking her at the front of the room, the man in the back row was gone.

Just gone. The seat empty. No memory of him standing up. No sound of him leaving.

Lana smiled and shook the moderator's hand and accepted the polite scattered applause and unplugged her laptop and packed up her bag, all of it on autopilot, while a small, expert voice in the back of her head said the word *predator* and refused to take it back.

By the time she made it down to the hotel bar, the voice was a little softer. By the time she had a glass of bourbon in her hand, the voice was almost gone.

But it wasn't quite gone.

Lana sat on a stool at the long, dim bar, watching condensation slide down the side of her glass, and tried to convince herself she was being paranoid.

She was being paranoid, in a sense... She was just not being paranoid *enough.*

Chapter 2: A Series of Unfortunate Events

Marlon Kade was sweating through his shirt.

Not the polite kind of sweat, the businessman-in-the-elevator-after-a-jog kind, but the deep, soaking, glandular kind that started at the base of the spine and climbed. His white dress shirt had a half-moon of gray spreading out from each armpit and a wider, darker patch creeping down his back like a tide line. He sat at a corner table in the Drummond Hotel bar with his back to the wall and his eyes on the door, and he held a tumbler of single-malt Scotch in his right hand the way a drowning man holds a piece of driftwood.

He had been here for forty-six minutes.

In sixteen more minutes, his contact at the FBI's Chicago field office was going to walk through the door and order a club soda and sit down across from him, and Marlon Kade was going to slide a small black flash drive across the polished oak of the bar table, and he was going to be, for the first time in eleven years, a free man.

Eleven years. Eleven years of running the false-invoice operation for Stanton Industries' shell holdings. Eleven years of watching numbers move from one offshore account to another and knowing exactly where the money came from, and exactly what the money was for, and exactly who got hurt to make it. Eleven years of being a useful man to a very dangerous one. Eleven years of pretending he hadn't noticed any of it.

Then his daughter had turned sixteen, and she had come home from school one Tuesday with her lower lip split open from a fistfight she had started, and when he had asked her why, she had looked him in the face and said, *Because some kid said you worked for crooks, Dad. And he was wrong, right? Tell me he was wrong.*

He hadn't answered her. He had just held her, and she had cried on his shirt, and he had felt the floor of his life sag a quarter-inch under his feet, and he had decided, then, that he was going to find a way out.

The flash drive in his pocket was the way out.

It contained eleven years of evidence. Account numbers. Wire transfer logs. Internal memos, the ones with names on them. Photographs of meetings that had never officially happened. A small audio file of Marcus Stanton himself, on a phone call, saying things that would put him in a federal prison for the rest of his life.

Sixteen minutes.

Marlon took a long pull of his Scotch and risked a glance toward the bar.

A man in a black suit was sitting at the far end of it. Tailored. Composed. Working a small tumbler of bourbon with the patient absence of a man who was waiting for a bus, or a meal, or a person. He was not looking at Marlon. He was not looking at anything. He was simply present, in the way that some men were simply present, the way a stove was present in a kitchen, the way a loaded firearm was present on a table.

Marlon's stomach dropped.

He had never seen the man before. He had heard about him. Once, two years ago, in a private elevator with one of Stanton's lieutenants, after a third drink had loosened a tongue that should have stayed in its mouth. *There's a man,* the lieutenant had said, slurring slightly, *Marcus's man, but more than Marcus's man, you understand? He cleans. He doesn't do anything else. He just cleans. And when the cleaner shows up, you know things have gotten away from someone.*

Marlon had asked, idly, what the cleaner's name was.

The lieutenant had laughed without any humor in his face and said, *Mr. Halloran. We just call him Mr. Halloran. Don't ever ask anyone else, Marlon. Pretend I didn't tell you that name.*

Marlon had pretended.

Now, in the corner of the Drummond's bar, sweating through a hundred-and-eighty-dollar shirt, he was looking at a man in a tailored black suit at the end of the bar, and he understood, with the cold clarity of a man whose blood pressure had just dropped twenty points, that the cleaner had shown up.

He fumbled for his phone with hands that did not entirely belong to him anymore. He swiped to the contact. He was just about to tap the green call button, was just about to tell his FBI contact to *not come, abort, abort, the meeting is burned,* when the bar's lights flickered, and the front door of the lounge opened, and a young woman in a hoodie and dark jeans walked in.

Marlon had no way to know it. But the moment that young woman crossed the threshold, his sixteen minutes ran out.

* * *

Lana Harper stood inside the doorway of the Drummond's hotel bar and did the visual sweep she always did when she walked into a strange room. Two exits, one main and one through the kitchen. Twenty-one patrons, give or take. Three bartenders. A bus station, a dishwashing alcove. The lights were low, amber, expensive. Soft jazz from speakers she could not see. The kind of bar that wanted you to spend a hundred and forty dollars on dinner and feel sophisticated about it. The kind of bar where, somewhere in the last five years, a designer with strong opinions had ripped out the original heavy iron chains on the chandeliers and put in thin modern aircraft cable, because thin modern aircraft cable was what the magazines were doing this year, and a hundred-year-old hotel bar that had no business hosting this kind of design choice was now, quietly, hosting it anyway. Lana noticed this in the way she noticed everything. She filed it under: *somebody's going to regret that, eventually.*

She walked to the bar, slid onto a stool four down from the only other person currently sitting there, ordered a Maker's Mark neat, and nursed it.

She told herself, again, that the man in the back row of her conference talk had just been a corporate security guy. She told herself that her brain was tired and her dream had wound her up and her father's voice on the phone was sitting heavier on her chest than it usually did. She told herself that one drink would settle her down and she would Uber home and watch a stupid show until she fell asleep.

She did not look around the bar to see if the man from the conference was here.

She had decided, in the elevator down, that she was not going to give him the satisfaction. He was probably an attendee. He was probably gone. She was a grown woman who could have one drink in a hotel bar without checking under every table for the boogeyman.

She did not see Mr. Halloran at the end of the bar. She did not see Marlon Kade in the corner. Her brain was logging a half-dozen low-priority threat indicators and was politely declining to escalate them, because Lana had decided, in the elevator, to stop being weird tonight.

Her brain would later file a formal complaint about being overruled.

She was halfway through the bourbon when she noticed the server.

He was a kid. Twenty one at most. Lean, anxious, the kind of skinny that hadn't filled out yet. He was navigating the room with a tray of three cocktails balanced just slightly above his shoulder, and Lana could tell from a single look at his shoulders that this was the kid's third week on the job and he had not yet developed the muscle memory for a tray. He was tense. He was overthinking it. He was watching the drinks instead of watching the room.

Lana was so caught up in feeling sympathetic for the kid that she did not, until it was happening, notice his trajectory.

It happened the way these things happen.

A woman in a low-cut dress reached out to flag the kid down. Her elbow caught the edge of the tray. The cocktails skated. Two of them recovered. The third, a blood-orange margarita in a wide-bowled coupe glass, leapt off the tray with a kind of weightless grace and arced through the air in a perfect, slow-motion parabola of pinkish liquid that ended directly in the center of Marlon Kade's chest.

The glass hit the table next, bounced once, and shattered.

The bar went briefly, completely silent.

Then Marlon Kade screamed.

Not a yelp. Not a curse. A full, frothing, blood-pressure-spiking scream. He surged up out of his chair with the cocktail dripping down his shirt and his face going the color of an angry beet. The chair fell over backward. Three people at the next table flinched away.

"This shirt cost more than you make in a week, you little punk!"

He grabbed the kid's wrist. The kid's tray hit the floor. The kid's eyes went wide and wet.

"Sir, I, I'm so sorry, I.."

"You're sorry?" Marlon's voice had gone up an octave. "You're sorry? You stupid, useless.."

Lana had already set down her glass.

She had not made a conscious decision to do so. Her hands had simply put the bourbon down, neatly, on the cocktail napkin, and slid off the barstool, and started walking. By the time her brain caught up, her body was four steps into the bar.

Two things, in those four steps, registered in the analytical back-channel of her mind that had never stopped paying attention.

The first thing was that Marlon Kade's free hand, the one that wasn't crushing the kid's wrist, had drifted toward the inside pocket of his suit jacket in a small, automatic motion. Not the motion of a man reaching for a wallet. The motion of a man reaching for a tool.

The second thing was that she could see, from this angle, the edge of a small leather sheath inside the jacket. And the handle, just barely visible above the sheath's lip, was serrated in a way that no kitchen knife had ever been serrated. It was a working knife. It was the kind of knife a man carried because he expected to use it on a person.

Marlon Kade was not a businessman who had snapped over a stained shirt.

Marlon Kade was a man with a knife and a problem.

Lana arrived at his table.

"Hey, Hulk," she said, in the voice she used on Kevin during sparring drills. "Take a breath. The kid's young. Let him go."

Marlon's head snapped around. His eyes locked onto her. They were wide, the whites showing all the way around the iris, and not because of the cocktail. He was a man whose adrenaline was already at red-line for reasons that had nothing to do with this room. The cocktail had not started this. The cocktail had only been the spark on already-soaked tinder.

He released the kid's wrist.

The kid stumbled backward and disappeared behind a passing bartender.

Marlon turned the full weight of his attention onto Lana.

"You bitch," he breathed. "You should mind your own fucking business."

His right hand was already in his jacket.

The knife came out small and ugly. Three inches of serrated edge. A handle wrapped in black grip tape. Held low, point forward, in the kind of grip that was not for show. He had used this knife before. He knew what to do with it.

The bar around them, already quiet, went somehow quieter. Somebody whispered *oh my god.* A chair scraped. People started moving away.

Lana, in the still place at the center of her own skull, registered three things in rapid sequence.

The knife was a working knife. The man with the knife was not a drunken businessman. The man with the knife was scared, and a scared man with a knife was the most dangerous animal in any room.

She did not move backward.

Eighteen years of training had taught her that backward, against a knife, was the wrong direction. A knife was a close-range weapon. The longer your range, the more advantage your attacker had to charge into. Distance was not safety. Distance was just *time for the bad thing to happen.*

You had to be either very far away from a knife, or very close to it.

She was already inside the bad space. She decided, in the half-second she had, to commit.

"Okay," she said, very calmly. "Okay, sir, I am going to ask you, very nicely, to put the knife down."

Marlon Kade lunged.

* * *

The lunge was clean. He had used a knife on a person before. The blade tracked low, aimed at her belly, where a slash would open her up in a way she would not survive a hospital trip from.

Lana did exactly what eighteen years of repetition had taught her to do.

She did not step back.

She stepped *off-line*, a small, fast pivot at a forty-five-degree angle that took her body out of the path of the blade while keeping her inside his striking range. Her left hand swept down across her body in a cross-body block, the heel of her palm clipping his wrist hard enough to deflect the knife further off-line. Her right knee came up at the same moment and drove into his short ribs.

The strike connected with the soft place just below the bottom rib, where there was no bone to protect the diaphragm. Marlon Kade folded around her knee with a sound that came out of him in two parts: first the *whoof* of all his air leaving his body, then a high, surprised wheeze.

She did not stop. The textbook said you did not stop.

She stepped through the strike, her hip rotating, and her body completed the motion her training had drilled into her ten thousand times. She redirected his blade arm down and across, using his own forward momentum, and his legs tangled with the leg of his own overturned chair, and he went down sideways into a barstool with a crash that made every bottle behind the bar shiver in sympathy.

The knife did not leave his hand.

That was the thing about working knives and the people who carried them. They knew the value of holding on.

Lana stepped back, set her stance, and watched him pull himself up onto one knee, the blade still in his fist.

The bar had cleared a wide circle around the two of them. The bartender had vanished. Somebody, somewhere, was yelling *call 911, call 911,* in the voice of a person who had assumed somebody else had already done it.

Marlon's eyes were still wide. But behind the panic now, there was something else. There was something focused. He had measured her. He had felt the knee strike. He had made a calculation that he was still bigger than her, that he was still armed, and that the next exchange was going to be different.

He came up off the knee with his weight shifting forward, and the blade came up in a clean upward slash aimed at her throat.

Lana caught a glint of metal at the edge of her vision.

The drinks tray. The kid's drinks tray, fallen on the floor when Marlon had let him go. Round, chrome, restaurant-grade, about the diameter of a dinner plate.

She caught it on the bounce of one foot and brought it up flat across her chest as the blade came in, and the serrated edge hit the chrome with the sharp metallic *clang* of a hammer striking an anvil.

The blade rebounded off the tray.

The knife flew out of Marlon's hand and tumbled, end over end, across the room, and lodged with a small, decorous *plnk* into the soil of an enormous potted ficus tree by the entrance to the bar.

There was a brief, unscheduled moment of total silence in which everyone in the room simultaneously processed the sight of a serrated combat knife sticking out of the dirt of a houseplant.

Then somebody behind Lana actually laughed. A single short bark, immediately stifled, the way people laugh in church when something inappropriate happens.

Marlon Kade, weaponless, sweat-soaked, eyes huge, saw his only advantage skitter across the bar and embed in landscaping. Some animal, lizard-brained part of him decided, in that instant, that the next correct move was to rush her.

He rushed her.

Lana did not meet him head-on. She pivoted again, planting her left foot, and as he barreled past where she had been standing, she snapped a side kick into the back of his trailing knee. The whole point of a side kick to the back of the knee was that it didn't matter how big the man was. The joint hyperextended. The leg buckled. Marlon Kade went down hard, all two hundred and forty pounds of him, and crashed into a low table covered in champagne flutes.

The flutes erupted. Glass everywhere. The table's white tablecloth ripped half off, and as it did, it dragged the heavy velvet curtain that ran along the wall behind it. The curtain swept sideways, and the heavy fringed bottom of it landed across the open flame of a copper-pot sterno that had been quietly keeping a charcuterie warmer warm.

The curtain caught fire.

It caught fast. It caught in the way velvet catches when it has not been treated for fire safety since whatever decade had decided the Drummond Hotel was going to keep being the Drummond Hotel.

Flame ran up the curtain like a signal flare.

Somebody screamed. Smoke alarms began to wail. And then, with the sweet, theatrical timing of a building that had been waiting for a cue, the fire suppression system of the Drummond Hotel's bar engaged.

The sprinklers came on.

Cold water hit the room in a thousand simultaneous arcs.

Lana stood in the middle of the suddenly-monsooning bar, drenched in the first three seconds, watching the flame die on the curtain with a hiss, and her brain, in the small clear voice of a person who has decided that this is fine, said:

Not my fault. None of this is my fault.

That was when she noticed the chandelier.

The Drummond's bar had a centerpiece chandelier directly above the spot where she and Marlon Kade had been doing their unauthorized choreography. Wrought brass, three feet across, hung with crystal pendants that were probably real and probably cost more than her car. It hung from the ceiling on a single thin steel suspension cable, anchored into the original 1923 hardwood by a flush ceiling mount. The original heavy iron chain that had once held the fixture had been removed during the bar's last fashionable renovation, replaced by aircraft-grade cable that was sleeker, cleaner, and considerably less rated for direct fire impingement.

She looked up at it because the sprinklers were spraying water directly onto it and the crystal was throwing rainbows in the strobing red of the fire alarm and the whole thing was, briefly, beautiful in a way that made her heart do something inconvenient.

She did not look up at it for very long.

But she looked up long enough to see the cable.

The cable was running directly through the column of orange-yellow flame coming up off the burning velvet curtain.

Thin steel, taking direct fire impingement at the rate of approximately one second per second, while holding three feet of brass and crystal at the end of it. There was, even to the small detached part of Lana's brain that had been doing physics homework when the rest of her had been doing other things, exactly one outcome to that arrangement.

The cable, by Lana's quick estimate, had about four seconds of cooperation left in it.

Her heart did not have time to ask why.

Marlon Kade was crawling. He had landed in the wreckage of the champagne table and was pulling himself up across broken glass with bleeding palms, and his eyes were on the ficus tree, and the knife sticking out of its dirt. He was making for the knife. He had decided this was not over. He had decided that if he could just reach the knife, he could still finish what he had started.

He pulled himself to a half-crouch. Took one staggering step. Then another. His weight shifted forward.

The cable gave.

There was a single sharp metallic twang, the sound of a steel cable under load suddenly not being under load. The upper end of the cable whipped up against the ceiling. The lower end, with three feet of brass and crystal at the bottom of it and nothing holding it anymore, did what gravity asked of it.

The chandelier dropped.

It dropped immediately, with no swing and no grace, three feet of brass and crystal coming down at once with the precision of a thing that had simply stopped being held up.

It came down directly on Marlon Kade.

Lana, who had already started stepping backward by pure reflex, stopped at a safe distance and watched the impact. The brass body of the chandelier struck Marlon between the shoulder blades and drove him face-down into the broken glass of the champagne table. The crystal pendants kept swinging for a second after the body came to rest, ringing softly against each other in the strobing red light.

Marlon Kade did not get up.

He did not move.

He was not, in any meaningful sense of the word, going to.

The sprinklers kept spraying. The fire alarm kept wailing. Lana stood in the middle of the soaked, smoking, shimmering bar with water running off her hair into her eyes and looked down at the body of a man she had not, in any direct sense, killed.

She had not stabbed him. She had not strangled him. She had not pushed him under the chandelier.

The chandelier had been an accident.

The accident had been *hers.*

And there was, at the end of the bar, a man who knew exactly that, and who was deciding, on the spot, what it was going to mean for him.

A small, very old piece of Lana, the piece that had spent her entire life doing pattern recognition on rooms full of strangers, lifted its head and said, in a quiet, urgent voice: *You are inside something, Lana. The man at the end of the bar is going to use what just happened. You need to leave this room right now.*

She did not move.

She could not have said, in that moment, why she did not move.

She would understand, in retrospect, that her body was waiting. That her body had clocked, somewhere in the chaos of the last forty seconds, that there was one other person in this room who was not running, not screaming, not flinching from the spray of the sprinklers, not doing any of the things a normal patron of a hotel bar would do during a fire alarm and a homicide.

There was one person who was simply standing very still at the end of the bar, watching her, the way a man watches a horse he has just bought run for the first time on its new track.

She turned her head, very slowly, and met Mr. Halloran's eyes.

* * *

He walked toward her through the spray of the sprinklers like a man walking through light rain in a city he owned.

His tailored black suit was not getting wet, exactly. The water hit him and seemed to politely re-route around him. Lana, dripping and shivering, had time to register this as the kind of detail that made her brain want to lie down and reassess its assumptions about physics.

He stopped six feet from her. His hands were in his suit pockets. He did not look at the body. He looked, with mild, pleasant interest, at her.

"Impressive," he said. The voice was warm and dry and slightly amused. "Unorthodox, but effective."

Lana opened her mouth.

She did not know what she was going to say.

He moved past her, with the same elegance, and stooped at the ficus. He plucked the serrated knife out of the soil and turned it over in his hand once, twice, examining it, then dropped it into a small velvet pouch he produced from inside his jacket. He tucked the pouch back into his jacket like a man pocketing a cigar.

Then he turned back to her, and from the same jacket, produced a small black velvet pouch.

The pouch was small. The pouch was the size of a deck of cards. The pouch should not, on first glance, have caused her stomach to drop the way it dropped when she looked at it. Lana, who had been doing IT consulting long enough to recognize the silhouette of a flash drive in a velvet pouch when she saw one, did not need to ask what it was.

He set the pouch on the bar between them.

"Payment for services rendered," he said. "One million USD value, settled in Bitcoin. The wallet is on the drive. The seed phrase is on the slip in the pouch. Banks, as you can imagine, are not for transactions like ours."

Lana stared at the pouch.

She stared at Mr. Halloran.

The fire alarm was still screaming. The sprinklers were still raining. Somewhere, distantly, the sound of approaching sirens was beginning to thread itself into the larger noise.

"I think," Lana said, slowly, "there has been some kind of mix-up."

Mr. Halloran smiled. It was not a smile that involved his eyes.

"There has not."

"I.."

"The pickup," he said, "will be at eleven hundred hours tomorrow. Details to follow." He produced, from yet another pocket, a small black flip phone of the kind that no human being had carried voluntarily since 2007. He set it beside the pouch. "This is your contact line. Keep it on. Do not use it to call your mother."

The word *mother* landed in Lana's chest like a thrown rock.

She did not know why.

Mr. Halloran noticed. Mr. Halloran noticed everything. The very faint, almost-not-there flicker in the corner of his mouth said that he had filed the reaction away for later consideration.

"Until tomorrow, Sophia," he said.

He turned. He walked, unhurried, through the spray, toward the kitchen exit at the back of the bar.

It was at this point that Lana noticed the two men in dark coveralls.

They were entering the bar through the same kitchen door Mr. Halloran was now exiting. They moved past him without acknowledgment, the way coworkers passed each other in a hallway at a job they had been doing for years. They were carrying small black cases. One of them was already pulling a digital camera out of his case and crouching beside the chandelier. The other was kneeling beside Marlon Kade's body. He was, Lana saw, very efficiently going through the dead man's pockets with gloved hands.

He found something. A small black flash drive. He held it up to his partner.

The partner nodded, very slightly, and went back to photographing the chandelier.

Lana, soaking wet, holding a small velvet pouch with a million dollars in Bitcoin inside it and a cell phone that belonged to someone who was not her, watched two strangers calmly take apart the scene of her not-quite-crime as if she was no longer in the room.

She understood, in a single clean moment of clarity, that she had not committed a crime. There was not going to be a crime. There was not going to be a 911 report, a police interview, an incident, a name. The Drummond Hotel was, right now, having an unfortunate accident with its century-old wiring, which had ignited a flash fire above the bar's centerpiece chandelier, weakening the suspension cable to the point of failure and dropping the fixture on a guest who had been having a medical event in the bar. The cable, by the time the fire department arrived, would look exactly like what it actually was: a thin modern aircraft cable that had been entirely the wrong rigging for a hundred-year-old building, and that had taken a brief and unusually hot fire that nobody who had specified it for the renovation had ever imagined it would have to handle. The knife and anything else that needed disappearing would be in the velvet pouch in Mr. Halloran's jacket pocket.

She, Lana Harper, was not going to appear in any record of this evening.

She was, instead, going to walk out of this hotel with a flash drive worth a million dollars, and a phone, and a name that was not hers, and a debt to a man she did not know, in a transaction she had not agreed to, with a partner she could not negotiate with.

Lana picked up the pouch.

It was lighter than a million dollars had any business being.

She walked, dripping, through the spraying remains of the Drummond's bar. She walked past the cleanup crew. She walked past the body. She walked through the kitchen, which was empty, the staff having all evacuated through the rear emergency exit when the fire alarm started, and the cleanup crew not having bothered to stop them.

She walked out the rear emergency exit into a service alley behind the hotel.

The sirens were closer now. Two streets over, maybe one. She had ninety seconds, maybe less.

She stood in the alley with the pouch zipped into the inside pocket of her jacket and looked up at a narrow strip of night sky between the building and the dumpster, and she let herself, for one single second, register that she was carrying a flash drive worth a million dollars she had not earned for a job she had not done because somebody, somewhere, had mistaken her for somebody else.

The little black flip phone in her hand began to vibrate.

She stared at it.

It vibrated again.

The screen read: NEW MESSAGE.

She thumbed it open.

Welcome back, Sophia.

Lana Harper, IT consultant of Chicago, age twenty-nine, owner of one cat and one motorcycle and a small business in cyber security, looked at the message, and the message looked back at her, and she understood, with the cold clarity of a person standing in an alley with a million dollars she had not asked for, that something extremely large had just happened to her, and she did not, yet, know what.

Who the hell is Sophia? she thought.

Two streets over, she heard the siren cut out as the first fire engine arrived at the front of the hotel.

She started walking.

Chapter 3: The Chandelier Assassin

The safe house was a third-floor walkup over a Polish bakery on the north side, and at six in the morning, the smell of warm rye bread came through the floorboards in a way that, on better days, Sophia found comforting.

Today she was bleeding onto her own kitchen table, and it did not smell like much of anything.

The gash on her left forearm had reopened during the night, the way she had known it would. She had cleaned it three times, sutured it once, butterfly-taped it twice, and the deep cut still wanted to remind her that a man with a serrated curved blade had nearly opened her arm to the bone six days ago in a rooftop garden in Lyon, and that her body, like every body, kept the score.

She sat at the small table in her safe house's kitchen, in a black tank top and tactical pants, and re-dressed the wound with the focused, untroubled efficiency of a woman who had been re-dressing her own wounds since she was thirteen years old. Iodine. Antibiotic ointment. Fresh gauze. A single roll of self-adhering medical wrap. She did not flinch. She did not curse. She did the work, and when the work was done, she straightened her arm twice to test the range of motion, and she reached for her coffee, which had gone cold.

She drank it anyway.

The laptop on the table beside her had been chiming for the last ten minutes.

Sophia had been ignoring it because she had been bleeding, and one thing at a time. Now, with her arm wrapped and the coffee cold and the bakery downstairs starting to fill the apartment with the smell of pierogi dough, she pulled the laptop in front of her and opened the alerts.

She read the first alert.

She read the second alert.

She read the third alert.

Her face did not change. Sophia Harper's face had not, in any meaningful way, changed in fifteen years. There were people in the trade who had started calling her *the iron woman*, not because they had ever seen her stay calm under pressure, but because they had never seen her do anything else.

Her face did not change. Her hands did, slightly. Both of them flattened, palms-down, on the surface of the table, with the precise, deliberate slowness of a woman placing a glass of water down before she did something stupid with it.

The first alert was a dark web bulletin, posted to a forum she monitored, that was less a forum than a kind of trade publication for people whose trade did not have a public-facing brochure. The bulletin had two embedded images and a short text caption.

The first image was a still from a hotel security camera, time-stamped 9:47 the previous evening. The image was grainy and the angle was bad. The image showed a young woman in a hoodie standing in the middle of a partially-flooded hotel bar, water running down her hair, looking up at a fallen chandelier and a body. The image had been zoomed in and clarified by someone who knew what they were doing. The young woman's face was perfectly clear.

The face was Sophia's face.

The face was, of course, also Lana's face. They had the same face. They had been born with the same face. They had spent the first six and twelve years of their respective lives in front of mirrors that returned the same face. The face was the central, immutable fact of being a Harper twin, the thing you grew up with and the thing you never quite stopped being startled by when you saw it on someone else.

The second image was a grainier still from the same camera, taken six seconds earlier in the same incident, in which the same young woman could be seen executing what was, even in low resolution, an unmistakable and technically clean side kick to the back of a man's knee.

The text caption read:

SOPHIA HARPER: THE CHANDELIER ASSASSIN. NEW METHODS. SAME DEADLY RESULTS.

The bulletin had three hundred and seventy comments on it.

Sophia closed her eyes for a long second.

She had built her entire career on the principle that she did not exist.

She was, to civilians and to law enforcement and to the news cycle, a ghost. Her face was not in any database. Her name was not on any list. The handful of intelligence agencies who knew the name *Sophia* did not know the face that went with it, and the much larger number of agencies who knew the face from grainy stills of finished work did not know what to call it. Within the trade, *Sophia* was a name spoken in lowered voices, a ghost they all knew the shape of even if none had seen her in person. *That* was the trade-side reputation. That was the thing she had cultivated for fifteen years. That was the thing that kept her alive.

Her sister, who did not know what her sister was, had just put her face on the dark web in the middle of a contract kill, with a side kick that was *visibly* her side kick because they had taken the same first three years of taekwondo from the same instructor before their mother had died and Sophia had stopped going to lessons.

Lana, Sophia thought, with the slow, deep, weary affection of an older sister who had spent her entire life trying not to be the older sister, *what have you done to me.*

She opened the second alert.

The second alert was an internal Stanton Industries communication that Sophia, through a back channel that had taken her four years to build, had been intercepting for the last eighteen months. The intercept was patchy. She got, on average, one message in five. This was a message she had gotten.

The message was a contract notice. The contract was on a man named Lucas Deveraux. The pickup window was between ten in the morning and two in the afternoon, the day of, at an Uptown café whose location was given in coordinates and whose address Sophia recognized immediately.

The contractor of record was listed as *S.*

She had not been contacted about this contract.

She had not accepted this contract.

She had not been *offered* this contract, because the contractor of record was *S,* which was the trade tag the Stanton organization used internally for *Sophia,* and *Sophia* was not the kind of contractor you offered things to. You set things in front of *Sophia,* and *Sophia* either did the thing or did not, and you found out which one she had done by observing the world for changes.

Stanton's people thought Sophia had taken a contract last night.

Stanton's people had now offered Sophia, a contract that Sophia was not aware of, on a man Sophia had been trying to reach for two months because *Lucas Deveraux,* whoever he was, had, six weeks ago, started moving very large amounts of money out of Stanton's offshore shell companies in a pattern that Sophia's analyst friend in Zurich had described, professionally, as *suicidally clumsy and morally beautiful.*

Lucas Deveraux was running.

Stanton's people had finally figured out who was running.

And they had, through the bizarre fog of misidentifying her sister, just put a contract on him with the wrong sister.

Sophia read the third alert.

The third alert was an automated cell tower ping confirming that a particular SIM card, one she had been tracking for nearly three years, had pinged from a cell tower at the corner of West Fulton and North Sangamon. That SIM card belonged to one specific phone, in the pocket of one specific man, and the man wore a tailored black suit, and the man's name was Henrik Vanek, and the trade called him Mr. Halloran.

He had been at the Drummond Hotel last night.

He had been standing twenty feet from her sister.

Sophia picked up her coffee, looked at it, set it down again, and calmly picked up the small ceramic mug and threw it, hard, against the wall over her sink. The mug did not shatter so much as it briefly pretended to be a small grenade. Coffee and ceramic shrapnel everywhere.

Pixel, had Pixel been in the apartment, would have judged her.

But Pixel was three blocks away in another woman's apartment, in another woman's life, and Sophia Harper had not seen her sister in person in fifteen years, and her sister had just walked into the worst possible night of her life, and Sophia Harper, professional ghost, was now, abruptly, no longer a ghost.

She got up.

She started packing.

* * *

Lana Harper sat at her kitchen counter in damp pajamas and ate pancakes that tasted like cardboard.

She had cooked them on autopilot. She had cracked the eggs, whisked the batter, melted the butter, plated and syruped the stack, all on autopilot, because somewhere on the long damp Uber ride home from the Drummond Hotel last night her brain had decided that the only way through the next several hours was to perform the rituals of a normal human until she felt like one again.

She had taken a forty-minute shower. She had thrown her clothes in the trash. She had thrown her shoes in the trash. She had stood under the hot water until her skin was angry and the steam had filled the bathroom and the smell of the chandelier and the sprinklers and Marlon Kade's last bad minute had been, mostly, washed off her.

She had not, at any point, plugged in the drive.

The pouch was sitting on her workbench. It had been sitting on her workbench for nine hours. It was a small black velvet pouch, perfectly nondescript, the kind of pouch a jeweler used for a single nice ring. Inside it was a flash drive, a small square of cardstock with a twelve-word seed phrase written on it in fountain pen, and nothing else. It was sitting on her workbench between her soldering iron and the framed photograph of her father, and it was, in Lana's increasingly frayed estimation, radiating menace at her like a low-grade thermal output that had no business coming off something the size of a deck of cards.

Pixel, who had already opinions about damp pajamas at seven in the morning, was making them known by sitting on the corner of the counter and watching her eat pancakes with the grim focus of a forensic auditor.

"I know," Lana said, around a mouthful. "I know, buddy."

Pixel stared.

"I have made a series of choices," she said.

Pixel stared.

"I will be honest with you, Pixel," Lana said. "I do not have a plan."

Pixel, slowly, stood up, walked across the counter, and knocked the bottle of maple syrup off the edge with a single, clean swipe of his paw. The bottle landed on the kitchen tile with the wet *thud* of a thing that did not have the decency to break. Syrup began to seep, slowly, across the floor.

"That's fair," Lana said.

She got up to mop the syrup. She was halfway through the cleanup when her phone, the real one, rang.

DAD, the screen said.

Her stomach, which had been performing well above expectations, dropped through the floor.

She stared at the phone for two rings. She thought, with an honesty she rarely allowed herself, about not picking up.

She picked up.

"Hey, old man."

"Hey, kiddo."

His voice was the same. His voice was the same as it had been yesterday afternoon when she had been on her back under the Triumph and the world had still made sense. His voice was warm and gravelly and it was so familiar that it felt, this morning, like a betrayal.

"You up early," he said. "Or up late?"

"Up early. Getting ahead of the day."

"You always say that."

"It's always true."

He chuckled. The chuckle bent into a small cough, and the small cough straightened back into a chuckle, and Lana closed her eyes.

"How was the conference?" he said.

"Conference was fine. Talk went well. Two job offers in the lobby afterward, both terrible."

"My girl."

"How are you?"

"Oh, you know. Bert at the shop is making me crazy. He's convinced his wife is poisoning him. I told him, Bert, your wife is not poisoning you, you are seventy-one years old and you eat onion rings for lunch every day, the issue is not the wife. He didn't take it well."

She laughed. She laughed in a way that felt, in her own chest, like she was laughing in a foreign language.

"Lana." His voice changed. The chuckle was gone. "You okay?"

"I'm fine, Dad."

The pause on the line was longer than it should have been.

She had lied to her father exactly once, ever, that she could remember. She had been seventeen. She had told him she was studying at a friend's house and she had instead been at a punk show downtown and a boy named Devin had given her a beer, and she had felt so guilty about the lie that she had thrown up in a parking lot and called her father at midnight and confessed, and her father had picked her up and bought her a milkshake and not punished her, and she had never, in twelve years, lied to him again.

She had lied to him just now. She had said *I'm fine,* and the words had been a lie, and her body had not punished her for it. The words had come out smooth and easy, the way a coin slides into a slot.

She felt, more than anything else she had felt that morning, profoundly, terrifyingly grown up.

"...okay, kiddo," her father said. "You take care of yourself today, you hear me?"

"I will."

"Take a long ride this weekend."

"I will."

"Love you."

"Love you too, Dad."

She put the phone down on the counter very gently, the way one puts down a glass of water one is afraid to spill, and she stood very still in her kitchen with the syrup on the floor and the pouch on the workbench, and she did not, for almost a minute, breathe.

Then the *other* phone began to vibrate.

The little black flip phone was sitting beside the pouch where she had left it. It had been silent since she had brought it home. It was vibrating now in a slow, patient pattern: *brrrt, brrrt, brrrt.* Like a heartbeat.

Lana walked across the kitchen.

She stood over the pouch.

The phone kept vibrating.

She picked it up. She flipped it open. She did not say anything. She just held it to her ear.

For a long moment there was nothing on the line except a faint, expensive silence, the kind of silence that came from the inside of a high-end vehicle with a satellite uplink.

Then Mr. Halloran's voice said, "Good morning, Sophia."

Lana's mouth opened.

She closed it.

She thought, in that small still place at the center of her own skull, about hanging up. She thought about taking the phone outside and putting it under the wheel of the next passing truck. She thought about taking the phone, the pouch, and the keys to her bike, and getting on a flight to anywhere that did not have a Drummond Hotel.

She thought about two men in dark coveralls, calmly removing a flash drive from the pocket of a dead man.

She thought about the cable and the twang.

She thought about the way Mr. Halloran had said *do not use it to call your mother,* and the way the word *mother* had landed in her chest like a rock thrown from a long way off.

She did not hang up.

"There has been," Lana said, in as steady a voice as she could manage, "a misunderstanding."

"There has not."

"My name is not Sophia."

There was, on the other end of the line, the briefest pause. The kind of pause a man takes when he is briefly entertaining a piece of information he had not expected.

Then Mr. Halloran said, "Charming."

Lana closed her eyes.

"Listen to me, Sophia," he said. The voice was warm and dry and slightly amused, the way it had been in the bar, and it was somehow more frightening on a phone, where she could not see the man behind it. "Your reputation precedes you. Your work precedes you. We have been waiting some time for the opportunity to work together, and last night was, if I may say, an excellent introduction. Your aesthetic, in particular, was a delight. The chandelier was a flourish I will be remembering for some time."

The aesthetic was an *accident,* Lana thought. The chandelier had been an accident waiting for the right night. *I just happened to be there for it.* She did not say this. She had begun, despite herself, to listen.

"You are, however," Mr. Halloran continued, "a contractor of mine, and contractors of mine have a schedule. I am sending you a follow-up assignment. I expect it executed today. I will not insult you by repeating the financial terms. Your reputation, again, precedes you."

"I won't," Lana said.

"You will."

"I won't," she said again, and her voice, to her own surprise, did not shake. "Whatever you think I am, I'm not. I don't kill people. Last night was an accident."

The silence on the other end was, this time, a very different silence.

It was the silence of a man who was, for the first time, considering whether the thing he was holding was the thing he had thought it was.

Then Mr. Halloran said, in a voice of such warm, pitying patience that it made Lana's teeth itch, "Sophia. I will give you, as a courtesy, one piece of advice. Failure is not an option. I do not mean this in the figurative way that men in suits mean it on television. I mean this in the literal way that men in my position mean it when they are placing a contract in the hand of a contractor. The target is a man who has, in the last ninety days, taken a great deal of money that does not belong to him, and made a series of small, foolish decisions that have brought him to a public café in your city today. Either you will retrieve what he has taken, and ensure that he no longer represents an organizational risk, or someone else will be sent to do both of those things on your behalf. The second option will cost you significantly more than the first. Are we clear?"

Lana stared at the pouch on her workbench.

She thought about Lucas Deveraux, whoever he was. She thought about a man in an Uptown café, drinking a coffee, about to be killed.

She thought, with a clarity that was new to her, that *someone else will be sent to do both of those things on your behalf* did not just mean someone else would kill Lucas Deveraux. It also meant something quieter, something Mr. Halloran had not stated outright because men like Mr. Halloran never stated such things outright. *Someone else* would also be sent to clean up *Sophia,* if Sophia turned out to be the kind of contractor who had, for whatever sentimental reason, declined to do her job.

There was no version of this morning in which Lana Harper hung up the phone and went back to her pancakes.

"...we're clear," Lana said.

"Excellent. Watch your phone. Pickup details in two minutes."

The line went dead.

Lana stood in her kitchen with the burner phone in her hand and the pouch on her workbench and the syrup still seeping across her tile, and she did not, for a long moment, feel anything at all.

The phone in her hand buzzed.

A text. From a number that had no number, in the way certain numbers in her life had stopped having numbers.

Target: Lucas Deveraux. Location: Uptown Café, 1814 N. Damen. Window: 1100 to 1400. Objective: Recover assets. Eliminate.

Beneath the text, a photograph.

The photograph was a tight zoomed-in image of a man at a small marble table by a café window, in mid-sip of a latte. He was in his mid-thirties. Slick suit. Expensive watch. He was looking at his phone and his face was the face of a man who had not slept in six nights and had not yet decided whether to admit, even to himself, that he was running for his life.

The photograph was time-stamped *eleven seconds ago.*

They were watching him right now.

Lana looked at the photograph for a long, long time.

She did not, she realized, see a target.

She saw a man who looked exactly like Marlon Kade had looked in the bar last night, in the moments before Marlon Kade had made the choice that had killed him. Lucas Deveraux had the same posture. The same constant sideways flicker of the eyes. The same hunched shoulders of a man who had finally understood what kind of room he had been sitting in, all this time, and who had only just now, far too late, started looking for the door.

Lucas Deveraux was about to die in approximately three hours. He was going to die whether Lana showed up or not. He was going to die whether Lana said yes to Mr. Halloran or said no. He was going to die because he had taken something that did not belong to him, and the people who owned that thing had, two minutes ago, called the contractor they intended to use to clean him up, and the contractor they intended to use to clean him up was Lana, and Lana was not going to do it.

Which meant that, if Lana did not go to the café, Lucas Deveraux was going to die at the hands of whoever Mr. Halloran sent next.

And if Lana did go to the café, Lucas Deveraux had a chance.

She set the phone down on the workbench. She looked at the photograph one more time. She took a deep, slow breath.

"Pixel," she said.

Pixel, who was now working at a strand of dried syrup on his paw, ignored her.

"Pixel," she said again. "I'm going to do something stupid."

Pixel licked his paw.

"I am going to go to a café," Lana said, "and I am going to not kill a man. And I am going to hope very hard that a different person, who is allegedly me, doesn't show up in the meantime."

She said this out loud to her cat, in her kitchen, at twenty after seven in the morning, and the words sounded, in her own ears, like the kind of sentence a person heard themselves say in the moment just before their life stopped being the thing it had been.

She left the syrup on the floor.

She left the pancakes on the counter.

She did not, this time, take the pouch.

She put on her dark hoodie and her best running shoes and the keys to her car, and she left the apartment, and she did not look back, and the burner phone, in the pocket of her hoodie, buzzed once more before she made it down the stairs.

She did not check it.

She already knew what it said.

Failure is not an option.

She started the car and pulled out into the cold morning, and the city, indifferent and full of people who did not know her name or any of her names, opened up in front of her like a long, patient mouth.

Chapter 4: Oat Milk and Assassins

The Uptown Café occupied the ground floor of a renovated brownstone on the kind of leafy north-side street that real estate listings described as *charming, walkable, and lovingly preserved.* It had a hand-painted sign, brass-rimmed front windows, three small wrought-iron tables on the sidewalk, and the kind of menu where every drink came with a small adjective in front of it. *The artisan latte. The mindful matcha. The intentional cortado.*

It was, Lana thought, exactly the kind of café where a man who had stolen millions of dollars from a global criminal enterprise would absolutely go to wait for somebody.

She was parked across the street and half a block down, in her own beat-up Honda Civic, the hood of her dark grey sweatshirt up, a paper cup of gas-station coffee gone cold on the dash. She had been there for an hour and twenty minutes. She had watched the morning crowd come and go. She had watched a young woman walk a small white dog past her car five separate times in increasingly dramatic outfits, which Lana suspected meant either the woman was on a long phone call or the dog was lying about needing to go out. She had counted twenty-three patrons enter the café and seventeen leave it. She had eaten one granola bar from her glove compartment, which had expired in 2022 but tasted essentially the same as a granola bar would have tasted in 2022, which was to say, not great.

She was also doing her best not to look at the man through the front window.

Lucas Deveraux was at a small marble table by the window, just as he had been in the photograph Mr. Halloran had sent her. He was wearing the same slick suit. He was wearing the same expensive watch. He was on the same untouched latte, although the latte's foam had collapsed into a sad beige film at some point in the last forty minutes.

He was not, as far as Lana could see, doing anything criminal.

He was checking his phone. He was setting his phone down. He was picking the phone back up. He was looking out the window at every car that passed. He was staring blankly at the door every time the bell over it rang. He was the worst stakeout subject Lana had ever observed, and Lana, in her professional capacity, had observed several, including one CFO who had embezzled three million dollars from a logistics firm and who had been, at the moment of his arrest, hiding in an Olive Garden.

Lucas Deveraux was a man waiting for someone to save him.

Lucas Deveraux was, unfortunately, going to be saved by Lana, and Lana was not feeling especially saved-up that morning.

She watched him pick up his phone for the eighth time. She watched him put it down. She watched him take a sip of the latte, grimace, and put the cup down. She watched him glance over his shoulder at the door, and then, in a small, jerky motion, glance over his other shoulder at the kitchen pass.

He was not waiting on a coffee date. He was looking for exits.

Okay, Lucas, Lana thought. *I see you. You see you. Everyone in this café has, at this point, seen you. That makes the next ninety minutes interesting.*

A meter maid in a small white truck rolled up alongside her car and tapped on the window.

Lana, who had grown up in Chicago and who knew a great many things about how to live her life but who had never once successfully argued with a Chicago parking enforcement officer, rolled down her window with the bright apologetic smile of a person who had never broken a single law in her entire life.

"Move it along, sweetheart," the woman said. "You can't sit in a residential zone for an hour and a half."

"Of course," Lana said. "Sorry, I was just, uh, waiting for a friend."

"Wait somewhere else."

Lana started the car. She drove around the block. She parked, illegally, in a loading zone half a block in the opposite direction, where she had the worse angle but, critically, no immediate meter maid.

Her burner phone vibrated in the center console.

She picked it up, flipped it open, and looked at the screen.

It was a new photograph. Lucas Deveraux. At his table. Sipping his latte. Time-stamped *forty-one seconds ago.*

Below the photo, five words. *Failure is not an option.*

Lana looked up sharply at the café window. From this new angle, she could see Lucas's table at a shallower oblique. She could see the patrons around him. She could see the man in the dark green jacket sitting at the table directly behind Lucas's left shoulder, who had a phone in his hand and who had not, in the time Lana had been watching, looked at his phone except to take a single, well-framed photograph of the back of Lucas Deveraux's head.

The man with the phone, whose face Lana now memorized in the half-second before he looked back down at the table, was not eating. He had a coffee in front of him. He had a small leather portfolio case open beside it, in the manner of a businessman pretending to take notes. The portfolio case was open just enough to show a sliver of black metal under the leather flap that had no business being inside a leather portfolio case.

There was a second man at a table on the other side of the café, near the kitchen pass. He was reading a newspaper. He had not turned a page in the time Lana had been watching. His coffee, like the first man's coffee, was full.

They had been here longer than Lana.

They were not waiting for Lucas to leave. They were waiting for *Sophia* to arrive, and for Sophia to do her work, and then they were going to clean up after Sophia, the way professional crews cleaned up after expensive contractors who could not be trusted to handle the disposal of their own targets without leaving fingerprints.

Lana, sitting in her illegal Civic in her loading zone, with the burner phone on her thigh and the photo of Lucas Deveraux still glowing on its tiny screen, had the small, unwelcome epiphany that her plan, which was to *observe and improvise,* had a serious flaw, which was that her plan was *observe and improvise.*

She made a small frustrated sound.

She zipped her hoodie up to her chin.

She got out of the car and crossed the street.

* * *

The bell over the Uptown Café's door went *ding* in a way that, to Lana's nervous ear, sounded like a church bell at a funeral.

She did not look at Lucas. She did not look at the man with the portfolio. She did not look at the man with the newspaper. She walked, with the casual unhurried air of a woman who had been here a hundred times, up to the counter, and she ordered the largest available coffee, black, and she did not, when the barista asked her if she wanted oat milk, immediately answer.

She was thinking about the layout of the café.

The café was long and narrow. The counter ran along the right-hand wall, with the espresso machines and the pastry case and the two visible employees behind it. The tables were on the left, in two rows: the window-side row with five small marble two-tops, and the inner row with four larger four-top tables. Lucas was at the third window table from the front. The man with the portfolio was at the fourth window table, directly behind Lucas. The man with the newspaper was at the inner table closest to the kitchen pass. There was a third employee in the back, visible through the pass, doing something to a tray of muffins.

Three civilians at other tables. A woman on a laptop. Two college-aged guys sharing a plate. A young mother with a stroller and a toddler.

The toddler complicated things.

"Ma'am? Oat milk?"

Lana refocused. "Yes, please. Lots of it. And, um, can you put it in a separate cup? On the side? My stomach's been weird."

The barista, a kid with three nose rings and the patient face of a person who had heard far worse requests at this counter, nodded and reached for a small carafe.

Lana paid in cash. She tipped well. She accepted her enormous black coffee, hot enough to feel through the cardboard sleeve, and the small separate cup of oat milk, also hot, in the careful pressed-paper cup.

She walked, slowly, with one cup in each hand, toward Lucas Deveraux's table.

This was, she reflected, the moment her plan committed.

She had, walking up to the counter, run through the entire sequence in her head, the way she walked her students through forms before a tournament. Step 1: Intercept. Step 2: Escalate the distraction. Step 3: Non-lethal force, applied to the assets first, the muscle second. Step 4: Disarm and extract.

It was a clean four-step plan. It had the rare advantage of being possible. It had the disadvantage of requiring her to start it by tripping over a four-year-old.

She walked past the stroller.

She made a small, theatrical, well-rehearsed *whoops.*

The cup of oat milk left her hand.

Hot oat milk arced through the air with the kind of slow-motion grace that only oat milk possessed, because oat milk was thicker than dairy milk and behaved, in flight, more like a sauce. The arc cleared the stroller, cleared the toddler, cleared the table belonging to the two college kids, and landed in a startlingly precise splash directly across the open leather portfolio of the man at the fourth window table.

The man, who had been pretending to take notes, stood up so fast his chair tipped backward into the table behind him. His shirt was beige. His shirt was now also beige in some places and hot-oat-milk-translucent in others. The leather portfolio was, in his lap, beginning to ooze.

"What the.."

"OH MY GOD, I am SO sorry," Lana said, in the voice of a woman whose worst day was now, she insisted, his day. She was already moving. She was already at the table, the napkin holder in her hand, tearing napkins out of it with ferocious helpful energy. "Oh my god, oh my GOD, I am the worst, I tripped, I literally tripped on absolutely nothing, oh my god is that *leather*, I ruined your *leather*.."

She was pressing napkins against the portfolio. She was, in the same motion, tilting the portfolio toward herself just enough to look inside it for the half-second it took her brain to confirm what she had suspected.

It was a Glock 19. It was in a custom foam cutout. It was, helpfully for the man, threaded for a suppressor.

Step One: Intercept.

She had successfully intercepted.

"Just step away," the man was saying, his hand already moving toward the portfolio's inner flap. "Just step away, ma'am, I will handle this.."

Lucas Deveraux, two feet behind the man, had stopped sipping his latte. He was watching the scene unfold with the wide-eyed, slow horror of a man who had just realized that the tablecloth in front of him had a pattern that, when you looked at it for long enough, became a face.

Lana's eyes flicked to Lucas. Her right hand was still flapping napkins. Her left hand was now, casually, wrapped around the heavy ceramic sugar dispenser at the corner of the man's table.

Step Two: Escalate the distraction.

She raised the sugar dispenser, in apparent helpful frantic chaos, and brought it down on the man's table with a gesture that was supposed to be *dabbing at the spill* and was actually *spinning the dispenser one full rotation.* The lid, which had been loose, flew off. White granular sugar erupted across the table, the man's lap, and the leather portfolio.

The man made a noise of pure animal grievance.

"Oh my GOD," Lana said, "oh my GOD I'm not even, this is not, I am having such a bad day.."

Behind her, the second man, the one with the newspaper, had stood up. She saw him in her peripheral vision. He was moving along the inner row of tables. His right hand was sliding inside his jacket.

She did not turn to look at him.

She turned, instead, to Lucas, and in a voice loud enough that everyone in the café heard it but pitched in the panicked register of a customer apologizing for a spill, she said, "Sir, I am so sorry, can I get you anything, do you need to step away from this disaster zone, I am literally a walking, oh my god, are you okay.."

She locked eyes with him.

She held the eye contact for one full second.

She mouthed, very clearly, the single word *RUN.*

Lucas Deveraux's face, which had gone from confusion to wide-eyed horror to wide-eyed comprehension in three seconds, did the thing she needed it to do. His brain, which had been waiting for this signal for six bad nights, accepted the assignment. He pushed back from his table. He stood up. He turned. He did not, mercifully, run *into* anything. He ran, in a ducking, half-crouching scramble, toward the kitchen pass at the back of the café.

The man with the newspaper, three tables away, broke into a sprint after him.

The man with the portfolio, oat-milk-soaked and sugar-crusted, drew his Glock.

Lana, standing two feet from him, holding a still-very-hot eighteen-ounce coffee, did the thing the thing required.

Step Three: Non-lethal force.

She turned her wrist and dumped the contents of the cup directly onto the man's gun hand and forearm.

The coffee hit him in a solid hot column from his wrist to his elbow.

The man's hand did not magically open. The man's fingers did not loosen. The hot coffee did not, in some Hollywood way, disable him. What it did was something more specific, more medical, and more ugly. It triggered an involuntary reflexive contraction of the muscles in his hand and forearm in response to acute thermal injury. His grip tightened, hard, then, in the next half-second, when his nervous system caught up to the actual heat of the burn, his entire hand spasmed open.

The Glock dropped.

It dropped because his hand had no choice.

The man bellowed and clutched his forearm, and the Glock hit the floor between them, and Lana stepped on it, hard, and slid her foot backward, sending the gun skidding under the next table where a college kid was now staring at it with an expression of pure existential bafflement.

The man, in genuine pain, swung at her with his uninjured left hand.

Lana ducked. She caught his wrist as it came past, redirected the punch downward, and as his weight shifted forward, she pivoted her hips and used his own momentum to flip him over the small marble table. He crashed into the window glass, did not break it, but bounced off it with the satisfying *whoomp* of a man who had not braced for a window. He slid down to the floor in a heap of sugar and oat milk and ruined leather.

She turned, fast, toward the back of the café.

The man with the newspaper had reached the kitchen pass. Lucas Deveraux had made it through. The third employee, the one who had been doing something to muffins, had vanished, presumably out the back. The man with the newspaper was now in pursuit, his right hand inside his jacket, moving with the efficient gait of a man who had done this before and who knew that the kitchen exit only led to one alley and that he could intercept his target there.

Lana grabbed the broom.

The broom was leaning against the wall by the pastry case, where the barista had, in some happier moment of the morning, been sweeping. It was a long-handled push broom, restaurant-grade, stiff bristles, solid hardwood handle. Lana grabbed it with both hands and ran.

Step Four: Disarm and extract.

She caught up with the man with the newspaper just as he was passing through the kitchen pass. She did not have time for grace. She did not, in this moment, have any of her dojo's measured technique left in her toolkit. What she had was a six-foot wooden pole and the muscle memory of a third-degree black belt who had, over the last eighteen years, been hit in the face with a six-foot wooden pole more times than she cared to count.

She brought the broom around in a wide horizontal sweep at the height of his left ankle.

The man's left foot came up in the middle of his stride. The broom handle caught his ankle on the upswing and continued its travel. His ankle, now redirected sideways with the full momentum of his stride, pulled his entire body off-balance. He stumbled. His shoulder hit the door frame of the kitchen pass.

She did not give him the half-second he needed to recover.

She reversed the broom and brought the butt of the handle, hard, into the back of his right knee. The same strike she had used on Marlon Kade the night before. Different man, same joint, same outcome. His leg buckled. He went down on one knee. As he came down, his right hand finally cleared his jacket, and a Glock 19, identical to the first one, came up in his fist.

Lana brought the bristle end of the broom around in a sharp arc and slapped the gun out of his hand.

It clattered into the kitchen, somewhere out of sight.

The man, now disarmed, on one knee, half through a doorway, looked up at her.

He was not panicked. He was assessing. He was, even kneeling, calculating his next move. He was, she understood with a small cold wave at the base of her spine, a professional, and the broom and the slip-and-fall were not going to work on him a second time.

She did not let him have a second time.

She brought the broom handle around and drove the butt, with both hands, into his chin in a clean rising strike. His head snapped back. The back of his skull connected with the door frame of the kitchen pass. His eyes did the slow roll-up of a man whose nervous system had elected to take a recess.

He slumped forward against the door frame.

Lana stood over him, breathing hard, the broom still in her hands, in a kitchen pass full of muffin trays, with her hood up and her heart somewhere in her throat.

She stepped over the man.

She walked, quickly, through the kitchen, past the abandoned muffins, past the open back door, and into the alley.

* * *

The alley behind the Uptown Café smelled, predictably, of cooking grease, dumpster, and the particular sharp wet smell of Chicago alley in late spring. The pavement was slick. The morning was overcast. A delivery van was parked at the far end. There were two large green dumpsters. There was a fire escape ladder hanging down from the second floor of the brownstone, and there was, between the dumpsters and the fire escape, Lucas Deveraux, doubled over with his hands on his knees, gasping like a man who had not run more than ten consecutive steps since he was fifteen.

There was also, six feet from Lucas, a woman in a black tank top and tactical pants, standing very still, with a pistol in a low ready hold.

Lana stopped short.

The woman was facing her.

The woman had Lana's face.

She had Lana's face the way Lana had Lana's face, which was to say, with the perfect, identical correctness that came from sharing a zygote. Same nose. Same eyes. Same line of the jaw. Slightly shorter hair, cut shorter and harder, and a thin pale scar through the left eyebrow that Lana did not have, and a kind of way of standing that Lana absolutely did not have. The woman did not stand the way Lana stood. The woman stood the way a knife stood when it was leaning against a wall, point down, balanced, capable at any moment of doing the thing knives did.

The woman's eyes met Lana's eyes.

Something in Lana's chest came open.

It came open in a way she had not expected, in a way she had not prepared for, in a way that her therapist, several years ago, had once described as *the body remembering things the mind has chosen not to.* It came open and a single, clean, completely unbidden phrase rose up in her throat from somewhere very deep, in a voice that was not quite hers, in a voice that was, she realized with a jolt, a voice from her dream:

Bet you can't catch me, Lana.

Lana said, very quietly, "You."

The woman closed her eyes for one second.

When she opened them, her face was the iron face of a professional, and her voice was the iron voice of a professional, and the professional was, very obviously, furious.

"You absolute, total, walking disaster," Sophia Harper said, "of a sister."

Lana's mouth made a few unsuccessful attempts at words.

Behind her, in the kitchen, somebody was groaning.

Behind Sophia, at the far end of the alley, an engine started.

Sophia's eyes flicked, fast and professional, over Lana's shoulder. Then over her own. Then she said, in a clipped voice that brooked no argument, "Get him in the car. Now."

"Whose car.."

"Mine. End of the alley. Black sedan. MOVE, Lana."

Lucas, who had been listening to this exchange with the slack-jawed expression of a man being introduced to a parallel universe, started moving. Lana grabbed his elbow and pulled him along. Sophia did not turn her back on the alley mouth where the engine had started. She walked, smoothly, backward, her pistol still in low ready, sweeping the corner.

The black sedan was a four-year-old Lincoln, exactly the kind of car nobody noticed, parked exactly where Sophia had said it would be. Lana wrenched the back door open and shoved Lucas in. She started to climb in after him, then thought better of it, and got into the front passenger seat instead. Sophia slid into the driver's side, dropped the pistol into a holster in the center console with one fluid motion, and put the car in gear.

The engine at the other end of the alley revved. A black SUV nosed in around the corner, blocking the exit Sophia had been driving toward.

"Hold on," Sophia said.

She put the car in reverse.

The Lincoln shot backward down the alley at a speed Lana would not have previously believed a sedan could achieve in reverse. Lana, who had not yet buckled her seatbelt, was thrown forward into the dash and then sideways into the door. Lucas, in the back, made a sound that was less a word and more a small whistling exhalation.

Sophia hit the alley's far entrance going forty miles an hour in reverse, swung the wheel hard, used the parking brake to slide the rear end around in a textbook backward J-turn, and was, twenty seconds later, doing fifty miles per hour the right way down a residential street that had not, until that moment, expected to host a chase scene.

The black SUV came out of the alley behind them and accelerated.

Lana found her seatbelt.

"Okay," she said, in a voice that was higher and faster than she had intended, "okay, hi, hello, I have a lot of questions."

"Save them."

"You are alive."

"Yes."

"You are my sister."

"Yes."

"You have been alive my entire life."

"...yes."

"What in the absolute, hammered, baked, slow-roasted Christ.."

"Lana," Sophia said, and her voice had a hard edge that cut Lana off mid-rant, "I will explain everything. I will explain everything you have ever wanted explained. But right now, my entire life is on fire because you are wearing my face, and there is an SUV behind us, and we have approximately two minutes before they shoot the tires out, and I need you to be useful instead of cathartic."

Lana stared at her sister.

Her sister stared at the road.

Lucas, in the back, in a small voice, said, "...I'm Lucas."

"Hi, Lucas," Sophia said, without taking her eyes off the road. "Lana, the bag at your feet."

Lana reached down. There was a tactical bag in the footwell. She pulled it up onto her lap.

"Side pocket," Sophia said. "Caltrops. Open the window. Throw a handful behind us. Aim for the lane."

"...caltrops?"

"Caltrops. Little metal jacks. Don't argue."

Lana opened the side pocket. There were caltrops. They looked exactly like the caltrops she had read about in middle-school books on medieval warfare, which was an aesthetic detail she did not have time to appreciate. She powered the window down, twisted in her seat, and flung a generous handful out the back at a slightly upward angle.

She heard, three seconds later, the satisfying multiple *bangs* of an SUV's tires meeting four-pointed steel objects designed by a thousand years of military tradition to do exactly that.

The SUV slewed sideways. Smoke began pouring from its right rear wheel well.

"Oh," Lana said, with genuine delight, "oh, that's *fun*."

"Try not to enjoy it."

"I will not try."

Sophia, who had not, since she had picked Lana up at the alley, taken her eyes off the road, made a small sound that, in another woman, might have been the very front edge of a laugh. In Sophia, it was as close as it had ever come.

The Lincoln took the next corner at speed, then the corner after that, then a third, and within four minutes they were on a parkway heading north out of the city, with the SUV nowhere in their rearview.

Lana exhaled, slowly.

She put her hands flat on her thighs.

She turned her head and looked, for the first time properly, at her sister.

Up close, in profile, Sophia was both exactly Lana and entirely not Lana. Same face. Different posture. Different musculature. A long, faded scar on her left forearm. A fresher gash along the same arm, half-bandaged. Hands that were calloused in places Lana's hands were calloused, but more so. Eyes that were Lana's eyes but had seen things.

Sophia, without looking at her, said, quietly, "I missed you."

Lana's throat closed.

She did not, for several seconds, trust her voice.

When she did, all she could get out was: "...me too."

Sophia's hands tightened on the wheel. She did not look over.

Lucas, in the back, who had been watching this exchange with the held breath of a man who had been told he could not breathe yet, finally exhaled.

"...I am so confused," he whispered, to nobody in particular.

Sophia, eyes on the road, voice flat: "Welcome to the family, Lucas."

Lana turned her face to the window and tried very hard not to cry.

She did not, in fact, cry.

She just sat with her sister on a parkway heading north out of Chicago, with a stranger she had saved in the back seat, and a million dollars she had not earned in the apartment they were not going back to, and a man named Mr. Halloran, somewhere, learning that his contractor had not, after all, done her job.

The city, behind them, kept being the city.

The Lincoln kept going.

Chapter 5: The Kill Switch

The Lincoln crossed into the suburbs on autopilot the way a horse heads back to the barn, except the driver was Sophia Harper and the barn was, on principle, never the same place twice.

Sophia had been driving for eleven minutes without speaking. Her hands were at ten and two on the wheel. Her eyes were doing the thing Lana had only ever seen done by professional drivers and a particular breed of paranoid uncle: a continuous slow scan from the rearview to the passenger mirror to the road to the driver's mirror, every two seconds, like a metronome, in a pattern so steady that Lana had begun to find it soothing in spite of itself.

Lucas, in the back seat, had his head down between his knees and was practicing what appeared to be a yoga breathing exercise that he had perhaps last performed in a college wellness seminar. Every few breaths he made a small high sound that was not quite a whimper.

Lana, who had run out of things to say at *I missed you,* was watching the speedometer.

The speedometer was steady at four miles per hour over the limit. Not so much over that they would draw attention, not so little under that they would draw attention. Sophia drove the way Sophia did everything else, which was with the unblinking precision of a person who had been told at age twelve that mistakes were how people died, and who had taken that lesson to heart in a thoroughly unhelpful way.

"Where are we going?" Lana finally said.

"Not my safehouse."

"Why not?"

"Because it's mine."

"...I am going to need you to expand on that, Sophia."

Sophia's eyes flicked to the mirror. Flicked to the road. Flicked to the mirror again.

"I have six properties in this city," she said. "Three I would call safehouses. Two I would call boltholes. One is a maintenance shed that is technically a coffee table on top of a hatch, but it counts. I will burn through one of the boltholes today. I will not burn the safehouse. The safehouse is the one place in this city that nobody, on any side of any equation, is supposed to know exists. If I take you there, then you know it exists. If you know it exists, then anyone who watches you knows it exists. And in approximately one hour, there is going to be a great deal of professional attention on what you know and do not know, Lana. So no. We are not going to my safehouse."

Lana absorbed this.

"...you have six properties."

"I have six properties."

"In this city alone."

"In this city alone."

"I rent. I rent a one-bedroom over a Thai restaurant."

"I am aware."

"...you've been to my apartment?"

"Three times. The deadbolt is good. The window above the fire escape is not. You have a leak under the kitchen sink that is going to be expensive in about six months. Pixel has gained weight."

Lana stared at her.

"Eyes on the road," Sophia said, calmly, even though her own eyes had not left the road.

Lucas, in the back, made another small sound.

Lana opened her mouth to say something, possibly several somethings, when Sophia's eyes did a thing in the rearview that they had not, until that moment, done. The slow steady scan went sharp. The hands at ten and two tightened a quarter inch.

"Lana," Sophia said, in a voice that had gone, in the space of half a syllable, from conversational to operational, "I need you to look in the side mirror, casually, and tell me about the dark grey crossover at the back of the line."

Lana looked, casually, in the side mirror.

The dark grey crossover was four cars back. It was a Hyundai, or a Kia, or one of those other cars that was specifically engineered to be impossible to identify in a rearview at any distance. Two men in the front seats. The driver was wearing sunglasses on an overcast day. The passenger had his right hand resting on the dashboard, palm down, the way a man rested his hand on the dashboard when he had a sidearm in a thigh holster and did not want it to print against his jacket while he sat down.

"How long have they been with us?"

"Eight minutes. They picked us up two blocks after the parkway. They are not Stanton's first team. Stanton's first team is the SUV we left behind at the caltrops. These are second-tier, but they are competent."

"How can you tell?"

"Because the first team would have already tried something. These are pacing. They want to know where we are going more than they want to take us off the road."

"...so we don't let them know where we're going."

"Correct."

"Cool. Cool cool cool. What's the plan."

"The plan," Sophia said, "is the construction zone in three quarters of a mile. There is a half-finished overpass off Western. The contractor has been bankrupt for fourteen months. Nobody has poured concrete there since February. There are large concrete drainage pipes stacked along the south side of the work area that have been sitting there long enough to develop opinions. We are going to deposit some of those opinions onto the road. Get the bag. Open the side pocket again."

"More caltrops?"

"Different pocket. The black one."

Lana opened the black side pocket.

Inside was a small remote control, the kind that looked vaguely like a garage door opener, except that the casing was matte black and there were no labels on any of the buttons.

"...what does this do?"

"You'll see."

"Sophia. I love you. I have known you for fourteen minutes. I am going to need you to start telling me what the buttons on the magic box do."

Sophia, eyes still doing the metronome, said, "It triggers a small, shaped, professionally placed charge that I had Tomas put on the third pipe from the left in the second stack three days ago, when I started thinking it was about time someone needed to be chased through a construction zone. Press the red button when I tell you to press it. Not before."

Lana looked at the magic box.

"You," she said, slowly, "pre-positioned an explosive charge in a construction zone, three days ago, on the chance that you might someday need to chase someone through it."

"Yes."

"How many other charges have you pre-positioned in this city?"

"Lana."

"I'm just asking, as a citizen."

"Twenty-three," Sophia said. "Two of them in the parking garage of your dentist's office. Eyes on the road."

The Lincoln took the off-ramp at Western. The dark grey crossover took the same off-ramp four cars later. Sophia accelerated, smoothly, into the long divided street that paralleled the half-finished overpass. Construction barriers along the right shoulder. Orange cones. The skeleton of a viaduct rising up over the road in a forest of rebar and gray concrete.

Sophia clipped the first row of orange cones at fifty miles per hour. The Lincoln barely registered them.

The dark grey crossover followed.

Sophia braked, hard, and swung the wheel to the right. The Lincoln drifted, its rear end fishtailing politely, into the wide gravel access road that ran along the south side of the overpass project. The road was lined, on the right, by a long stack of unused concrete drainage pipes, each one about four feet in diameter and seven feet long, stacked in a pyramid configuration that, in better times, would have been steadied with chocks.

The chocks, Lana noticed, had been removed.

"Now, Lana. Now."

Lana pressed the red button.

The third pipe from the left, in the second stack, made a sound that was less an explosion than a polite, well-mannered *whump,* the sound of a charge designed by someone who knew exactly how much energy was required to do exactly one specific job. The shaped charge cut, cleanly, the rebar tie that had been holding the pipe in place. The pipe shifted half an inch. The pyramid above it, freed from its single point of structural integrity, paused.

Then the pyramid let go.

Concrete pipes the size of large dogs began to roll, with the gathering implacability of physics, down the gentle slope of the gravel access road, directly into the path of the dark grey crossover.

The dark grey crossover's driver had perhaps a second and a half to react. He swung the wheel hard to the left. The crossover went up onto two wheels, came down, and met the lead pipe with its right front quarter panel at thirty miles per hour. The pipe did not stop. The crossover did. There was an excellent crunching noise. The crossover slammed sideways into the concrete pillar of the half-built overpass and caved its passenger side in by approximately a foot.

Lana watched this in the side mirror.

Lana said, "Holy shit."

"Two more minutes," Sophia said. "There's a second car."

"There is always a second car."

"Yes. There is always a second car. Lana, I am going to need you to stop reacting and start observing. There is a black Toyota Highlander coming up our six o'clock. He has been trailing the grey at a hundred yards. He is now closing. He is closing fast. There is a service path under the overpass at the next gap in the pillars. The Highlander cannot fit. We can. Tell me when you can see him in the mirror."

Lana looked.

The black Toyota Highlander was closing fast, having decided, at the moment the grey crossover met its concrete pipe, that the time for pacing had ended.

"I see him."

"How far?"

"Eighty yards."

"Tell me when he's at fifty."

"...seventy. Sixty. Fifty."

Sophia did not slow down.

Sophia, accelerated, and at the moment the Lincoln approached a small gap in the line of concrete pillars, she swung the wheel hard to the right and the Lincoln shot, with about three inches of clearance on either side, between two concrete pillars and out onto a paved service path on the far side of the overpass. The path was a single lane wide. It had a low concrete barrier on each side. It dipped down into a service tunnel that ran under the overpass and came out, three hundred yards later, in the parking lot of a darkened, abandoned big-box store that had once been a Toys R Us.

The black Highlander, having been built for soccer mothers rather than tight-fit smuggling, did not make the gap.

Lana heard the sound of a Highlander failing to fit between two concrete pillars at fifty-five miles per hour. It was a sound she had not previously had occasion to hear. It was not a sound she would forget.

The Lincoln came out of the service tunnel into the cracked, weedy expanse of the abandoned Toys R Us parking lot. Sophia drove, slowly now, around the side of the building, past a graffitied loading dock, and up to a service entrance gate in a chain-link fence that, despite appearances, opened smoothly under the touch of a small black device Sophia produced from her pocket.

The fence closed behind them.

They were in the lower level of a parking garage attached to the abandoned Toys R Us, a level which, Lana noted, did not appear on any map she could remember of this part of the city.

Sophia killed the engine.

The garage was lit by a single buzzing fluorescent strip three rows over. The air smelled of damp concrete. Somewhere, a drip.

Nobody spoke.

The Lincoln's engine, cooling, made the small *tick-tick-tick* sound that engines made when they were collecting themselves after having been worked.

Sophia turned in her seat, slowly, and faced the back.

She looked at Lucas Deveraux.

Lucas Deveraux, who had been, for the last seven minutes, doing the yoga breathing with growing intensity, looked up.

Sophia said, "Talk. Now."

* * *

Lucas talked.

Lucas talked the way a man talked when he had been waiting for six months to talk, the way a man talked when the inside of his head had been a single, very loud, single-occupancy speech for so long that as soon as he had a license to let it out, it came out all in one long unbroken paragraph that he could not, even when he tried, get all the way through without his own voice catching on itself.

He was a senior data analyst at Stanton Industries. He had been there for nine years. He had started in their Chicago office as a junior associate doing forensic accounting on acquisition targets. He had moved up to senior analyst after three years. Six months ago, on a Wednesday afternoon, he had been auditing a routine quarterly reconciliation between two of Stanton's offshore subsidiaries when he had noticed an anomaly. A six-figure discrepancy that should have been noise but was, on inspection, a clean repeating pattern. The pattern had a structure he recognized from a fraud case study he had read in graduate school. He had pulled the thread. The thread had not stopped pulling.

The thread, as it turned out, was eleven years long.

Stanton Industries, the publicly-traded conglomerate where Lucas Deveraux had worked for nine years, had a network of seventeen offshore shell companies. Those shell companies had a network of two hundred and forty subsidiary entities. Those subsidiary entities had a network of approximately three thousand bank accounts in fourteen jurisdictions. Through that network, money flowed every day. Some of the money was legal. Most of the money was not. The money that was not legal came in from buyers Lucas had spent the last six months attempting, very carefully, to identify, and went out to sellers Lucas had spent the last six months attempting, very carefully, to also identify, and the buyers and the sellers were, with disturbing frequency, the same people, transacting with themselves through the network in patterns that, when you mapped them, formed a kind of accidental confession on the part of an entire criminal economy.

Lucas had mapped them.

Lucas had also, after about three months of mapping, started taking small amounts of money. Not for himself. He had kept ledgers. The small amounts were, in his head, evidence. He had moved them through a series of accounts of his own, in his name, with full documentation, with the intent that when he eventually went to the FBI, he could hand them not just the records but the seized funds. He had thought of it as an exhibit. He had thought of it as proof of intent.

He had also, in the act of taking the money, made noise that the people running the system noticed.

Six weeks ago, his immediate supervisor had stopped meeting his eyes in the elevator.

Four weeks ago, his desk had been searched while he was at lunch.

Two weeks ago, his cat had been killed.

Lucas's voice, when he said this, did the thing voices did. He had, he said, found the cat outside his apartment door in a small white box with a note that said, in printed block letters, *SEE? WE CAN COME INTO YOUR BUILDING.* He had sat on his bathroom floor for two hours. Then he had stood up. He had gone to his apartment safe. He had taken out the small black flash drive. He had taken out a small Glock 19 he had bought, illegally, in a parking lot on the South Side, six months earlier, in a moment of extremely bad judgment that he had immediately regretted and had also, since the cat, stopped regretting. He had packed a single small bag. He had not gone home for nine nights. He had been waiting, this morning, in the Uptown Café, for an FBI contact to whom he had been promised an introduction by a journalist friend of his late mentor.

The journalist friend's name was Max King.

Sophia, who had been listening with the still focus of a sniper, said, very softly, "Max."

Lucas blinked. "You know him?"

"Of him. By reputation. He worked with my mother."

The car went quiet.

Lana, who had been listening to her sister's voice without entirely registering its content, registered it now. She turned her head, slowly, toward Sophia. "...what?"

"Later," Sophia said.

"You said.."

"I said *later,* Lana. Lucas. The flash drive. Where is it?"

Lucas reached, with hands that had gone less steady the longer he had talked, into his front trouser pocket and produced a key ring. On the key ring were three keys, a small fob for a Toyota, a little plastic Captain America shield, and a small black flash drive about the size of a thumbnail.

He held it out.

Sophia took it.

Sophia turned in her seat and held the flash drive out to Lana.

"Crack it," Sophia said. "Now."

Lana took the drive.

"I'm going to need a laptop, Sophia."

"Trunk."

"Of course it's in the trunk."

"Black hardshell case under the spare. The password is *fifteen.*"

"...fifteen."

"Fifteen."

Lana got out of the car.

In the trunk, under a clean spare tire, in a black hardshell case secured with a four-digit combination lock, was a laptop. It was a Lenovo ThinkPad in a configuration Lana had only ever seen in product photos for tactical contractors. It had a fingerprint reader, a smart card slot, and an externally visible kill-switch toggle on the side panel that physically disconnected the camera and microphone at the hardware level. It also had, Lana noticed when she opened it, a small custom sticker on the lid that read NOT YOUR DAD'S LAPTOP.

Lana made a small noise that was somewhere between a laugh and a hiccup.

She brought the laptop into the back seat next to Lucas, plugged in the flash drive, sat cross-legged on the seat, and got to work.

* * *

The drive's outer encryption was civilian-grade. AES-256, password-protected, with a perfunctory key file that Lucas had hidden, with touching innocence, in the system's recycle bin. Lana was through the outer layer in nineteen minutes.

The inner encryption was harder. It was layered. Lucas had taken what was clearly a pre-existing Stanton-internal encryption schema and wrapped his own additional onion of personal protection around it, with the result that Lana spent the next forty minutes doing a kind of forensic archaeology, peeling Lucas's amateur layers off the outside in order to reach the professional layers underneath.

The professional layers, when she got to them, made her stop typing.

"Sophia," she said, very quietly.

Sophia, who had been watching the garage entrance through the driver's-side mirror with the unblinking patience of a cat at a mousehole, looked over.

"What?"

"Come look at this."

Sophia got out of the driver's seat and slid into the passenger seat beside Lana. She leaned over the screen. Her shoulder brushed Lana's shoulder. It was the first time, Lana realized in a small distant part of her brain, that they had touched.

The screen was full of directories.

The directories were named in Stanton's internal filing convention. They had been pulled, in their entirety, from a Stanton corporate server that Lucas had, at some point in his six-month investigation, had administrative access to. They were mirrored. They were complete.

Lana clicked into the first one.

Inside the first directory was a sub-directory tree that, when she expanded it, contained two hundred and forty-one folders, one for each subsidiary entity, organized by jurisdiction. Inside each of those folders were sub-folders organized by year. Inside each of those, by quarter. Inside each of those, by transaction.

Lana opened one of the transactions, at random, and the screen filled with a single PDF: a wire transfer record, in clean corporate formatting, between two banks she had never heard of, for the amount of three million two hundred thousand U.S. dollars. The memo line read SECURITY CONSULTING SERVICES, NIGER DELTA. The recipient was a company named Black Crescent Logistics.

She closed the PDF. She opened another transaction. The memo line on this one read FACILITATION, KIEV. She closed that one. She opened a third. The memo line read PAYROLL, KARACHI EVENTS. She did not close that one. She read it.

She read all of it.

When she finished, she sat back, very slowly, against the door.

"Sophia," she said.

"I know."

"Stanton Industries doesn't just launder money."

"I know."

"Stanton Industries has a *human resources department* for assassins. Indexed by political district."

"I know, Lana."

"They have a *spreadsheet,* Sophia. They have a spreadsheet with payroll codes. There is a *401(k) line item* on this. There is a 401(k) line item for a category that Lucas has tagged in the next column as *terminations.* What does *terminations* mean in this spreadsheet, Lucas?"

Lucas, who had been holding his breath, said, in a small voice, "...not employee terminations."

"NO, LUCAS. NOT EMPLOYEE TERMINATIONS."

"Lana," Sophia said. "Quieter."

Lana exhaled, slowly, and put her hands on the laptop's keyboard, and pulled herself together with the discipline of a woman who had, eighteen years earlier at age eleven, learned how to put herself together in front of an audience of teenage boys at a regional tournament after losing a round badly.

She kept exploring.

She found, in the third directory, the politicians. Not bribery records, exactly, although bribery records were also in there. The deeper file was a kind of relationship registry. Forty-seven names of sitting U.S. members of Congress. Eighty-three names of state-level officials. Ninety-six federal regulators. Twelve sitting federal judges. Each entry contained financial records, photographic surveillance, transcripts of phone calls, and what was, in some cases, very clearly extortion documentation. Every entry had a status marker. The status markers were, with disquieting consistency, three-letter codes. *COP. CLT. ACT.*

"Cooperative. Compliant. Active asset," Sophia said, reading over her shoulder.

"You know these abbreviations."

"I know the people who use these abbreviations. Keep going."

Lana kept going.

She found the buyer registry. She found the seller registry. She found the maps. She found the coded shipping manifests that she did not, in the time available, have the cipher to break, but which she could, by their structure, identify as movement of goods that were not soybeans. She found a sub-directory labeled *FAMILY,* which she did not open, because Lucas, who had been peering over her other shoulder, made a choked noise and said, "Lana, please don't," and she trusted that small choked noise more than she trusted her curiosity.

She did, eventually, find the thing.

It was at the bottom of the file tree, in a directory that was not, like all the others, named in the corporate filing convention. It had no jurisdiction code. It had no quarter. It had no year. It had a single name, and the name was a single word.

aegis.

Inside *aegis* was a single file.

The single file was 2.7 megabytes. It was a binary. It was encrypted, separately, in a way that the other files in the drive were not encrypted. It had a different cipher signature.

Lana looked at it for a long time.

"What is it?" Sophia said.

"It's not a document."

"What is it?"

"It's executable code. It's a program."

"What kind of program?"

Lana opened a terminal window and ran a passive analysis on the binary. She did not run the binary. She did not do anything to it that would, in any way, suggest to it that it had been examined. She read its surface signatures the way a careful archaeologist read the outside of a sealed urn.

The signatures came back.

Lana said, "...oh."

"What?"

"Sophia."

"What."

"This is a self-replicating destructive payload. With network propagation. Designed to authenticate against a specific class of high-value enterprise systems and, on authentication, execute a series of cascading destructive operations. Account zeroing.

File system wipe. Inter-system propagation through specific authenticated trust relationships. This is a kill switch. This is *Stanton's* kill switch. They built it as a suicide pill in case they were ever truly compromised. If their network was about to be seized by hostile parties, they would deploy this thing internally and it would burn their own house down before anyone else could walk through it."

Sophia stared at the screen.

"And we have it," Sophia said.

"And we have it."

"...what does that mean?"

"It means," Lana said, slowly, working it out as she went, "that we are holding their nuclear deterrent. The thing they were going to use on themselves if they ever had to. Lucas, I don't know if you understand what you took. This is not the books. The books are bad. The books are, frankly, federal-prison bad. But this. This is the failsafe. This is what they built to make sure that even if the books got out, the books would never matter, because the network would no longer exist. And you stole it."

Lucas, in the back, said, quietly, "...I did?"

"You absolutely did."

"I didn't... I just downloaded the directory. I downloaded everything. I didn't know what was in everything. I just thought, get the whole drive, sort it later."

"Lucas. You walked into a bank vault and you stole the bank vault."

"...yeah?"

"Yes, Lucas. Yes."

Lana turned to Sophia.

"We can use this," she said. "This is everything. Stanton's whole network has trust relationships with the Council infrastructure. If we deploy this from inside their network, it cascades. Bank accounts frozen. Communications cut. Black sites exposed. The whole thing collapses on itself."

Sophia's eyes had narrowed.

"There has to be a catch," Sophia said.

Lana ran the analysis a second time. She ran it a third time. She read the binary's authentication signatures. She read the propagation specifications. She read the deployment requirements.

Then she sat back, again, against the door.

"There's a catch."

"Of course there's a catch."

"This is a hardware-authenticated payload. It does not propagate over the public internet. It propagates over Stanton's own internal high-trust network, which is air-gapped. It can only be activated from a primary server hub. A direct network interface. With a physical handshake. Which means that if I want to use this thing, I cannot launch it from this parking garage. I cannot launch it from a coffee shop. I cannot launch it from a rented satellite uplink. I can launch it, exclusively, from a chair, sitting at a console, plugged into a fiber jack, inside one of Stanton's hub facilities. With a smart card. That is presumably in the pocket of someone we will need to relieve of it."

Sophia smiled.

It was not a wide smile. It was not a warm smile. But it was, Lana realized, the first time her sister's mouth had moved in that direction in their entire reunion.

"That," Sophia said, "is not a catch."

"What is it?"

"That is an objective."

Lana looked at her.

Sophia looked back.

"Sophia," Lana said, "I am an IT consultant. I am very good at being an IT consultant. I am, I have been told by several people, unusually good. I do not, as a rule, break into the fortified server hubs of multinational criminal conglomerates in order to insert physical media."

"You will."

"...I will?"

"Yes."

"Why?"

"Because they put your face on the dark web."

Lana opened her mouth.

She closed it.

She thought about her father's voice on the phone that morning. She thought about Mr. Halloran, calmly putting a small velvet pouch on a bar. She thought about Marlon Kade, eyes wide, sweating through his shirt, sixteen minutes from being free. She thought about a woman in a low-cut dress whose elbow had caught a tray, and a kid with three nose rings, and the bell over a café door, and the small fact that she was sitting in a parking garage in an abandoned big-box store with a man named Lucas and a sister named Sophia, and that there was no version of the next twenty-four hours in which she went home.

There was no home, anymore. There was only what came next.

"Yeah," Lana said, slowly. "Okay. Yeah."

Sophia nodded once, a small soldier's nod, and turned back toward the front of the car.

She reached into the side pocket of her tactical bag and pulled out a granola bar.

She handed it back over the seat to Lana.

"Eat," she said. "You haven't since the pancakes."

Lana took the granola bar.

She looked at it.

It was an unbranded, dense, honey-colored bar of the kind that came in fifty-count boxes from some kind of restaurant supply company. Oats. Almonds. A scattering of dark, suspicious lumps that Lana, on closer inspection, identified as raisins.

She started to peel the wrapper open.

"Wait," Sophia said.

Lana looked up.

Sophia was looking at her with a strange, careful expression.

"Do you still hate raisins?" Sophia said.

Lana stopped.

The granola bar was in her hand. Her fingers had paused on the wrapper. She felt, somewhere deep in her chest, the smallest possible adjustment, the way a tuning fork tuned to a frequency it had not heard in a long time.

"...what?" she said.

"Raisins. Do you still hate them?"

"I, um." Lana looked at the bar. "I don't *hate* them. I don't seek them out. But I don't, I,why?"

Sophia was quiet for a long moment. She was looking out the windshield, at the dark concrete pillars of the parking garage, at the single buzzing fluorescent light three rows over. Her hands were very still on her thighs.

"You used to pick them out," Sophia said. "When we were small. Whenever Mom packed us cookies, or oatmeal raisin cookies, or a granola bar with raisins. You used to pick them out, one at a time, with your little fingers. You used to stack them in a line on the side of your plate, end to end, like soldiers. Mom called it your raisin army."

Lana did not breathe.

"You don't remember."

Lana's voice, when it came, was very small.

"No."

"I know."

Sophia did not look at her. Sophia did not, as far as Lana could tell, breathe either, for a long moment.

Then Sophia reached out, slowly, and took the granola bar out of Lana's hand. She unwrapped it. She used a thumbnail and a fingernail and worked, with the same delicate untroubled efficiency Lana had seen in everything else her sister did, the dense honey-colored body of the bar, and she picked the raisins out, one at a time, and laid them in a small line on the dashboard.

There were, in the end, eleven of them.

Lana watched the line of raisins.

Lana did not, at any point, look up at her sister.

She thought, with a clarity that was new and sharp and not at all welcome, that she had spent twenty-three years calling something *the dream,* and that the dream wasa memory, and that the memory had a smaller hand in it, and that the smaller hand had been her own hand, holding her *older* sister's hand, and that the older sister was Sophia, and that her name, the smaller voice in the dream, the voice that had said *Bet you can't catch me, Lana,* had been Sophia.

Sophia had been the one running.

Sophia, who at twelve had been smarter than anyone gave her credit for, who had heard the engine pull away and gone very still beside her at the edge of the lawn. Sophia, who at twelve had said

Lana, hold on to my hand. Don't let go. Sophia, who had said it in a voice that was a grown-up's voice in a child's mouth, because Sophia, at twelve, had already been the older one, the one who held the smaller hand, the one who carried the silence at the end of a long summer afternoon.

Lana had been six.

Lana had let go of the hand.

Lana, somewhere in the long blank space of being six, had let go, and had not remembered letting go, and had spent twenty-three years being told, by her own father, by her own therapist, by her own brain, that the smaller hand in her dream had been the hand of someone who had not survived.

The smaller hand had been Sophia's.

The hand that held it had been Lana's.

Sophia, the entire time, had been alive.

Lana lifted her head, slowly, and looked at her sister.

Sophia was looking at the line of raisins on the dashboard.

Sophia's eyes were wet.

Sophia did not, in any other way, make a sound.

Lana reached out across the center console, very slowly, the way a person reached out to a strange dog or a piece of glass on a table, and she put her hand on top of her sister's hand, and her sister's hand turned, slowly, palm up, and their fingers tangled together with the same easy unthinking knot they had not made since 2002.

Neither of them said anything.

In the back, Lucas Deveraux, who had been holding very still for a long time, looked at the ceiling of the Lincoln, and decided that whatever was happening in the front seat was not, at this particular moment, his to be a part of.

After a while, Sophia said, very quietly, "So we stop running."

It was not a question.

Lana said, "Yeah."

"We hunt them."

"Yeah."

"Together."

Lana, who at twenty-nine had spent twenty-three years not knowing what she had lost, who had spent twenty-three years dreaming of a smaller hand and a wrong kind of smoke, who had spent the morning lying to her father for the second time in her life and walking out of an apartment she would not, in any meaningful sense, return to, looked at her sister and squeezed her sister's hand.

"Yeah," she said. "Together."

The fluorescent light, three rows over, kept buzzing.

The Lincoln kept ticking.

The line of eleven raisins, on the dashboard, kept being a small army.

And somewhere, in a city they could not, yet, see, Mr. Halloran was standing in a hallway with a phone to his ear, listening to a man on the other end tell him that the contractor named Sophia had not, in fact, been the contractor named Sophia, and that the situation had, in light of this development, become significantly more interesting.

Mr. Halloran, on the phone, smiled.

He had never, in his career, particularly enjoyed easy work.

Chapter 6: The Devil's Bargain

The Lakefront Motor Lodge had been built in 1974, had not been renovated in 1984, had been re-carpeted exactly once in 1996 in a color that the carpet manufacturer had, at the time, optimistically called *harvest gold,* and was currently being run by a small, leathery man named Ed who took cash, asked no questions, and was so disinterested in the existence of his guests that he had not, in Sophia's experience, even looked up from his crossword puzzle when she had walked into the office to extend their stay.

It was the third place Lana had slept in less than thirty-six hours.

She was not, in any technical sense of the word, sleeping.

She was sitting cross-legged on the second of the two queen beds, with the tactical laptop balanced on her thighs, with three cell phones arrayed around her in a small constellation, and with the expression of a woman who had been awake for so long that she had passed through tired and into the peculiar second-wind clarity that lived on the other side of it. The motel room smelled of stale cigarette smoke from before the smoking ban, mildew from the bathroom, and the cheap floral air freshener Sophia had plugged into the wall in a futile attempt to render the previous two odors theoretical rather than ambient.

It was three in the afternoon.

Outside the window, a parking lot. Beyond the parking lot, a four-lane road. Beyond the four-lane road, a strip mall containing a shuttered Pizza Hut and a still-operational nail salon called *Glamour Tips*. Beyond the strip mall, the rest of the country.

Lana, on the bed, was running an analysis she had run nineteen times.

The analysis was simple. She had the kill switch. She had the structure of Stanton's network. She had a mental list of every primary server hub she could identify from the documentation, which numbered forty-three globally, distributed across three continents and a small number of tax-friendly islands.

What she did not have was a way in.

The hubs were not connected to the public internet. The hubs did not respond to any kind of remote authentication. The hubs were physical fortresses, and even if she somehow managed to get into one, she would still need a smart card, and the smart card would need to be a current credentialed card belonging to a human being whose biometric data was on file with Stanton's internal systems, and that human being was not going to hand the card over willingly.

She had been around this loop nineteen times.

The loop did not, on the twentieth pass, become any more open at the top.

"You are doing it again," Sophia said, from the small motel-issue armchair by the window, where she had been sitting for two hours with a paperback novel she was not reading and a pistol she was not pretending to hide.

"Doing what."

"The thing where you stare at the screen and your jaw clenches and you start doing the small cracking thing with your knuckles."

"I don't crack my.."

"You do."

"...I don't notice when I do."

"I know. You started doing it when you were four. Mom used to put your hands in oven mitts to stop you. It didn't work."

Lana's hands, which had in fact been doing the cracking thing, paused.

She set them down, palms-flat, on the laptop.

There was a small thing happening in her chest that had started happening in the parking garage and had not, since, entirely stopped. She had decided, somewhere in the last twenty-four hours, that she was not going to give it room. There was too much on the laptop. There was too much in the parking lot beyond the window. There was a man named Lucas Deveraux currently snoring on the floor of the motel bathroom, where he had insisted on sleeping because, in his words, the floor felt like a place an assassin would not necessarily look first. There was, in particular, a man named Henrik Vanek, somewhere in this city, currently on the phone to his employer, who was beginning to assemble, from the shape of the previous twenty-four hours, the small number of discrete and unwelcome conclusions he was professionally obligated to assemble.

Lana had decided that she would have feelings about her dead sister having spent twenty-three years not being dead, in a small, careful, parceled-out way, on a schedule, when the mission permitted.

Sophia, who knew Lana, was respecting the schedule.

For now.

"I have the weapon," Lana said. "I do not have a target. I do not have a way *to* a target. I have spent the last two hours looking at a piece of malware so beautiful it makes me cry, and I have no door to put it through."

"You will," Sophia said.

"How."

"Because in approximately seven minutes, a man is going to knock on this door, and the man is going to give us a door."

Lana looked up.

"...I'm sorry?"

Sophia did not answer. Sophia was looking, very steadily, at the window, where the angle of the curtain showed a small triangular slice of the parking lot, and where a tan Ford F-150 had, eleven minutes earlier, pulled into the spot three down from theirs and idled with its engine running for ninety seconds before the driver had killed it and gotten out.

The driver had not, since getting out, walked toward the motel.

The driver had, instead, walked across the lot to the strip mall, gotten a coffee from a self-serve kiosk inside Glamour Tips, walked back across the lot, and was now leaning against the side of his truck, drinking the coffee, in the posture of a man who had not yet decided whether this was the moment or not.

"That," Sophia said, "is the man."

"Sophia."

"Mm."

"Why did you not, at any point in the last two hours, mention that we were waiting for a man."

"Because I was not certain he would come. He was deciding. He has finished deciding."

"And he is."

"A complication."

"Sophia."

"He knew our mother."

Lana, who had not, in the last twenty-four hours, found a stable position from which the world stopped surprising her, looked at her sister for a long second, and understood, in a clean way understanding sometimes worked, that there was a layer to this morning that she had not yet been let into.

"You don't trust him."

"I trust him to do the next correct thing. I do not trust him to do the *third* correct thing, because the third correct thing tends to involve other people's secrets and his temper, and his temper has, historically, been a reliability problem."

"What's his name?"

"Declan."

"Just Declan?"

"Just Declan."

"...of course."

Outside, the man at the truck finished his coffee, set the empty cup on the hood, and started walking, slowly, toward the door of the motel.

His knock, when it came thirty seconds later, was three quick, then one slow.

Sophia got up from the chair.

She did not draw the pistol. She did, however, set the safety to off and set the pistol down on the small particle-board nightstand within easy reach, in plain view of whoever was about to walk through the door, with a unhurried gesture that communicated, in the universal language of tradecraft, *I am not pointing this at you, but I would prefer that we both be aware of where it is, so that nothing happens in the next minute that we both, later, regret.*

She opened the door.

Declan walked in.

He was a tall man, taller than the doorframe wanted him to be, and he ducked slightly out of habit as he crossed the threshold. He was wearing a faded charcoal henley under an unstructured grey jacket and dark jeans, and he carried himself with the compactness of a man whose body had learned, a long time ago, to apologize to nothing and to no one. His hair was salt-and-pepper, silvered at the temples, cut shorter on the sides than on top in the careless style of a man who had once cared about how his hair was cut and had stopped caring some time before the silver had arrived. He had a small, faded white scar that ran horizontally through the right eyebrow and another one that started at the corner of his mouth and disappeared into the salt-and-pepper stubble of his jaw.

He smelled, faintly, of cedar and gunpowder and the kind of cologne that had not been advertised on television since the Reagan administration.

He looked, first, at Sophia.

He took her in, slowly, top to bottom, with the thoroughness of a man taking inventory. His eyes paused on the bandage on her left forearm. His eyes paused on the pistol on the nightstand. His eyes paused on her face, and something complicated flickered there, and he closed his mouth around whatever the something complicated had been about to say.

Then he looked at Lana.

His mouth, which had been a flat line, did, at the sight of Lana, a small thing.

The small thing was not a smile.

The small thing was the prelude to a thing that, in a different room, in a different decade, in a different body, might have been a smile. The thing about Declan, Lana decided in that same half second, was that he had calluses on his face. Whatever had been a smile, on Declan, twenty years ago, had been wrapped up and put away and only sometimes, when nobody was looking, was allowed to come out and see if the muscles still worked.

"Christ," he said, softly. "You really do have the same face."

"You knew her," Sophia said. Not a question.

"I knew *her,*" Declan said. "Helena."

The word, in the close quiet of the motel room, landed like a small stone in still water.

Lana did not, for several seconds, breathe.

Helena, she thought, very carefully, the way a person turned a word over with their tongue to see if it was the word they had been looking for. *Helena. Helena.*

The name did not, on first hearing, do what she had expected. It did not unlock anything in her chest. It did not bring back her mother's face, the way she had, at moments, hoped a name might. It only rang, the way a bell rang in an empty room, and the ringing was not warm or cold, it was just there, a sound that her body recognized without recognizing.

She had not heard the name spoken out loud in twenty-three years.

Her father had never said it. Her father had said *your mother* and *Mom* and, once, when very drunk, *the love of my entire life,* but he had never, in Lana's hearing, said the name *Helena.*

It had not occurred to Lana, until that exact moment, that this was strange.

Declan was looking at her.

Whatever he saw on her face, he was reading correctly.

"You haven't," he said, gently, "heard her name in a while."

Lana's voice, when it came, was very small. "No."

He nodded once, the slow nod of a man for whom this was not, in any meaningful way, surprising news.

"Okay," he said. "Okay."

He sat down, uninvited, in the small motel-issue armchair Sophia had vacated. He did not look at the pistol on the nightstand. He did not look at the laptop. He sat, with his hands open and resting on his thighs in the posture of a man who had spent twenty-some years learning how to be in rooms where people were deciding whether to trust him, and he waited.

Sophia closed the door.

Sophia walked, slowly, around behind the pistol on the nightstand. She did not pick it up. She placed her hand near it, without theatrics, and she said, "How did you find us."

"I didn't," Declan said. "You found me."

"...explain."

"Three years ago I left a marker in a forum we both used to read. Specific kind of marker. The kind that pings me when somebody else who knew her uses one of three of her old protocols. You used one of hers about fourteen hours ago, in a private channel I haven't seen lit up since 2009. I checked the timestamp, I checked the location, I checked the shape of the way you used it. I knew it was you. I drove."

"From where."

"Madison."

Sophia processed this.

"You have," she said, "been three hours away. For three years."

"I have been three hours away for eleven years, Sophia."

Sophia's face did something that Lana, who had now been studying her sister's face for thirty-some hours with the increasingly accurate eye of a younger sister catching up, identified as the first thing that approximated genuine surprise. Lana had not, until that moment, been entirely sure her sister could be surprised.

"You should have told me," Sophia said.

"You weren't ready to be told."

"That was not your call."

"It was, actually, exactly my call," he said, mildly. "You and I, the last time we spoke, were standing over the body of a man named Pierre, in a hotel suite in Lisbon, and you were nineteen, and you told me, in extremely clear terms, that you did not want me near you, and that the only thing I was good for was getting people killed, and that if I came near you again, you would put a bullet in me yourself. You have, since then, been an extremely competent professional. I believed you would put a bullet in me. I left you alone. I have, periodically, tried to verify you were alive, and I have, every time I have tried, found you had moved a property and I had to start over. I respected the distance. Which was difficult, because Helena would have killed me, twice, with her own hands, for letting you do this without me."

The room, for a moment, was very quiet.

Sophia did not, for a long time, say anything.

When she did, it was in a voice that Lana had not, until that moment, heard from her sister at all.

"...Declan."

"Yeah."

"I was nineteen."

"You were."

"I was nineteen and I had just watched a man die."

"You had."

"I should not have said that to you."

"You should not have. You did. You were nineteen. I forgave you, in Lisbon, before you had finished saying it. I have continued forgiving you, in absentia, for eleven years. I am here now because Helena's other daughter,", he gestured, briefly, at Lana, "just got recruited, by a man named Henrik Vanek, into a contract she did not take, and the situation has, in my estimation, exceeded the limits of what one of you, even one of you as good as you, can do alone. I am offering you my services. You will pay me appropriately, because I am not anyone's volunteer. But the price will be extremely reasonable, because Helena, in 2002, paid for a year of my life when nobody else would, and I have not, to my satisfaction, paid her back."

Sophia's hand was no longer near the pistol.

Sophia's hand was flat on the nightstand. Her knuckles had gone pale.

"What do you bring," she said.

"I bring," Declan said, "twenty-two years of having been in rooms that you have only ever been outside of, and the names of fourteen hub facilities in three regional networks that I personally helped Marcus Stanton set up between 2003 and 2008, and the locations of three of those hubs that are not, currently, on any defensive footing, because Stanton is consolidating after a public incident in a hotel bar last night and is, over the next forty-eight hours, going to be more vulnerable than he has been in nine years. I bring you a door, Sophia. I bring you a door with a key in the lock and a lock that has not been changed in five years because the man who would have changed it died in 2019 and Marcus has been too cheap to replace him."

Sophia let out, slowly, a breath.

"Okay," she said.

"Okay?"

"Okay."

Lana, who had been trying for several minutes to follow the unspoken language of a conversation between two people who clearly had a 2002 and a 2008 and a 2019 that she was not, in any way, party to, finally cleared her throat.

"I'm Lana," she said.

Declan looked at her.

The thing his face had been preparing to do, twelve minutes ago, finally did it. He smiled. It was a small smile. It was a slightly creaky smile, in the way of a hinge that had not been used in a while. But it was, unmistakably, a smile.

"I know who you are, Lana," Declan said. "Your mother used to talk about you for hours. You were her favorite topic."

"...what?"

"She talked about both of you. But you, the little one, you were the funny one. You used to put raisins on the side of your plate. She thought it was the best thing anyone had ever done."

Lana's eyes, without her permission, started doing the thing eyes did. She turned her face, casually, toward the window. She did not, at any point, lift a hand.

Sophia, behind her, said, quietly, "Declan. Sit down with us. Tell me about the door."

* * *

The door, as Declan laid it out across the small fake-wood-grain table in the motel room over the next half hour, was not, technically, a door. The door was a freight transfer.

Stanton Industries, in the publicly-traded portion of its business, ran a global logistics and shipping operation that moved approximately fourteen percent of the chartered freight in and out of the Great Lakes region. The logistics operation was real. The logistics operation was, in fact, fully legitimate, in the sense that all of its ships were licensed, all of its drivers were vetted, all of its customs paperwork was filed, and all of its accounting was clean.

The accounting was clean because Stanton's actual dirty money did not move through the logistics operation.

What Stanton's dirty money did, instead, was move through the *server infrastructure* that supported the logistics operation. Every container that moved through Stanton's terminals had a digital manifest. Every digital manifest passed through a particular set of servers. Every set of servers, when the logistics operation grew too large for centralized handling in 2008, had been distributed across a small number of regional hubs. And every regional hub, in a piece of operational efficiency that had seemed clever to Marcus Stanton in 2008 and was now, in 2025, the single weakest point in the entire criminal architecture, also handled the routine cryptographic key rotation for the *rest* of Stanton's network.

Which meant, in plain terms, that if you sat in a chair at one of those hubs, with the right smart card, plugged into the right fiber jack, you were not just connected to a freight server.

You were connected to the entire trust relationship matrix of Stanton's actual business.

You were exactly where Lana needed to be in order to deploy a self-replicating destructive payload.

The chair, the smart card, and the fiber jack, Declan said, were currently sitting in a freight terminal on the Calumet River, on the south side of the city, in a building marked HARBOR LOGISTICS GROUP, TERMINAL 4. The terminal was scheduled, in approximately fourteen hours, to receive a shipment of forty-seven containers from a registered Stanton subsidiary out of Singapore. The shipment would arrive at nine in the evening. The shipment would be processed through the digital manifest system between nine and midnight. During those three hours, Stanton's own credentialed people would be cycling through the hub on a rotating basis, with their smart cards on lanyards around their necks, doing their normal jobs.

One of those people was named Carl.

Carl, Declan said, was a logistics shift manager, mid-fifties, with an alimony problem, a daughter at Northwestern, and a habit of stepping out the back of the terminal for a cigarette every forty minutes. Carl carried his smart card on a lanyard. Carl took the lanyard off when he smoked, because the lanyard's clip had a tendency to catch in the zipper of his jacket. Carl set the lanyard down on the railing of the loading dock when he smoked.

Declan had, Declan said, observed Carl smoking on the loading dock railing with his lanyard set beside him, on three separate visits, over the course of the previous six weeks.

"You," Sophia said, "have been observing a logistics shift manager named Carl, on a loading dock, on the south side of Chicago, for six weeks."

"It's been kind of relaxing, actually. Carl is a very predictable man."

"You did not, at any point in the last six weeks, think to call me."

"You weren't ready."

"Declan."

"Sophia. I am not picking the fight you are picking."

Sophia closed her eyes.

She opened them.

She said, "Lay out the rest."

Declan laid out the rest.

The rest involved a perimeter fence Lana could disable in under three minutes, a security hub Lana could loop in under five, a rotating exterior patrol of two two-person teams that Sophia and Declan could neutralize without lethal force in approximately ninety seconds, a side entrance that opened with a magnetic stripe of the kind that was depressingly easy to forge, a hub control room that, once entered, would give Lana approximately forty-five minutes to do her work before any anomaly would be detected at the corporate level, and an exit through the loading dock back to a second vehicle Declan would have pre-staged on the south end of the property.

In exchange for delivering them the door, Declan asked for one specific thing.

He asked for a copy of the file Lana had already pulled out of the drive. The directory that Lucas had, in his small choked voice, asked Lana not to open. The one labeled *FAMILY.*

Sophia's face did not change.

Sophia's hand did not move.

Sophia, in a voice of great calm, said, "Why."

Declan, in a voice of equal calm, said, "Because there is a name in that directory that I have been looking for since 2014, and Stanton has been keeping it from me, and I am now, finally, in a position to ask politely."

Sophia studied him for a long, slow second.

"That name is not somebody I can hand you and expect you to stay on the team."

"I will stay on the team. I am not going freelance on this. I am asking for a copy of the file. I will read it after we are done with Marcus. I will then, after we are done with Marcus, ask permission to handle the name on my own time. You can say no. I will not, in that case, do it."

"Declan."

"Sophia."

"...you're asking me to trust you."

"I am asking you to trust me. Yes."

The motel room was very quiet.

Lucas, in the bathroom, snored, oblivious, on a green tile floor that had seen things.

Sophia looked at Declan for a long time.

Then she nodded, once.

"After Marcus," she said.

"After Marcus," he agreed.

He stood up.

He looked at his watch.

"Eight hours to position," he said. "I have a vehicle. I'll meet you at the staging point I've already cleared. I'll bring breaching tools, a backup sidearm for Sophia, a comms kit good enough for four channels, and a set of clothes for the redhead in the bathroom that don't make him look like he's selling insurance. Wake him up. Feed him. Find out if he can drive a stick."

"Why does he need to drive a stick?"

"Because the staged exit vehicle is a 1992 Toyota cargo van. Helena bought it. It is, somehow, still running. It only does manual."

He left.

Sophia closed the door behind him.

The room was, again, very quiet.

Lana looked at her sister.

"Helena," she said.

Sophia did not turn around.

"Helena," Sophia said. "Yes."

"That was the first time I've ever heard her name."

"I know."

Lana waited.

Sophia, after a moment, turned around.

Her face was the face Lana was beginning to learn, the iron face that had a small set of cracks in it that you could only see if you stood very close. "I will tell you about her. I promise. Not in this room."

"Why not in this room?"

"Because this room smells like 1996, and our mother deserves better."

That, despite everything, made Lana laugh. It was not a long laugh. It was not a healing laugh. It was the kind of laugh that escaped a person before they remembered they were not supposed to be laughing, and it felt, in her chest, like the first decent breath she had taken in a day.

Sophia, watching her, almost smiled.

"Get Lucas up," Sophia said. "And before we start. There is one thing I owe you."

"What."

Sophia walked across the room and sat down on the corner of the bed, beside Lana. She did not, this time, sit at a professional distance. She sat close enough that her shoulder was almost touching Lana's shoulder, and she set her hands on her knees, and she looked, for a moment, at the hideous harvest gold carpet, and she said, in a voice so quiet that Lana almost missed it,

"Dad is in a cabin in the Bitterroots in southwestern Montana."

Lana's breath caught.

"He has been there for fifteen years. He thinks he won the cabin in a lottery for retired auto mechanics that I created on the internet using a small amount of money and a website that I have, every year, renewed. He is in good health. He has a small dog. He has two next-door neighbors, both of whom have been on my payroll since 2010, and both of whom have told him, very convincingly, that they are old fishing buddies of the man he bought the cabin from. They cook him dinner twice a month. They check on him every morning. They have, in fifteen years, fired their sidearms exactly twice. Once at a coyote, which they did not hit. Once at a man, whom they did. The man is buried in a gully approximately three miles north of the cabin and was not, when they buried him, an immediate concern. Dad does not know about the man in the gully. Dad does not know about the sidearms. Dad does not know, in any form, that he has been protected. Dad has not been touched. Dad has had a pretty good fifteen years. He fishes a lot. He has gotten very good at woodcarving. He sometimes calls you on Sundays."

Lana stared at her sister.

Lana said, very slowly, in a voice that was almost not her own, "...you have been watching our father, for fifteen years."

"I have been protecting our father, for fifteen years."

"...why didn't you tell me."

"Because if you had known he was being protected, you would have visited. If you had visited, they would have followed you. If they had followed you, they would have found him. I left you with him, Lana, because you were safe with him as long as you did not know. He was not in any way fragile. He was simply a man with one daughter, in a cabin, fishing. The moment that became a man with two daughters being watched by an assassin, the math changed. I needed the math to stay the way it was."

Lana was crying, again. She was not loud about it. She had not, since the parking garage, been loud about any of it. She was crying the small dry crying of a woman who had run out of new feelings and was now recycling old ones.

"He's okay."

"He's okay."

"He's..."

"He's okay, Lana."

"I want to see him."

"I know you do."

"I can't see him."

"Not yet. But when this is done. I will take you to him. Both of us. Together. We will tell him. He will be confused, and then he will be furious with me, and then he will be very, very happy, and then he will ask if any of us would like a beer. In that order. I have run the simulation."

Lana laughed. The laughter, this time, came out wet.

She put her head, briefly, against her sister's shoulder.

Sophia, after a moment, put her arm around her.

Sophia held her there, for a long moment.

Then she said, gently, "Get Lucas up."

* * *

Lucas Deveraux, when woken, was startled, then disoriented, then briefly under the impression that he had been kidnapped. The fourth thing was a kind of sleepy resignation that Lana found, in her current emotional state, rather charming. She handed him coffee. He drank it. She handed him a piece of toast that Sophia, at some point, had produced from a small cooler in her duffle. He ate it. By the time they had walked him through the plan, the resignation had hardened into something like determination, in the way coffee and toast sometimes hardened resignation into determination.

He could not, it turned out, drive a stick.

He could, however, work a comms console.

That was, as Sophia pointed out, what they actually needed him for.

They sat him down at the small motel desk and Lana set up the comms terminal Declan had described, which was, when it arrived at five o'clock with Declan, a ruggedized tablet with a custom shell and four headset jacks and a small handheld auxiliary camera control. Lana walked Lucas through the interface for an hour. He picked it up with the speed of a man who had spent his career doing exactly this kind of work and who had, in the last six weeks, developed an extremely strong appreciation for the value of being indispensable to people with guns.

By six o'clock, he could route a call between three channels with one hand. By six-thirty, he could pan and zoom the auxiliary camera while taking a status update on the radio without losing the channel. By seven, he had, on his own, identified a potential routing issue in the comms map and proposed a workaround, which Sophia, after looking at it, accepted.

At seven-thirty, with the sun starting to do its end-of-spring thing in the west, Sophia knelt down beside Lucas's chair, and she said, in a voice Lana had not heard from her,

"Lucas. I need you to listen to me."

"Yeah," Lucas said.

"You are not, tonight, a passenger. You are not in the back of the van. You are the eyes. You are the voice. You see a patrol we don't see, you tell us. You see a problem on a camera, you tell us. You see anything that does not match the picture in your head of what is supposed to be happening in that yard, you say it out loud. Do you understand me?"

"...yeah."

"You are the guy in the chair, Lucas. You are essential. We do not do this without you."

Lucas Deveraux, who had spent six months running, who had spent fourteen days sleeping in motels, who had spent the last day and a half being told repeatedly by a series of well-armed strangers that he was at the center of his own particular catastrophe, looked at Sophia Harper. His eyes were wet. He did not, for a long moment, say anything.

Then he nodded.

"Okay," he said.

"Good," Sophia said.

She stood up.

She turned to Lana.

"You ready?"

Lana, who had spent the previous hour packing her own kit, who had loaded the kill switch onto a clean USB stick along with a sandbox runtime in case the smart card threw an unexpected challenge, who had repacked her hoodie and her running shoes and her tactical knife and the burner phone that had, since the parking garage, gone disturbingly silent, looked at her sister.

"No," Lana said.

"Good. Honest answer. Let's go."

* * *

Terminal 4 of Harbor Logistics Group occupied a fenced rectangle of approximately eleven acres on the south bank of the Calumet River, between a defunct grain elevator and an active scrap yard. It had four primary buildings: a main office, a maintenance shed, a hub server building, and a long low-slung warehouse on the river side where the freight came in. Three operational dockside cranes ran the length of the river side. A single rail spur ran in from the south. The whole property was lit, at night, by the kind of orange high-pressure sodium lamps that Chicago industrial operations had been buying in bulk since 1973, and the orange light gave the whole yard the appearance, in the dark, of a movie set for a film about the apocalypse.

The team approached from the southeast in two vehicles.

Lucas was in the cargo van, parked half a mile out, on a quiet residential side street that gave him a clean line of sight to the terminal's perimeter cameras through the auxiliary camera he was now controlling remotely from the passenger seat. The van had its headlights off. The van had its dome light disabled. Lucas had a headset on and a thermos of coffee at his elbow and the unmistakable, slightly hunted look of a man who had decided, in the last hour, to take this seriously and was now committed.

Lana, Sophia, and Declan were in the second vehicle, a battered grey sedan Declan had borrowed from someone he did not name, parked on the far side of the scrap yard. They left the sedan there. They went in over the southeast corner of the fence, where Declan had clipped the chain link three nights earlier and bent it back into place with a gardening tie, and where the cameras on the southeast tower had, fourteen hours earlier, started having an unexplained intermittent blackout that the on-shift IT contractor was, even now, on the phone trying to escalate.

The on-shift IT contractor, Sophia had noted, was Lana's accidental gift to the operation. She had been getting frustrated. She had been bored. She had, between three and four that afternoon, hacked the camera firmware on the southeast tower for fun.

"This is not a habit you can develop, Lana," Sophia had said, when Lana had told her what she had done.

"It worked, though."

"It is, useful. Don't do it again without telling me."

"Define *don't.*"

"Lana."

"Define *useful.*"

Sophia had not bothered to respond.

In the dark, at the southeast corner, the team slipped through the fence one at a time. Declan went first. Sophia second. Lana third. They crossed the gravel yard in a low crouch behind a row of dormant container chassis. Above them, the orange sodium lamps flickered and hummed.

In Lana's earpiece, Lucas's voice, calm and clear: "Two-man patrol northwest corner, walking south. ETA your position, four minutes. Second patrol on the river side, stationary at crane two. Camera coverage, you're clear in the gap between containers six and seven for the next eleven minutes."

"Copy," Sophia said.

"You're doing great, Lucas," Lana whispered.

"Don't talk to me," Lucas whispered back. "I am extremely focused."

Lana had to physically suppress a snort.

They reached the security hub at the south side of the office building. Declan held position at the corner. Sophia took the door. Lana plugged into the wall jack with a small cable from her kit. The hub's authentication challenge came up on her tablet. She had not, in advance, known what the challenge would be. She knew the family of challenges that Stanton's vendor used, and she knew the quirks of the firmware, and she knew the kind of side-channel attack that worked on this generation of hardware, and she knew, in the abstract, that she could probably get in.

In specific, it took her three minutes and eleven seconds.

The cameras went into a loop.

The motion sensors on the eastern perimeter went into a loop.

The badge readers on the side door of the hub server building went into a state where they would, for the next forty minutes, accept any badge as valid.

"We're ghosts," she breathed.

"Move."

They moved.

Across the yard. Behind the maintenance shed. Around the back of the warehouse. To the side door of the hub server building. Sophia put a hand against the door. The badge reader chirped. The lock disengaged. They were inside.

The hub server building was small. Two stories. The bottom floor was racks of equipment in a cold, fluorescent-lit room, with a heavy server cage in the center and a single workstation against the far wall. The workstation had a monitor, a keyboard, a mouse, and a single fiber jack labeled HUB-01. The chair in front of the workstation was empty.

The lanyard, with the smart card, was sitting on the corner of the desk.

Carl, by some grace of the gods of operational sloppiness, had not bothered to take the lanyard outside with him on his cigarette break.

Lana sat down at the chair.

She slotted the smart card.

She plugged in the USB stick.

The system, after a brief contemplative pause, accepted the credential.

The system displayed a logon.

Lana's hands were on the keyboard.

The kill switch was queued.

In her earpiece, Lucas's voice, suddenly tight: "Three black SUVs, just rolled through the front gate. Five minutes out. Nine, maybe ten guys. They're armed. They are not Carl's friends."

Sophia, calm, in Lana's other ear: "Lucas. How did they know."

"...I don't know. I don't know, I don't know, oh my god.."

"Lucas."

"Yeah, sorry, sorry, three SUVs, four men out of the lead vehicle, fanning out, six minutes from the building you're in if they hustle, the cameras are looped, they're coming in dark.."

Sophia, behind Lana, set her hand on Lana's shoulder.

"Forty minutes," Sophia said.

"I have forty minutes," Lana said.

"You have forty minutes. We hold them off. Use the time."

Lana started typing.

Outside, in the orange-lit yard, the first of nine men in tactical gear was crossing the gravel toward the side door of the hub server building, his weapon drawn.

The crane control tower, two hundred yards to the north, sat dark and silent above the river.

Declan, watching the SUVs through the corner of the office building, looked back at Sophia.

"Sophia," he said.

"What."

"Tell your kid sister, when she has a free hand, to think about the cranes."

In her chair, Lana, who had heard him, smiled for the first time since she had walked into the building, with the, focused, slightly unhinged smile of a woman whose hands were finally, after thirty-six hours, exactly where they belonged.

"Working on it," she said.

She kept typing.

The kill switch deployment protocol began to load.

The clock, for the first time since the chandelier had come down on Marlon Kade, began to tick in a direction Lana, for the first time, knew how to use.

Chapter 7: The Cascade Begins

The first man through the side door of the hub server building made it approximately one and a half steps into the room before Declan put him on the floor.

Declan did not, in his own description of his work, do flashy things. The man came through the doorway in the tactical-team approach posture, weapon shouldered, eyes scanning. Declan, who had been waiting against the wall to the right of the door at a height that put him below the man's shoulder line, did three things in a sequence that took less than a second and a half. He swept the muzzle of the rifle up and away from the room with the back of his left hand. He brought his right elbow down on the side of the man's neck just below the helmet line. He hooked his right foot around the man's ankle as the man's center of gravity went forward, and he rode the man down to the concrete floor in a controlled fall that ended with the man's face making a small, surprised acquaintance with the floor and Declan, kneeling on the man's back, taking the rifle out of his hands with the easy efficiency of a man taking groceries off a counter.

It was, Lana thought from her chair at the workstation, a strangely beautiful piece of work. It was also, Lana thought from her chair at the workstation, the first thing she had ever seen that had made her understand why Sophia, at nineteen, had stood in a Lisbon hotel suite and trusted this man with her life.

She did not have time to think about it for very long.

Sophia was already moving past the doorway in the other direction, low and silent, into the dark of the gravel yard. The second tactical man, who had been five paces behind the first, was just clearing the angle of the doorway when Sophia took him from his blind side with a forearm strike to the throat that rolled him sideways into the corner of the building, where she put him to sleep with a single knee against the carotid that, Lana noticed with a small clinical part of her brain, was textbook hand-to-hand: not the kind of strike that would kill a man, but the kind that would send him to a hospital with a headache and a brief, disorienting blank spot in his memory.

The two men were on the ground in less than five seconds.

Lana, in the chair, was three minutes into a forty-minute deployment, and the deployment was, even in those three minutes, beginning to tell her things.

The kill switch was loading. The kill switch was authenticating. The kill switch had, on first handshake with the hub's smart-card credential, accepted Carl's badge as legitimate within the local trust domain, and Lana had felt the small electric thrill of a system saying *yes* to her when it should have been saying *no*. She had begun the deployment protocol. The protocol had begun reaching out, the way the documentation had said it would, into the local tree of authenticated systems, and it had begun, file by file, queue by queue, account by account, to insert its little destructive hooks into the soft underside of Stanton Industries' regional financial architecture.

The protocol was working.

The protocol was working beautifully, with the kind of clean cascading authentication that Lana had only ever seen in textbook examples and a small number of academic papers she had read for fun in graduate school.

The protocol was also, Lana realized as she watched it propagate, *not propagating the way it was supposed to.*

It was supposed to climb.

It was supposed to leave the local hub, ride the trust relationships outward into Stanton's broader network, propagate to the other forty-two regional hubs, reach out from those hubs into Stanton's executive infrastructure, climb from the executive infrastructure into Stanton's encrypted communication network, and from the communication network out into the buyer-and-seller registry, and from the registry into the politicians, and from the politicians into the black sites, and from the black sites into the asset registry, until the entire criminal architecture of Stanton Industries was, in eight to twelve hours, a smoking hole in the ground.

What it was actually doing was sitting at the local hub and refusing to climb.

The cascade, after the first three layers of regional propagation, had hit a wall.

The wall was, Lana saw when she ran the trace, a higher-tier authentication challenge that the kill switch could not, with Carl's smart card, satisfy.

Carl was a logistics shift manager. Carl had local domain credentials. Carl could get the kill switch into every Stanton subsidiary in the Great Lakes region, into every shell-company financial account the region was responsible for managing, into every internal HR system, every payroll, every operational manifest, every shipping log, every freight contract, every account in every bank that the regional hub authenticated against.

Carl could not, with Carl's smart card, get the kill switch any higher than that.

Above Stanton Industries, Lana realized in a clean way that realizations sometimes worked, was something else.

Above Stanton Industries was a network that Stanton himself was a *client* of.

Lana had assumed, with the half-formed assumption of a person who had been working from a single afternoon's reading, that Stanton was the top of the tree. He was the CEO of the company on the books. He was the man whose name was in the holding-company registries. He was the architect of the network.

Stanton was not, it turned out, the architect of the network.

Stanton was a *user* of a network.

The network above him had its own credentials. The network above him had its own trust relationships. The network above him was, in this very moment, watching Lana's kill switch try to climb, and the network above him was refusing to authenticate her, and the network above him was, Lana could see in the trace logs, *responding.*

A higher-tier authentication request was, in real time, querying the dockyard hub.

Someone, somewhere, was logging in.

Lana stared at the screen.

"Sophia," she said into her earpiece.

"Busy," Sophia said.

"Sophia, the kill switch isn't going to climb."

A pause.

"What does that mean."

"It means Stanton's not the top. It means there's somebody else, and they have a credential I don't have, and they are *currently* logging into this hub from somewhere not in this hub, which is, I am not going to lie to you, deeply unsettling. They saw me. They are looking at me. They are about to lock me out."

Sophia's voice, on the comm, was the kind of calm that Lana had come to understand was Sophia's *worst* calm, the calm of a person preparing to do an unscheduled kind of violence.

"Can you finish the regional cascade before they lock you out?"

Lana looked at the trace.

The regional cascade was at sixty-eight percent. It was still propagating. Inside the perimeter of Stanton Industries' local domain, the kill switch was eating everything. Subsidiary accounts were going dark. Internal email was, in real time, beginning to bounce. The shipping manifest queue had stopped moving.

She had, by her estimation, four minutes before whoever was logging in from above shut the entire process down.

"Yes," she said. "I can finish the regional. I can't get higher. Stanton is going to feel this in his sleep. The Council, or whoever is up there, won't."

"Then finish the regional. I will take care of the Council later. Do not stop typing."

"Sophia."

"Yes."

"There are nine men outside this room."

"Lucas." Sophia's voice changed. "Talk to me. The cranes."

Lucas's voice, in Lana's other ear, slightly higher than it had been thirty seconds ago: "Cranes are dark. The control tower is at the north end of the yard, second floor of the maintenance shed, single guard outside the door, lights are on, his coffee is on the railing. Cranes one, two, and three are loaded with empty containers from this afternoon's shift. The hydraulics are still warm. If somebody started them up over the next ninety seconds, they would, mechanically speaking, do whatever that person told them to do."

"Lana."

"I hear it," Lana said.

"Can you?"

"While doing this? Yeah. The crane control system is on the same SCADA backbone as everything else in this yard. I am, at this moment, the local network. Give me thirty seconds."

She pulled up a second window. She did not stop the kill switch deployment. The kill switch deployment did not need her to babysit it; it needed her to not unplug the laptop. She let it run on its own clock. In the second window, she opened the SCADA interface for the Calumet River dockyard's industrial control systems. The interface was, like most industrial control systems, a piece of late-1990s software design philosophy that had been incrementally patched for twenty-five years and had never, in any meaningful sense, been redesigned. It had a single login. The single login was *operator.* The password, Lana discovered after the first three guesses, was *operator1.*

She made a small, despairing noise.

"Are we okay," Declan said, behind her.

"I am *furious,*" Lana said, "that I am here at all, given that the password to a forty-million-dollar industrial control system is *operator1.*"

"Use the anger. Drive the cranes."

She drove the cranes.

She did not do anything dramatic. She did not, despite the temptation, attempt to send a four-ton container directly onto a tactical team. She did, however, identify the three cranes' last queued sequences, override the queues with a freshly written set of instructions, and execute. Crane one's boom began to swing, slowly, ninety degrees to its right. Crane two began to lower its empty container directly into the path of the gravel road that led from the front gate to the loading dock area. Crane three, which was at the north end of the yard, began to extend its boom in a full pivot back toward the southwest, in the direction of the maintenance shed and, more usefully, in the direction of the four tactical men who had just begun crossing the gravel between the office building and the hub server building.

The cranes, all three of them, came on at the same time, and the orange-lit yard suddenly contained the rumbling, groaning, building-sized presence of three industrial machines that had been entirely silent thirty seconds earlier, doing things that had not, in their queued schedules, been on their list of things to do.

Outside, men shouted.

Outside, the shape of the assault changed, the way the shape of assaults always changed when the people running them had to suddenly account for an entire moving variable they had not, in their planning, accounted for.

The four tactical men crossing the gravel between buildings stopped. One of them looked up at the boom of crane three, which was now, in the orange light, swinging visibly through an arc that would, in approximately fifteen seconds, intersect with the patch of gravel they were standing on. The man did the math. The man broke and ran for the cover of the maintenance shed, taking the other three with him.

The boom did not, in fact, hit them.

Lana had not, in setting the queue, intended for it to hit them. She had merely intended for it to plausibly *threaten* to hit them, in a way that no rational professional would willingly stand under. The boom continued past the patch of gravel and continued through its arc, and the four men, having committed to running for the maintenance shed, were now, by their own choice, on the wrong side of crane three's boom and on the wrong side of crane two's lowered container, and were, in operational terms, on the far side of the yard from the hub server building, separated from their target by an industrial obstacle course of their own making.

"That is going to buy us four minutes," Sophia said, in Lana's ear.

"I'll take four minutes. The kill switch is at eighty-one percent."

"They will, in approximately ninety seconds, recover and start coming around the long way. Lucas, the side gate."

"They have the side gate covered," Lucas said. "There are still two men with the lead SUV. They are watching the south side of the property. They know we're not going out the front."

"Declan."

"Yeah."

"The transformer."

There was a pause.

"You sure."

"Yes. Lana?"

"Yes?"

"How is your relationship with sudden, complete darkness."

"...cordial."

"Improve it."

Declan moved.

He went back to the side door of the hub server building. He paused at the corner. He pulled, from a pocket of his jacket, a small device that looked like a child's toy walkie-talkie, which Lana remembered Sophia describing as a paired remote for a charge that Declan had pre-positioned. He toggled a small switch. He spoke into his comm.

"Lucas. Do me a favor. Tell me the moment the second-shift IT contractor leaves the eastern blockhouse."

A pause.

"He is leaving the eastern blockhouse," Lucas said. "Right now. He is, uh, he is putting on a high-visibility vest. He is walking out toward the southeastern fence."

"Good. He's going to check the camera tower. He is a civilian. He will make it to the fence and stop. Tell me when he's at the fence."

A pause.

"He's at the fence."

"Excellent."

Declan pressed the button.

There was, somewhere out in the orange-lit dark beyond the perimeter of the dockyard, a clean *thump,* the kind of sound a high-end concert speaker made when the bass came in. Lana felt it in her chest more than she heard it.

The lights in the hub server building did not flicker.

Then, as if some invisible hand had thrown a single immense switch, every sodium lamp in the eleven-acre dockyard went out.

The orange light, which had been continuous, was simply *gone.*

The cranes, mid-cycle, made a series of sad, disappointed mechanical sounds and stopped where they were, leaving their queued instructions hanging in the air.

The badge readers went dark. The cameras went dark. The motion sensors went dark. The hub server building's overhead fluorescents, which were on a separate uninterruptible power supply, flickered, then resolved into a slightly dimmer version of themselves, the way fluorescents did when they realized they had been promoted to sole light source.

Lana's laptop, which was on the same UPS, did not flinch.

The kill switch deployment continued.

In Lana's ear, Lucas, sounding deeply stressed: "Bye-bye, power grid. You okay in there?"

"We're up," Lana confirmed. "UPS held. I have, give me a second, eighty-nine percent."

"Tactical team on the gravel just lost their night vision," Lucas said. "Their gear was tied to the local power for charging. Two of them are switching to handhelds. One of them is yelling at his radio. The radio doesn't work, by the way."

"That is also the local cellular tower," Lana said. "I bricked it. They are now operating, technically speaking, in the past."

"You bricked the cellular tower."

"I bricked the cellular tower for a six-block radius. I will probably regret that. Let's keep moving."

The kill switch hit ninety-three percent.

Outside the hub building, the four tactical men who had been pinned by the cranes had, in the dark, regrouped and were now coming around the long way, moving in pairs, working off handhelds. Lana could hear the crunch of gravel. Sophia, who had come back inside the building during the transformer detonation, was at the doorway with the rifle Declan had taken off the first man, and she was waiting.

Lucas's voice in Lana's ear: "Lead pair, fourteen yards out. Second pair, twenty. They're going to clear and stack on the door. Get ready."

"Lana. How long."

"Forty seconds."

"Declan. Smoke."

"Already."

Lana heard, through the open door of the hub building, the small percussive *whump* of a thrown smoke grenade hitting gravel. White smoke, in the dim spillover of the building's emergency lights, began to bloom across the doorway.

"Lana. Thirty seconds."

"Twenty-eight."

"Wrap it. Get ready to move."

"Twenty."

The first tactical man came through the smoke.

Sophia was already moving.

Lana did not look up from her screen.

She heard, behind her, the clean sounds of professional violence: a brief impact, a body hitting the floor, a second impact, a second body. Sophia was not, in this moment, being merciful. She was not killing, but she was no longer concerned about hospitalization. The kill switch, ten seconds from completing, had become the only thing that mattered, and the only thing Sophia was now interested in was making sure nothing in the next ten seconds touched Lana's chair.

The kill switch hit one hundred percent.

The screen, after a small pause, displayed two lines.

REGIONAL CASCADE: COMPLETE. GLOBAL PROPAGATION: BLOCKED. AUTHENTICATION FAILURE AT TIER-2.

Underneath those lines, in smaller text:

EXTERNAL AUTHENTICATION CHALLENGE FROM CREDENTIAL VANEK.H@PRINCIPAL. SESSION TERMINATED. LOCAL HUB QUARANTINED.

Lana stared at the screen for one full second.

She read the line a second time.

She read the line a third time.

VANEK.H.

Henrik Vanek.

She had, in the last two minutes, been *personally observed,* via real-time authentication trace, by Mr. Halloran.

He had, somewhere in this city, just told a server to kick her out, with his own credential, on his own initiative, in his own name.

He was not, then, just Stanton's enforcer.

He was, she understood with a cold wave at the base of her spine, *credentialed at a higher tier than Marcus Stanton.*

He was, in some structural way, *above* his employer.

Sophia, Lana thought, and then she said it out loud. "Sophia."

"Tell me you're done."

"I'm done. I'm done. We have to go. I know who's at the top of the network."

"Tell me in the van."

Lana yanked the smart card. She yanked the USB stick. She slammed the laptop closed and stuffed it into the tactical bag and stood up, and as she stood up, she looked, for the first time in eight minutes, at her sister.

Sophia was standing in the middle of the room. She was holding the rifle in one hand. Her other hand, at her side, was wet to the wrist with somebody else's blood. There were three bodies on the floor in a rough triangle around the doorway, one of them moving, two of them not. The smoke was still drifting in. The fluorescents above were still humming. Sophia was looking at Lana the way Sophia, in 2002, must have looked at the door of the family home when she had been twelve and Lana had been six and the smaller hand had still been in hers.

"Move," Sophia said.

Lana moved.

* * *

The cargo van was a 1992 Toyota that was, as Declan had promised, somehow still running.

It also smelled, very strongly, of motor oil and old gun-cleaning solvent and, faintly, of cardamom, which Lana would, much later, learn was Helena's preferred scent, and which Sophia, in 2010, had absorbed into the upholstery by leaving a sachet of cardamom pods in the glove compartment for two and a half years for reasons she had never, in the moment, articulated to herself.

Lucas drove.

Lucas could not, technically, drive a stick. Lucas was, in the present moment, *learning* to drive a stick, in the dark, in the middle of an active crisis, with three armed people in the back of his van and the ruins of an industrial dockyard fifty yards behind him. He stalled the van twice in the first thirty seconds. He did not stall it a third time. He did not, on the next gear shift, grind anything beyond the limits of a 1992 transmission's tolerance for being abused. By the time they hit the four-lane road that ran north along the river, he was, if not smooth, then at least functional, with the white-knuckled focus of a man whose understanding of the clutch had been built, in real time, on his own desperate need.

In the back, Sophia was field-dressing a graze along her own ribs that she had not, until they were in the van, mentioned. The graze was not serious. The graze was, however, *new*, and Lana, who had just watched her sister move three armed men out of a doorway with mostly bare hands and a borrowed rifle, understood that she had not seen the entire fight.

Declan was watching the road behind them through the rear window.

"They're not following," he said, after two minutes. "They have one functional vehicle. The other two are on the wrong side of the cranes. They will take, at minimum, fifteen minutes to assemble pursuit. By that point we will be twelve miles away in a different vehicle. The cleanup crew will get to the dockyard before pursuit does."

"Cleanup crew?" Lucas said, from the front.

"There is always a cleanup crew, Lucas."

"Of course."

Lana, in the back, set the laptop on her thighs. She opened it. She had, in the last sixty seconds of her deployment, captured a snapshot of the kill switch's propagation log. She had also, on the way out the door, copied the trace of the external authentication challenge that had locked her out. She wanted, very badly, to look at both of these things at once.

She also wanted, very badly, to look at her sister, who was bleeding onto a 1992 Toyota cargo van that had once belonged to their mother.

The looking at her sister was not, at this moment, productive. The looking at the laptop was. She looked at the laptop.

The propagation log was beautiful.

Within Stanton Industries' regional perimeter, the cascade had been *total.*

Every one of the forty-three regional hubs that fell under Stanton's local domain had been compromised. Every operational subsidiary had been compromised. Every shell account in the Great Lakes region was now, as of approximately ninety seconds ago, displaying balances of zero in the actual Stanton accounting systems, because the kill switch had, as designed, zeroed them. The shipping manifest queue for the Singapore freight that was, even now, arriving at the dockyard had been replaced with seventeen thousand individual line items each labeled, for reasons Lana could not yet diagnose, *cabbage*.

She paused on the cabbage thing. That was, presumably, Stanton's people's idea of a deniability mechanism, an internal inside joke that meant *manifest corrupted, unrecoverable*. Of course it was cabbage. Of course it was.

The point, though, was that Stanton Industries, as Stanton Industries existed in the regional financial systems of fourteen jurisdictions, was, as of this moment, *gone*.

He still had his executive infrastructure. He still had his communications. He still had his black sites and his asset registry and his politicians.

But everything underneath those things, the regional financial layer that funded all of it, had just imploded.

Marcus Stanton was going to wake up, in approximately six hours, to find that his entire operational network in the western hemisphere had been zeroed, and that the people who had done it had, in his own files, his current internal codes, and the schematic of his own kill switch, which he had not, in the last twelve years, ever told anyone outside his innermost circle existed.

He was going to, Lana realized with a horrible thrill, panic.

He was going to consolidate.

He was going to pull every remaining asset he had into one place, and that place was going to be a place that he, personally, considered untouchable, and that place was going to be the place where he kept his last, best credentials.

Including, presumably, the credentials that would let her finish the cascade.

"Sophia," Lana said.

"Mm."

"I have to tell you something. Three things, actually."

"Three is a lot, Lana."

"One. The kill switch worked, but it only got Stanton's regional. He still has executive. He still has his black sites. He still has his communications."

"...that is not catastrophic. That is the best partial cascade I would have predicted from a single dockyard hub."

"Two. There is a second tier above Stanton. There is a network *above* his network that he, personally, does not have credentials for. Whatever they are, they own him. He is a tenant."

Sophia paused in her field dressing.

She did not look up.

"...go on."

"Three. The tier above him sent a real-time authentication challenge to the hub at the moment my cascade hit their boundary, and the credential that issued the challenge was logged in the system as VANEK.H@PRINCIPAL. They locked me out. With his name. *Henrik Vanek* is not Stanton's enforcer, Sophia. Henrik Vanek is the tier above Stanton, *acting as* Stanton's enforcer. He is, structurally, his employer's representative inside Stanton's organization. The man we have been calling Mr. Halloran is, in the architecture of this thing, *above* the man whose company he ostensibly works for."

The van went very quiet.

In the front, Lucas said, "...I have decided I am going to focus on driving. I will not be participating in this conversation."

"That's fair, Lucas," Lana said. "Drive."

Sophia finished the bandage on her ribs, slowly, with hands that had gone, Lana noticed, very still.

Sophia said, "That changes everything."

"Yeah."

"He has not been Stanton's man this whole time."

"No. He has been somebody else's, with Stanton on his portfolio."

"He is a *placement*."

"Yes."

"Helena," Sophia said, softly, "used to talk about placements. She used to say. 'Lana, the way you tell a real network from a pretend network is, you find the man who is in everybody's company and on nobody's payroll. Find him. He is the network. The companies are window dressing.'"

"...she said that to me?"

"She said it to you, when you were five. You were not listening. You were trying to feed your applesauce to a stuffed bear."

Lana made a small, helpless noise.

Sophia's hands were still very still.

She looked, after a moment, at Declan, in the seat beside her.

"Did you know?" she said.

"Did I know what."

"Did you know that Vanek was a placement."

Declan considered the question for a long second.

He answered it carefully.

"I knew Henrik Vanek was not, by training, Marcus Stanton's man. I knew he had been in the world before Marcus had been in the world, and that he had a longer pedigree than Marcus, and that there were stories about him from before Marcus had even started Stanton Industries. I did not know who his actual principal was. Nobody, in any room I have ever been in, has known. Vanek is a name. Vanek's principal is not a name. Vanek's principal is the *absence* of a name, and the absence is the giveaway."

"Helena would have known," Sophia said.

"Helena was working on it," Declan said, "the year she died."

The van went quiet again.

It was, Lana would think later, the first moment of the rest of the war.

Lana, who had, twenty minutes earlier, pulled off the most successful cybernetic strike of her professional life, who had reduced a regional crime network to a smoking pile of rebooted servers, who had personally cost Marcus Stanton, in the next six hours, an unrecoverable hundreds of millions of dollars in operational liquidity, looked at her sister and her sister's old friend in the back of an ancient Toyota van and understood, finally, the size of what they had walked into.

Marcus Stanton was not the dragon.

Marcus Stanton was a *vassal* of the dragon.

The dragon had a representative who had walked into a hotel bar two nights ago, mistaken Lana for Sophia, and decided, on the spot, that the situation was *amusing*. The dragon's representative had paid a million dollars in Bitcoin for an accidental death. The dragon's representative had, twenty minutes ago, watched Lana from a chair somewhere across the world and locked her out of his real network with the casual ease of a man closing a window.

The dragon, whoever the dragon was, was real.

The dragon had not, yet, been named.

But the dragon had, in the last twenty minutes, *seen* her, and the dragon was now, somewhere, having a conversation with someone about her that she would, over the next several days, find extremely unpleasant.

"Okay," Lana said, slowly. "Okay. So what do we do."

Sophia, after a long moment, said, "We finish Stanton."

"He's already finished, Sophia. The regional is gone. He can't.."

"He can't operate. But he can still hide. He can still consolidate. He can still walk away with the credentials I now know he has been holding for his principal. Stanton's executive infrastructure is going to run to the place he keeps his last secrets. We follow it. We take Stanton, with his head still attached and his mouth still working. We walk Stanton up the ladder. We make him show us the dragon."

"You want to *interrogate* him."

"I want to interrogate him, then I want to put him in front of a sitting federal grand jury, and then I want to spend an evening with whoever Vanek's actual principal turns out to be. In that order."

Declan, mildly, "That is a tall order, Sophia."

"It is the order, Declan."

Declan inclined his head. "It is the order."

Lana leaned her head back against the side panel of the van. The cardamom smell was all around her. Outside the rear window, the orange glow of the dockyard had receded into the city skyline, indistinguishable now from any other glow, any other distant fire. Lucas, in the front, downshifted, found the gear, did not stall, and accelerated up the ramp onto the highway.

In the back of the van, the tactical laptop made a small sound.

Lana looked at it.

A new message had appeared on the screen.

The message was not, this time, a propagation log. The message was not, this time, a system response.

The message was a single line of text, in white on black, in a small fixed-width font, in the secure messaging channel that the tactical laptop had been configured to receive.

The line read: *Well done, Sophia. Or shall I say, Lana? Henrik.*

Lana stared at it.

The cursor blinked under it, patient, courteous, the way Henrik Vanek did everything else.

Then a second line appeared.

Your father called you four times today. You did not answer. He is worried.

The blood in Lana's body, in the back of the cardamom-smelling van, did the thing blood did when somebody three thousand miles away showed you that they knew where your father lived.

She did not, for several seconds, breathe.

Sophia, who had seen the look on her sister's face, leaned over and read the screen.

Sophia's expression did not change.

Sophia took the laptop. Sophia closed the laptop. Sophia did not, by any visible sign, react.

"Lana," Sophia said, very calmly. "Listen to me."

"He's at the cabin, Sophia, he's.."

"Lana. Listen. The cabin is fine. He has not seen the cabin. He has not been to the cabin. He has access to your phone log because your phone is in your apartment, and your apartment is being watched, and the man on the phone is your father because your father called your phone four times today. He does not know where the cabin is. The cabin is *not on any record* that he can reach. The cabin was bought through the lottery shell I built. The lottery shell does not exist on paper. There is no path from your apartment to that cabin."

"You're sure."

"Lana. I built it. There is no path."

"...okay."

"He is showing off. He is doing what he does. He is letting you know that he sees you. He is not letting you know that he sees Dad. He cannot see Dad."

"You're sure, Sophia."

"I have been sure for fifteen years, Lana. That is the whole point of fifteen years."

Lana exhaled. It came out shaky.

"I have to call him."

"You will. Not from this van. Not on this network. Not tonight. Tomorrow. From a clean line. From a clean place. We will get you there."

"Okay."

"Okay?"

"Okay."

Sophia, after a long moment, did something Lana had not seen her sister do, in any of the previous thirty-eight hours of their reunion.

Sophia put a hand on Lana's hand, on her thigh.

She left it there.

The van rolled north, into the dark, and the city slipped behind them, and Lucas, who had been listening to every word of the previous conversation, navigated his way through three highway interchanges in a 1992 stick-shift cargo van without stalling, while the laptop sat closed on Lana's lap with the message from Henrik Vanek inside it, and Declan, in the back beside Sophia, watched the road behind them through the rear window, and the cardamom smell did not, at any point, fade.

Somewhere, in a city Lana could not see, in a building Lana would never enter, a man was sitting in a leather chair in front of a wall of monitors, sipping a small glass of something amber, watching one of those monitors quietly cycle through the trace of the cascade Lana had just executed, and finding the whole thing, in his careful, unhurried way, *interesting.*

The monitor's title bar was empty. There was no name at the top of the screen. There was only a small black icon that was, in another context, a stylized representation of an open eye.

The man in the leather chair set his glass down.

He picked up a phone.

He said, in a voice nobody in the van could hear, "Henrik. Bring me what's left of Marcus. And then I would like to meet his hacker. Personally."

He did not raise his voice.

He did not, in any way, sound angry.

He sounded the way a man sounded when he had, at long last, found a piece of work that was going to be worth his time.

Chapter 8: The Ripple Effect

The bolthole was the second floor of a defunct print shop on a side street in the Bridgeport neighborhood, above a still-functional kosher deli that had been operating, by Sophia's account, since 1962, under the same family, with the same recipe for the matzo ball soup, which was good news for them because the deli's owners had a strict policy of not asking questions about the man who paid the rent on the second floor in cash every January, a man named *Rosenfeld* whom none of them had ever actually met.

The print shop had been dark since 2017. The press on the ground floor was rusted into place and would never run again. The second floor had concrete walls, a tile floor that had seen industrial chemicals and was therefore extremely easy to clean, two windows that opened onto a fire escape Sophia had personally upgraded in 2019 with a quick-release crash bar, and one door at the top of a wooden staircase that the deli's owners thought led to a storage closet.

It was, Lana decided as she came up the stairs, the kind of room you chose when you had thought, in advance, about what kind of room you might someday need.

The room contained one folding metal chair, bolted to the tile, in the middle of the floor.

The chair contained one tactical contractor.

The tactical contractor was a man in his early thirties with a shaved head and the kind of disciplined, half-conscious look of a man who had, in the last hour, taken a rifle butt to the temple and been zip-tied into the back of a 1992 Toyota cargo van and driven across half a city without being told where he was going. His tactical vest had been removed. His helmet had been removed. His earpiece had been removed. He had been left, by Declan, with his clothes, his boots, and the small cuts on his hands from being put on the floor of a hub server building two hours earlier.

His name, on the dog tag they had found in his vest pocket, was COLE, J.

Cole, J. was beginning to come back to consciousness when they brought him up the stairs.

Declan dragged the chair he was zip-tied to into a slightly different position and turned on the room's single overhead light, which was bright in the sourceless industrial way of fluorescent fixtures everywhere, and which produced, on Cole's face, an expression that had progressed from disorientation to the practiced blank of a professional who had been trained, somewhere, in what to do when this happened.

Sophia was standing in the corner of the room. She was not, this time, holding a weapon. She had her arms folded. She had the iron face on. She was, in essence, *backdrop.*

Lana was at the small folding table by the window with the laptop open and a comms headset on, with Lucas's voice, three blocks away in a fresh vehicle Declan had arranged, in her ear at low volume.

Declan was the one who pulled up the second folding chair, sat down across from Cole, J. with the casual weight of a man sitting down to a long lunch, and said, in the voice of a friendly uncle, "How are you feeling, Cole?"

Cole did not respond.

Declan waited.

"I am going to tell you what I know about you," Declan said, after a moment. "I am not going to tell you in order to threaten you. I am going to tell you because telling you tends to save us all some time. Your name is Joseph Cole. You are thirty-one years old. You served two tours in Afghanistan with the 75th Ranger Regiment, and you took your honorable discharge in 2018. You have been working for a private security contractor called Allegiant Vector for the last six and a half years. Allegiant Vector is, on paper, a security firm. In practice, Allegiant Vector takes contracts from a small number of high-end clients, most of whom would be embarrassed to be named on the same page as their security firm. You have, in the last six and a half years, deployed in support of three of those clients. You have been on Stanton Industries' rotation for fourteen months. Tonight was your fourth deployment for Stanton. Your previous three were uneventful. Tonight was not."

Cole's eyes tracked Declan's face. Cole did not say anything.

"I am not, Cole, going to ask you anything you have been trained to refuse to answer. I will not ask you about your team. I will not ask you about your protocols. I will not ask you for names. The reason I will not ask you about those things is that I do not need them. I have, in front of me, a young woman with a laptop, and the young woman has, in the last two hours, gutted Stanton Industries' regional financial network in a way that has, by this point, started informing the people who employ you that your contract is, almost certainly, no longer valid. They have not yet told you. They will not, in fact, tell you. They will, instead, send a small team of professionals to the building you are currently sitting in, and they will silence you, and they will silence whatever conversation we have been having, and they will be very thorough."

Cole's jaw moved.

"I am, in fact," Declan continued, "about ninety minutes from being right about that. I am offering you a deal. I am going to ask you exactly two questions. You are going to answer them or not answer them, as your professional ethics dictate. Whether you answer them or not, when I am done, I am going to put you in the back of the van that brought you here. I am going to drive you to a city park three miles from here. I am going to leave you there with your hands free, your phone in your pocket, and a small amount of cash. You will then, I expect, have approximately forty minutes before someone who is no longer your friend finds you. I would suggest you spend those forty minutes going somewhere that is neither your home nor your girlfriend's apartment. Your team has, I am sorry to tell you, become liabilities. There is, in that sense, no longer a *back* for any of you to go to."

The silence in the room was long.

Cole, after a long beat, in a voice that was only a little hoarse, said, "What are the two questions."

"The first question. When were you briefed about the cleanup crew."

Cole's eyes flickered.

"I don't know about a cleanup crew."

"Cole."

"I don't."

"Cole. There is, by your own organization's protocols, a cleanup crew. There is always a cleanup crew. Tonight, I am told, the cleanup crew is something more interesting than you have previously dealt with. The cleanup crew tonight is not your firm's cleanup crew. The cleanup crew tonight is somebody else's cleanup crew. They were not, I am willing to bet, on your operational map when you breached the dockyard. They are not, I am willing to bet, on your radio traffic. You did not, I am willing to bet, recognize the men who came in behind you when the lights went out. You assumed they were yours. They were not yours."

Cole's face did something complicated.

He said, "...I saw a second team."

"Yes."

"They didn't ID. They went straight for the wounded."

"Yes."

"...I didn't recognize their gear."

"No. You didn't. You were not supposed to. You were supposed to engage your target, and you were not supposed to *be there* when the second team did its work, because the second team's work was meant to clean up the failure of *your* team. Whoever was running your op tonight, Cole, was not running your op for Stanton. They were running it for somebody who has been waiting for Stanton to fail, who has been waiting for a specific *kind* of failure tonight, and who needed a tactical engagement they could plausibly clean up. You walked into a kill box. The kill box was not for us. The kill box was for *you.*"

Cole stared at Declan.

Cole, after a long moment, said, "...Christ."

"Yes," Declan said, gently. "Christ."

The room was, for a small moment, the kind of quiet that happens when a man's understanding of his recent life is rearranging itself in his face.

"The second question," Declan said. "What name did your handler use, when he gave you tonight's brief, that you did not recognize."

Cole, who had stopped looking at Declan and had started looking at the bolted floor, did not answer for a long time.

When he did, he said, "Aegis."

Declan's face did not change.

Lana, at the table, did the still thing her face did when something landed.

Aegis.

She had seen the word once before, in a directory at the bottom of Lucas's flash drive, beside a single binary that had, four hours later, gutted the regional financial architecture of one of the world's largest privately-held criminal enterprises.

Aegis was, on Lucas's flash drive, the *kill switch.*

Aegis was, on Cole's brief tonight, the *operation.*

Stanton's people had told their tactical contractors, in the brief that had sent Cole to the dockyard, that they were responding to an *Aegis* event.

Aegis was not the name of the kill switch.

Aegis was the name of the *crisis protocol* that the kill switch had been designed to trigger.

Stanton had a doomsday plan.

When the doomsday plan went off, Stanton's people knew to mobilize.

When Stanton's people mobilized, they walked into a *cleanup operation* that was set up, in advance, by somebody else.

Stanton's people had, tonight, *been the target of their own crisis protocol.*

Lana, at the table, set both hands flat on the laptop and breathed.

"Sophia," she said.

"I heard."

"Sophia, the crisis protocol is engineered to, the moment it triggers, bring all of Stanton's most trusted tactical contractors into the open, where Henrik's people can sweep them. Stanton has been carrying his own assassins on his payroll without knowing. Henrik's principal has, this whole time, been waiting for Stanton to mess up, so he could clean Stanton out without lifting a finger himself."

"I know," Sophia said.

"This is, like, *exquisite* corporate strategy, Sophia."

"I know, Lana."

Cole, in the chair, looked at Declan.

Cole said, "Are you going to actually let me out of here."

Declan considered him.

"That," he said, "depends on whether the people coming for you give us forty minutes."

It was at that moment that Lucas's voice, in Lana's ear, went tight.

"Lana. Two SUVs. Coming up the alley."

* * *

The first thing the team did was pull Cole's chair sideways out of the line of fire from the door at the top of the staircase. They did this without speaking.

Sophia took the southwest corner. Declan took the door. Lana, who had been at the small table by the window, dragged the table on its side across the angle of the doorway and dropped behind it with the laptop in one hand and Sophia's spare pistol, which Sophia had pressed into her palm the moment Lucas had spoken, in the other.

Cole, for the first time in the conversation, looked frightened.

"I am not going to shoot you, Cole," Sophia said, quietly. "I would prefer that you not be in this room when this happens."

"...I would also prefer that."

"Tough."

Outside, in Lana's ear, Lucas: "Both SUVs. Front and back of the building. Six men out of the lead. Four out of the second. They are not, I want to stress, the same kind of professional. The lead team is wearing Allegiant Vector's vests. The second team is not wearing anything. They are in dark plain jackets. They are extremely calm. They are coming in through the kosher deli."

Sophia, in the corner, exhaled.

"Two teams," she said.

"Yes," Declan said. "Right on schedule. Marcus's people, and Henrik's principal's people."

"Sophia," Lana said. "I want to point out that there are, downstairs, civilians in a working deli."

"I know," Sophia said. "Lucas. The deli."

Lucas, sounding stressed: "I, um, I called the deli's number eight minutes ago. I told them their gas line was reading a leak on a remote sensor. They have evacuated. Three customers, two staff, the whole family. They are across the street at the dry cleaner. They are fine. The kosher deli is empty."

"...Lucas," Lana said.

"I had a feeling."

"Lucas."

"I have been getting feelings, Lana. About things."

"You called the deli."

"I called the deli."

Sophia, in the corner, did not allow her face to do anything, but Lana saw the corner of her sister's mouth move in a way that was, for Sophia, extremely close to a laugh.

"Lucas," Sophia said, "the moment you tell me that, I am giving you a raise."

"I would like a raise."

"You will get one."

"Are we going to die now."

"Probably not. Stay where you are. Do not, under any circumstances, drive over here. Do you copy."

"...copy."

The boots on the stairs started a moment later.

The boots were Allegiant Vector boots. The boots came up the wooden staircase in the practiced two-by-two stack of a tactical breach, and the lead boots reached the door at the top of the stairs, and the lead boots did the small distinctive *shuffle* that boots did when they were stacking on a door for entry, and Declan, who had been waiting for that particular sound, made a small gesture to Sophia.

Sophia put her hand on the heavy steel rod of the door's reinforcing bar.

Declan put his hand on the trigger of the rifle he had taken off the first man at the dockyard.

The door blew inward.

The breaching charge was small, professional, and well-placed. It took the lock and a small shower of splinters with it, leaving the door itself swinging inward on its remaining hinge. Two Allegiant Vector contractors came through, fast, weapons up.

They had, Lana realized later, perhaps three quarters of a second to register that the room they had entered was not the room they had been briefed to enter.

The room they had been briefed to enter was, presumably, full of confused civilians in the middle of an interrogation, and Cole, J., zip-tied to a chair, and a small number of distractable amateurs.

The room they actually entered contained Sophia Harper, who was already moving.

Sophia moved without taking the first contractor's weapon. She moved past it, the way she had moved past the rifle of the first man at the dockyard, redirecting the muzzle up and away as she swept inside the man's lead arm. Her right elbow connected with his throat. Her left hand drove his rifle barrel into the doorframe. He made a small choked sound and went down, taking his weapon with him in a way that meant his weapon was no longer pointing into the room.

The second contractor was a fraction of a second behind him.

The second contractor was, Lana would think later, the one who almost lived.

He came through the doorway in a clcancr posture, weapon shouldered, and he saw Sophia at exactly the same moment that Declan, from his blind side, caught the muzzle of the rifle Declan had taken off the first dockyard man and brought it down sideways across the contractor's wrists with a strike that broke the contractor's grip on his own weapon. The contractor's pistol came up next, in his other hand, and he was, in his own assessment, about to be the man who fixed the situation, when a third man came through the doorway behind him.

The third man was not Allegiant Vector.

The third man was not wearing a vest. The third man was wearing a dark plain jacket.

The third man shot the second man in the back of the head from a distance of approximately three feet, with a suppressed pistol, in a single quiet *fwip* that was less a gunshot than a stapler closing.

The second contractor went down.

The third man stepped over him without breaking stride.

He did not raise his weapon at Sophia.

He did not raise his weapon at Declan.

He did not raise his weapon at Lana.

He raised his weapon, instead, at Cole, J., who was zip-tied to the bolted folding chair in the middle of the room, who had been watching the door with his eyes wide and his mouth half-open, and who had not, in any meaningful sense, ever been a threat to anyone in the room who had not already been put on the floor.

The third man was about to put a bullet through the side of Cole's head.

He was, in the act of squeezing the trigger when Declan, with the economy of a man who had not, in eleven years, lost his sense of when to interrupt a homicide, shot the third man in the side of the chest with the rifle.

The third man dropped.

Cole, in the chair, made a small sound that, Lana realized, was the sound a man made when he understood, for the first time, that he had been told the truth.

A fourth man came through the doorway.

The fourth man was also in the dark plain jacket. The fourth man saw, in the half-second of his entry, three things he had not been briefed for: Sophia Harper in his line of sight, the third man on the floor, and the nominal subject of his entire operation, Cole, J., still alive in his chair. The fourth man did, with admirable professionalism, the calculation of a contractor who had just realized that the situation had progressed beyond what his operational parameters tolerated.

He threw a smoke grenade.

The grenade hit the tile floor and bloomed.

White smoke filled the room in approximately three seconds.

Sophia, in the smoke, was already moving toward the door.

Declan, in the smoke, was already moving toward Cole.

Lana, behind the table, was already on the floor, crawling toward the fire escape window.

The fourth man, whose face Lana had seen for less than a second, did not enter the room. The fourth man did, however, fire two rounds blindly into the smoke, and one of those rounds, by sheer probability, struck the laptop on the floor next to Lana's elbow and detonated its hard drive in a small, surprised electronic *pop.*

Lana, in the smoke, made a noise that, in another context, would have been classified as a wail.

"Lana!" Sophia, sharp.

"I'm okay! The laptop's not okay!"

"Did you have a backup."

"I had THREE backups. THE BACKUPS ARE IN A DIFFERENT BUILDING."

"...we'll get them."

"Sophia, I am extremely upset right now."

"Lana."

"Yeah."

"Window. Now."

Lana went for the window.

Declan, behind her, was cutting Cole's zip ties with a tactical knife and dragging Cole, who had now passed all the way through *frightened* and into *deeply compliant,* toward the same window. Sophia, at the doorway, had taken a position behind the splintered remains of the door and was, with cold efficient bursts, holding the staircase against the fourth man and the fifth man and however many men were behind them, in a way that was buying the rest of them the seconds they needed to reach the window.

Lana hit the fire escape with one foot.

She turned, in that motion, to look back at the room.

The smoke was at chest height. Through it, in the strobing dimness of the bare overhead bulb, she could see a figure at the bottom of the stairwell, looking up, watching the doorway. The figure was tall. The figure was wearing a tailored black suit. The figure's hair was perfect, even in the haze. The figure had a single hand resting, casually, on the bannister.

The figure was notin the room.

The figure was not entering.

The figure was, instead, standing at the foot of the stairs, watching the chaos at the top, with the unhurried focus of a man at a museum looking at a painting he had been told, in advance, was going to be interesting.

His eyes met hers.

Henrik Vanek, in the smoke, did the smallest possible thing.

He inclined his head.

Not a nod. Not a salute. An acknowledgment. The kind of acknowledgment one professional gave another, across a crowded room, when there was, between them, an unspoken agreement that a thing was being done, and that it was being done cleanly, and that, for the moment, the people in the room were not, in any direct sense, the people who were going to do anything about it.

He raised one finger, then, and tapped his own temple, twice, lightly. The way a man tapped his temple when he was telling another professional, *I see you. I will remember.*

Then he turned, and he walked, unhurried, down the stairs into the dark of the kosher deli, and he was gone.

He had not, at any point, fired a weapon.

He had not, at any point, done anything except stand at the bottom of a staircase and watch a man named Cole, J. fail to die, and a young woman named Lana Harper succeed in not dying, and a fourth contractor in a plain dark jacket fire two rounds into smoke and miss.

He had let them live.

He had not let them live by accident.

Lana stood on the fire escape with one hand on the railing and watched him go, and she understood, in a small clean way, that whatever the next several days were going to be, they were going to be played according to a different set of rules than she had assumed she was playing.

She was not, to Henrik Vanek, a target.

She was, to Henrik Vanek, *interesting.*

She was being collected.

* * *

The team made it out across two rooftops, down a delivery alley behind a laundromat, and into a Honda CR-V that Declan had pre-positioned three streets away.

Cole, J. came with them.

Cole, J. was, at this point, no longer in any meaningful sense their prisoner. Cole, J. was a man who had, in the last forty-five minutes, watched his employer attempt to murder him, watched a stranger save his life for reasons he did not understand, and learned that the people he had been working for had been, as a category, somebody else's bait. He was sitting in the back seat of the Honda CR-V between Declan and Sophia with his hands free, his face slightly slack, and his eyes on the road like a man who had just remembered that the road existed.

Lucas, from his vehicle, met them three blocks east at a designated rendezvous parking lot, and they consolidated. Sophia took Lucas's car. Declan took the CR-V. Cole was, Sophia decided, going with Declan.

"You are letting him go," Lana said, as they redistributed gear.

"I am giving him a head start," Sophia said. "Declan will drive him out to a freeway exit and hand him a phone with two numbers in the contacts. The first number is a man in St. Louis who Helena, at one point, made a habit of giving second chances to. The second number is, in case the first number does not pick up, a different man in Pittsburgh. Neither of those men are the kind of person you go to in order to keep doing the work he was doing. They are the kind of person you go to in order to *stop* doing the work. He will, if he is sensible, take the help. If he is not sensible, he will be picked up by Henrik's people inside of three days. We have done what we owe. He is no longer our problem."

Cole, J., who was watching Sophia from the back seat of the CR-V, said, quietly, "...thank you."

Sophia did not look at him.

Sophia said, "Don't thank me, Cole. Just don't be in the next room."

Cole nodded.

Declan, behind the wheel of the CR-V, looked at Sophia.

"I'll meet you at the place," he said.

"At the place," she agreed.

He pulled out of the lot.

Lana, in the passenger seat of Lucas's car, watched the CR-V's taillights disappear up the access road.

"What place," she said.

"A different place," Sophia said. "The bolthole is burned. I have, in this region, four left. We are going to a fifth that is not, technically, mine, but which the owner has agreed, for tonight, to let us use."

"...who is the owner."

"A friend."

"Sophia."

"Lana, I love you, and I am also, at this moment, deeply tired of being asked questions whose answers have been, for fifteen years, a function of my own personal operational security. I will tell you about the friend when we get there. Lucas, drive. Take Stockton north."

Lucas drove.

Lucas, who had been quiet through most of the redistribution, said, "Did we win, just now? Or did we lose."

Lana thought about it.

Lana said, "We didn't die. The kill switch took out Stanton's regional. Henrik knows where I'm not. Cole is going to live, probably. And I lost a laptop with three years of side projects on it that I am going to grieve for the rest of my life. So that's three for, two against, and one personal. I'm calling it a draw."

"Henrik knows where you are," Sophia said. "Lana. He sent you a message. He has been one step ahead of us all night. He is not, in the operational sense, *behind* us."

"...that's fair."

"He is also," Sophia said, "choosing not to act on it. Which is its own information. He could have killed us in that print shop. He didn't. He could have killed Cole. He didn't. He could have prevented the entire operation from happening, given that he had access to the dockyard's authentication systems three hours before we did. He didn't. He is not doing what he could be doing. Which means he is doing something else. Which means we don't yet understand what game he is playing."

The car was quiet for a moment.

"...he likes us," Lana said, slowly.

Sophia did not answer.

"He likes us, Sophia. He thinks we're interesting. He is *enjoying* this."

"...that is, I think, an accurate read."

"Which means his principal, the man in the leather chair, the actual head of all this, is the one running the cleanup. Henrik is, you know, a fan."

"Yes."

"That is a really upsetting thing to know about the man who is currently following us."

"Yes."

The car turned onto Stockton.

In the back seat, Sophia took out a fresh phone, the kind that came in a sealed plastic clamshell, that she had purchased six hours earlier in a gas station on the way out of the dockyard area, and she activated it, and she typed a brief text into it, and she sent it.

The text said, "Use the cottage. I'll explain later."

She put the phone away.

Lana watched her sister's hand, in the dark, do the precise motion of a woman who had, fifteen years ago, decided that she was going to live the rest of her life with both of her hands free.

"Sophia."

"What."

"I want to call Dad."

"I know."

"From the new place."

"From the new place. Tomorrow. Clean line. I will set it up."

"...okay."

"Lana."

"What."

"He is okay. I keep telling you this. He is okay."

"I know."

"I am sorry that I cannot, at this exact moment, prove it to you by handing you the phone."

"I know, Sophia."

The car kept going.

The night kept going.

Somewhere in the city behind them, a fourth man in a dark plain jacket was finishing his report to his handler, and the handler was finishing his report to a man in a leather chair, and the man in the leather chair was making a series of small decisions about the next ninety-six hours, with the patient attention of a man who had been waiting, for the last four years, for exactly this kind of opportunity.

Stanton Industries, in the regional sense, had ceased to exist at approximately ten-fifty p.m. central time.

By approximately one in the morning, the financial trades that had been triggered by the kill switch's regional cascade had begun to ripple outward into the legitimate banking system, and a small number of regional financial regulators in three jurisdictions were beginning to receive automated alerts that they did not, yet, know what to do with.

By approximately three in the morning, Marcus Stanton, asleep in his Alpine fortress on a continent Lana had not yet visited, was going to be woken by a phone call.

By approximately seven in the morning, he was going to have lost everything except the credentials he had hidden in a small, very clever vault in the wall of his personal office.

By approximately ten in the morning, the man in the leather chair would call him, courteously, on his personal line, and ask him to come for dinner.

Marcus Stanton, who had spent twenty-two years running a multinational criminal enterprise without ever once, properly, understanding which of his subordinates was actually his employer, was, in approximately seven hours, going to receive the kind of dinner invitation that men in his line of work understood to be the last conversation of their lives.

Lana, in the passenger seat of Lucas's car, did not yet know any of this.

She knew that her father was alive.

She knew that her sister was alive.

She knew that there was a man in a leather chair who had, in the last six hours, become aware of her existence in a way that was the worst kind of awareness, and that the man in the leather chair had a name she did not, yet, know.

She knew that she needed sleep.

The car rolled through a stoplight, and the streetlights came up over them in a slow rhythmic pulse, and Lana closed her eyes for the first time since she had woken up in her loft bed forty hours ago, and she let, for thirty seconds, the rhythm of the streetlights pass over her face like a small mercy.

Sophia, in the back seat, watching her sister's face in the mirror, did not, for those thirty seconds, look away.

Chapter 9: The Fortress

The cottage was on a small wooded property forty minutes north of the city, off a county road, behind a gate that looked, from the road, like the kind of gate a person bought at a Tractor Supply and put up to keep teenagers from drinking in their woodlot.

The gate was, in fact, a steel-core security gate with a hardened transponder, a pressure-plate spike strip beneath the gravel, and a small camera mounted in the trunk of an oak tree thirty yards inside the property. Sophia waved a small fob at the camera. The gate opened. Lucas, driving, did not, by any visible sign, register that he had just passed through several thousand dollars of concealed defensive infrastructure.

The cottage itself was a single-story log structure with a green metal roof, a wraparound porch, and a stone chimney with a curl of woodsmoke rising from it. There were two cars parked under a canvas-roofed carport. A grey shorthair cat sat on the railing of the porch, watching their approach with the unimpressed steady stare of a cat who had seen a great many strangers come up this gravel drive and had developed opinions.

The cat reminded Lana, with a sudden hard ache she had not been ready for, of Pixel.

She had not, in the last forty hours, allowed herself to think about Pixel.

She still did not allow herself to think about Pixel. She filed Pixel away, again, in the careful drawer in her chest where she had been filing the things she could not, in this exact moment, afford to feel. She was getting good at filing. Sophia, she suspected, had been good at filing for a very long time.

The door of the cottage opened.

A woman stepped out onto the porch.

She was perhaps seventy. She was small, compact, wearing a dark sweater and tan corduroy pants and reading glasses pushed up into her short white hair. She had the slightly amused face of a woman who had, at some point in her life, decided that the world was largely ridiculous and that she had survived it by paying close attention. She did not, in any visible way, react to the four strangers getting out of a Honda Civic in her driveway.

She did, however, look at Sophia for a long second.

Then she said, in a voice that had the faint trace of an accent Lana could not, on first hearing, place, "You look terrible, sweetheart."

"Hi, Margit," Sophia said.

"Inside, all of you. The kettle is on. Hands and faces, the bathroom is the second door on the right. The man with the bandages on his arm goes first." She looked at Declan. "Hello, Declan. You owe me eight hundred dollars from 2014."

Declan, mildly, "I have it on me, Margit."

"I know. Inside."

They went inside.

* * *

The cottage was warm.

It smelled of woodsmoke and chicken broth and the particular dusty herbal smell of a house where someone had been drying something in bunches from the kitchen ceiling for years. There was a kitchen at the back, a living room at the front with a worn leather couch and two armchairs and a lit fire in the stone fireplace, and three doors leading off a short hallway, one of which Margit had, with an unhurried herding gesture, indicated as the bathroom.

She did not, on the way in, ask any of them their names.

Lana noticed this. Lana noticed a great many things about Margit, in the first ninety seconds, and Lana was beginning to understand that Margit had, at some point in her life, also been someone who paid attention to a great many things.

There was, on the wall above the fireplace, a small framed black-and-white photograph of two women in their thirties at what looked like the railing of a Mediterranean ferry. One of the women was, unmistakably, a younger Margit. The other woman was a tall, slim brunette with sharp cheekbones and a laughing mouth, leaning her elbow on Margit's shoulder.

The other woman, Lana realized in a clean way realizations had recently been working, was a woman Lana had never seen, in her conscious memory, before in her life, and Lana knew her face anyway.

The other woman was their mother.

Lana stopped, in the hallway, in front of the photograph.

She did not, at first, breathe.

Behind her, in the kitchen, Margit's voice, quiet but pitched to carry: "That was Helena, in 1998. We were in Greece. She was supposed to be working. She was working. She was also, that day, drinking an extremely large glass of wine and laughing at me, because I had just been seasick over the railing of the ferry. She found my seasickness deeply funny. Helena was a great person, sweetheart, but her sense of humor was a *little* mean."

Lana's throat closed.

Margit appeared, at her elbow, with a steaming mug.

"Drink this," Margit said, gently. "It is broth. There is salt in it. You have been crying without realizing it. The salt will help."

Lana, wordlessly, took the mug.

She stood, for a long moment, in the hallway of a stranger's cottage, in front of a photograph of her mother, and she drank the broth.

Margit, beside her, did not say anything else.

After a while, Margit said, "I will give you the photograph, when you leave. It is yours. She would have wanted you to have it. I have many others."

"...you knew her well."

"I knew her very well. I trained with her. I lost her. And then I helped your sister find her way to a man named Janos Mariakos, in Hungary, in 2003, and I have been your sister's..." She paused, tilted her head, considering, "...stage mother. For the last twenty-two years. It is not a glamorous role. Your sister is, between us, a difficult kid."

Sophia, from the kitchen, said dryly, "I can hear you, Margit."

"You were *meant* to."

Lana, despite everything, laughed.

She laughed a small, wet, surprised laugh, and Margit, beside her, patted her elbow, and Margit said, quietly, "Sit. Eat. We have, your sister tells me, a fortress to take by morning."

* * *

The plan, as the team laid it out around Margit's kitchen table over reheated chicken soup and slices of dark rye bread, was the kind of plan that only made sense if you had run out of better plans, which was, in essence, where the team was.

Marcus Stanton, by Lana's analysis of the regional cascade, had retreated. He had not retreated to a city. He had retreated to a fortified residence in the Austrian Alps, in the Hohe Tauern region southwest of Innsbruck, on a property he had acquired in 2009 from the estate of a defunct Liechtensteiner industrialist and had, in the years since, retrofitted with the kind of security system one bought when one had given up the question of whether one was, technically, a member of organized crime.

He had taken his executive infrastructure with him. He had taken, in particular, the three credentials he was, at this point, almost certainly carrying on his person, including the one credential the team needed: a higher-tier authentication token that would let Lana finish what the dockyard cascade had started. With Marcus's tier-two credential, Lana could push the kill switch out of Stanton's domain and into the Council's network. The cascade would no longer stop at the boundary. It would climb.

He had also, by Declan's read of the chatter, accepted a dinner invitation for the following evening at an undisclosed location with a man whose name Marcus did not, yet, fully appreciate.

The dinner was Marcus's death.

The team's job, over the next sixteen hours, was to get to him before the dinner.

"You want," Margit said, mildly, from her chair at the head of the table, "to break into a fortified Austrian villa, abduct a man in his own home, take a credential off him, deploy the credential, and exfiltrate. In sixteen hours."

"Yes."

"From here."

"Yes."

"...Sophia. Sweetheart. This is a very ambitious plan."

"Margit, I know."

"You will need an aircraft."

"I know."

"You will need an aircraft on the ground in Austria within the next nine hours. You will need ground transport at the destination. You will need accurate building schematics, which Marcus has been paranoid enough to keep off any public registry, and which you will not, simply by walking up to the villa, be able to reverse-engineer in the time available."

"I know."

"You will need," Margit said, picking up her tea, "a friend in the air."

"Margit."

"Mmm."

"Will you call him."

Margit considered her tea.

She set the tea down.

She looked, with great fondness, at Sophia. Then she looked, with the same fondness, at Lana, who had been at the table for forty minutes and who had not, in those forty minutes, said anything beyond *yes* and *no* and *thank you for the broth.*

Then Margit said, "For Helena's daughters. Yes. I will call him."

She went out onto the porch.

She did not come back for nineteen minutes.

When she came back, she had a folded piece of paper in her hand. She set it on the table in front of Sophia.

The paper had, in a neat hand, an address in Indiana, a pilot's name, a tail number, a fuel report, and a note: *Wheels up at 0530. Fuel for direct to LOWI. Arrange ground transport from there. Tell Sophia I want my dinner back. Yannick.*

Sophia closed her eyes.

She opened them.

She said, "Margit."

"He has been waiting," Margit said, "for a reason. You are giving him a reason. Do not be mawkish. Eat your soup."

Sophia, after a long moment, ate her soup.

Lana, who had, twenty minutes earlier, decided that she was going to spend the rest of her life being grateful to Margit, ate her soup too.

* * *

There was, before they left the cottage, the call to Dad.

Margit set Lana up in the back study, on a hardline phone that ran out through a buried cable to a fiber junction box that Sophia, three years earlier, had personally walked the cable for. The phone, Margit promised, was as clean as any phone in the country. It would route through three switchboards and two satellite hops and would arrive on the cabin's end as a generic local exchange somewhere in Helena, Montana.

Lana sat in the small wood-paneled study with the phone in her hand for ninety seconds before she could make herself dial.

Her father picked up on the second ring.

"Lana?" His voice, instantly, was tight. "Kiddo, I have been calling you. Are you okay?"

"I'm okay, Dad."

"Don't lie to me."

She closed her eyes.

She thought about the chandelier and the pouch and the parking garage and the granola bar with the line of eleven raisins. She thought about Henrik Vanek tapping his temple in the smoke. She thought about her sister, alive, asleep against the wall of a kitchen in a stranger's cottage. She thought about the man in the leather chair, sitting somewhere in a building she would never see, knowing her name.

She thought about her father's cough.

"I'm not okay, Dad," she said. "But I'm safe. I'm with people I trust. I can't tell you where I am, and I can't tell you what I'm doing. I can tell you that it's, that I am, that it is going to be a few days before I can talk to you again. And I am not, when I do talk to you again, going to be the same person you knew yesterday."

The line was quiet.

Her father, in the long, slow way her father had, said, "Kiddo."

"Yeah, Dad."

"You found her, didn't you."

The world stopped.

Lana, in the small study, in Margit's cottage, in a county forty minutes north of Chicago, with a steaming mug of broth going cold on the desk beside her, said, in a voice that was not quite her own, "...what?"

"Your sister," her father said. "You found her. Or she found you."

Lana could not, for a moment, make any words come out of her mouth.

"Dad."

"Yeah, kiddo."

"You knew."

"I knew."

"You.."

"I knew," he said, gently. "I have known for, oh, a long time, kiddo. There was a man, in 2010, who came to the shop. He fixed a problem I didn't know I had. He said he was a friend of Helena's. He said your sister was alive. He said your sister had told him to tell me, that she was sorry, but that we could not talk about it, and that I had to go on as if I did not know, because if I behaved differently, it would put you in danger. He said your sister would, when the time came, find a way to tell you herself. I have been waiting for her to find that way for fifteen years, Lana. I figured it would happen sometime. I figured I would know when it did, because you would call me, in the middle of a Tuesday, and your voice would sound exactly the way your voice sounds right now."

Lana, in the small study, was crying without making any sound.

She had, at some point, put her hand over her mouth.

She took it away.

"Dad."

"I love you, kiddo."

"You knew."

"I knew."

"I'm so sorry."

"For what?"

"For not knowing. For all the times she could have come back and you could have, and you didn't, and we never.."

"Lana," her father said. "Stop. She did the right thing. So did I. So did you. The math, sweetheart. The math is the math. You don't apologize for the math."

She laughed. The laughter came out as a small wet sob.

"That," she said, "is exactly what she said."

"That," her father said, "is because your mother used to say it."

The line was, for a long moment, only the sound of two people not talking.

Then her father said, very gently, "Kiddo. Whatever you have to do. Do it. Be careful. Come home when you can. I have a six-pack in the fridge that has been waiting for fifteen years. We will, all three of us, drink it on the porch."

"Yeah, Dad."

"...tell her I miss her. Tell her I'm proud. Tell her she still owes me for the dent in the F-150 from 1998."

"I will, Dad. I will tell her exactly that."

"Love you."

"Love you too, Dad."

She hung up.

She sat in the small wood-paneled study for several minutes. Her hand, on the phone receiver, did not move. The mug of broth, on the desk, finished going cold.

When she finally stood up, and walked back out into the kitchen of the cottage, Sophia was there, leaning against the doorframe with her arms folded, with the kind of careful blank face Sophia wore when Sophia was doing something other than being blank.

Sophia, when Lana came out, did not say anything.

Lana, walking past her sister, said, very quietly, "He knew. He has known since 2010."

Sophia did not, immediately, react.

Then her sister, very slowly, exhaled. The exhale was the longest one Lana had heard from her, since the parking garage.

Sophia said, in a voice that was almost a question, "...Mariakos."

Lana, who did not know the name well enough to know what it meant in this context, simply nodded.

"He told me he wouldn't."

"...I think," Lana said, "he made a judgment call."

Sophia closed her eyes.

She put her forehead, briefly, against the doorframe.

She said, in a voice that had a small, complicated wet sound in it, "...I'm so glad."

That, in the small kitchen of Margit's cottage, was where Lana put her arms around her sister, and her sister, after a long moment, put her arms back, and they stood there, in the doorway, while in the living room Lucas pretended to read a magazine and Declan pretended to clean a rifle and Margit, in the kitchen, did not, in any meaningful sense, pretend anything at all.

* * *

The flight to LOWI, which was the airport code for Innsbruck, was nine hours and seventeen minutes long, and was, by the standards of cargo flights chartered by retired smugglers for old friends of the dead, comfortable.

Yannick was a sixty-eight-year-old former Belgian air-freight pilot with a single gold tooth and the cheerful weather-worn face of a man who had during his career flown things across borders that he was not, technically, supposed to be flying across borders, and who had retired into the kind of small-airfield charter business that allowed him to do exactly that as a hobby. He greeted Sophia at the airfield in Indiana with a great enveloping hug. He greeted Declan with a handshake and a wink. He greeted Lana, after a brief assessment, with a nod and a grave, "You look like your mother. I am sorry for your loss." He greeted Lucas, with even more gravity, with: "You look like a man who has not, until tonight, been on a small aircraft. Sit in the front. Watch the horizon. Do not vomit on the avionics."

Lucas, miserably, did not vomit on the avionics.

The plane was a Beechcraft King Air 350, a twin turboprop with a long range and a fuselage that had been, at some point in the late 1990s, refitted with a small enclosed cargo area in the rear. The cargo area was, on this particular flight, occupied by four passengers, six tactical bags, three rifles, two pistols, a complete drone control suite, the laptop replacement Lana had pulled from a secondary cache at Margit's cottage, and a very small dog named Brunhilde who belonged to Yannick and who did not, in Yannick's opinion, fly well alone.

Brunhilde, an aging dachshund with one cloudy eye, slept in Lana's lap for most of the flight.

Lana, scratching behind the dog's ears in the small, dim, droning quiet of the cabin, with her sister asleep against her shoulder for the first time in her conscious life, looked out the small oval window at the clouds passing under them in the dark and tried to think about nothing.

She thought, instead, about her mother.

She thought about a woman on a ferry railing in Greece in 1998, drinking a large glass of wine, laughing at her seasick friend.

She thought about a porch on a summer afternoon, where her mother had once told her, allegedly, that a real network was the man on everybody's company and nobody's payroll, while she had been five and feeding applesauce to a stuffed bear.

She thought about the line of eleven raisins on the dashboard of a Lincoln Town Car.

She thought about her mother and her father and her sister and her cat and Henrik Vanek, in approximately that order, and the order kept rearranging itself, and at some point she fell asleep, and Brunhilde, who did not, in Yannick's accurate assessment, fly well alone, slept against Lana's belly, and Lana did not dream, for the first time in three days, about anything at all.

* * *

The plane landed at LOWI at sixteen hundred local time, which was midmorning back in Chicago, and which gave the team approximately twelve hours of European daylight before the operation needed to be in motion.

Yannick passed them through customs with a small sealed envelope and a chuckle of which Lana wanted, very badly, to know the contents.

Their ground transport was a battered grey Land Rover Defender, parked in the long-term lot, which Margit's contact had pre-positioned three weeks earlier. It had, Sophia confirmed, half a tank of fuel, a clean set of papers, and a hidden compartment under the rear cargo deck that contained six pre-positioned lockboxes Sophia had not, in over a year, had occasion to open.

Declan drove.

The road climbed, out of Innsbruck, through the long wide green valley of the Inn, past small farms with snow on their pasture corners and small towns with onion-domed churches, into the foothills, and from the foothills into the proper mountains. The road narrowed. The treeline rose. Then they turned off the main road, onto a smaller road, and from the smaller road onto a gravel track, and from the gravel track onto the kind of unmaintained service path that did not, technically, appear on most published maps of the region.

The service path climbed for an hour.

It ended at a small avalanche-control hut, at fifteen hundred meters of elevation, on the western flank of a peak Yannick had, before takeoff, marked on Sophia's printed map with a small handwritten X.

The team parked. They unloaded. They strapped on packs. They began to walk.

The walk was five miles.

The walk was, in Lana's professional estimation, the worst five miles of her life.

She had hiked before. She had hiked in California and the Rockies and once, in college, on the Appalachian Trail with three friends and a series of regrettable nutritional choices. She had, despite a sedentary career in front of monitors, kept her body in the kind of shape required by an active dojo practice and an unforgiving sister-in-the-rearview imaginary judgment.

Her body, after thirty-six straight hours of action, on three hours of plane sleep, in real Alpine snow at altitude, in tactical boots she had not, until the previous evening, owned, did not, on the trail, perform to the standard her ego had assumed.

She was not, in any technical sense, struggling. She was keeping pace. She was, on the climbs, breathing harder than her sister was breathing. She was, on the descents, occasionally needing to plant her hand against a rock to steady herself in a way that Sophia, two paces ahead, was not. She was, in essence, *adequate.*

Sophia was a snow leopard.

Declan, twenty years older than both of them, was somehow, also, a snow leopard.

Lucas, behind Lana, was the second-worst hiker on the planet.

"Don't tell me about it," Lucas said, when Lana glanced back at him after a particularly steep section. "I know. I am aware. My boots are not designed for this. I am not designed for this. I will be standing, when I die, but I will be standing only because falling down is now, after the last hour, more tiring than continuing to walk. Do not, Lana, give me a sympathetic look. Pity is the only thing that will, at this point, finish me."

Lana, despite herself, laughed.

The trail crested a ridge.

Below them, three hundred feet down a sheer cliff, on a narrow shelf of rock that jutted out over a glacial valley, was the villa.

It was, Lana realized as she looked at it, the kind of building that wealthy paranoid men in the early 1920s had built for themselves when they had decided that no other rich person was, by their lights, paranoid enough.

It was three stories of jagged glass and pale grey local stone, clinging to the cliff like a barnacle. A long dark slate roof. Floodlights at intervals along the perimeter, which had begun, with the dropping sun, to come on in a slow staggered cycle. A helipad on the north side. A walled courtyard on the south side, with what appeared, even from this distance, to be a private chapel. A single approach road switchbacking up from the valley floor in three long zigzags, with a guard station at the first switchback.

The villa was not, by any measure Lana could observe, defensible against a serious military assault.

It was, by every measure Lana could observe, profoundly defensible against any number of more interesting kinds of approach.

It was, in essence, exactly the kind of house a man who did not believe in armies hid in.

The team set up the ice cave.

The ice cave was not, technically, an ice cave. It was a small natural overhang in the rock face on the far side of the ridge, screened from the villa's sightlines by a cluster of windswept pines, with enough flat stone underneath to set up Lucas's monitors and a small pop-up thermal tent that would, Sophia promised, raise the local temperature inside by approximately ten degrees Celsius.

Lucas, who had not stopped shivering since they had crossed sixteen hundred meters of elevation, looked at the thermal tent the way a saint looked at the gates of heaven.

"Get your guy in the chair set up, Lucas," Sophia said, gently. "You have eight hours."

Lucas got his guy in the chair set up.

He did it, despite the cold, with the practiced efficiency of a man who had been the guy in the chair for one operation now and who had, in that operation, come to understand the architecture of the work he was being asked to do. The drone control suite came up. The thermal cameras came up. The radio mesh came up. He had, within twenty minutes, three live thermal feeds on the villa, two live drone surveillance loops above its rooftops, and a clean radio circuit to Sophia, Declan, and Lana on three separated channels.

The drones, when Lucas brought them up to operational altitude, immediately encountered company.

Three patrol drones, of a model Lana recognized as Stanton's standard surveillance unit, were running a slow rotating pattern around the villa's perimeter at two hundred meters of altitude, in twenty-minute loops.

"Three drones," Lucas confirmed. "They're on a trust mesh. They're going to recognize each other. They are not going to recognize me. They are going to engage anything they don't recognize."

"Lana."

"On it," Lana said.

The drone takedown was, in operational terms, the gentlest piece of work Lana had done in three days. The patrol drones spoke a proprietary version of a publicly documented mesh protocol that

Stanton's vendor had, with the casual hubris of a vendor who had never imagined a counterparty would do their homework, secured with a single shared signing key. Lana had pulled the signing key out of the dockyard authentication trace before the kill switch had locked her out. She did not now have to break into the drone mesh. She could, in a literal sense, ask the mesh, politely, to add her drone as a member.

The mesh, after a brief contemplative pause, accepted Lucas's drone as a fourth member.

Lucas's drone, in its first act as a member of Stanton's patrol mesh, immediately began transmitting a small malformed telemetry packet that the mesh's older firmware had never, in its lifecycle of slow incremental patches, been hardened against. The malformed packet was a piece of mathematical poetry that Lana had spent, over the course of the flight from Indiana, the better part of three hours composing. The packet did not crash the mesh. The packet caused, instead, a slow, gentle, cascading misallocation of the mesh's GPS coordinate cache, in which each member drone was, very gradually, told, with increasing confidence, that it was approximately twelve meters lower in altitude than it was actually flying.

Drone one, fifteen minutes later, in a routine bank around the villa's western corner, flew, with great confidence, into the side of a pine tree.

Drone two, eleven minutes after that, encountered a similar disagreement with reality and clipped the cliff face below the villa's helipad.

Drone three, with the slow inevitability of a system that had stopped being able to disagree with itself, drifted, gently, over the villa's south wall and made very polite contact with the courtyard's marble fountain.

The mesh registered three lost members.

The mesh, by its own protocols, could not request reinforcements without an alert from the central security console.

The central security console, on the ground floor of the villa, was being monitored by a man who had, in the last twenty minutes, been distracted by a series of small power fluctuations in the building's HVAC system, which was a separate and unrelated piece of mischief Lana had triggered on his smart thermostat through a vendor backdoor she had spent the previous afternoon reading about.

The mesh, in essence, simply went quiet.

Stanton's villa was, as of nineteen hundred local time, *unwatched.*

Sophia, watching the cameras from Lucas's monitor, did not, in any way, smile.

She did, however, exhale.

She turned to Declan.

She said, "Perimeter."

He nodded.

The two of them moved out across the snow, into the long Alpine dusk, like a pair of ghosts who had, at some point, agreed not to be seen.

* * *

The two perimeter guards were dispatched in a way that, Lana saw on the thermal feed, took less than ninety seconds.

The first guard was at the southwest tower, drinking from a small thermos. Sophia approached him from his left blind, took the thermos out of his hand without spilling it, set it on the railing of the parapet, and put him to sleep with a bare-handed strike to the carotid that left him slumped against the wall in the unhurried posture of a man who had simply, after a long shift, decided to take a brief rest.

The second guard was at the northeast service entry, smoking. Declan came up the loading ramp behind him, hooked his free hand around the man's mouth before the cigarette finished its arc to his lips, and brought the man down quietly into the snow beside the ramp. The cigarette, dropped, hissed out in a small puff of melted snow.

Both bodies were dragged into the small concealed shadow of the helipad's storage shed, where the cold would, Sophia said, keep them in the same condition they were in for at least four hours. Both bodies were zip-tied. Both bodies had their radios removed and dumped in a snowbank.

The team, less than three minutes after the perimeter began, was at the service entrance.

The service entrance was, as Declan had described, a steel-clad door with a magnetic stripe reader, a backup PIN pad, and a small biometric panel that read, over a layer of glass, the right index finger of any of the fourteen people in Stanton's executive trust ring who were authorized to enter the villa from this particular point.

Lana sat down on the icy concrete of the loading ramp and opened her tactical bag.

She had, in the bag, three things specifically for the biometric panel.

The first was a small custom forging kit she had assembled, on the airplane, from the dockyard authentication trace. The trace had, in the wreckage of the kill switch's locked-out propagation, included, in a small careless piece of error logging, the public-facing biometric template of one of Stanton's senior executives, which had been used to validate his own session about six hours earlier on the day before the cascade. The template was not, by itself, a fingerprint. The template was a hashed mathematical representation of a fingerprint, which was, by the standards of this generation of biometric scanner, supposed to be irreversible.

The template was not, in fact, irreversible.

It was difficult to reverse. It was, on the scale of difficulties Lana had encountered in the last seventy-two hours, *medium.*

She had, on the plane, reversed it.

She had then, with the reversed template, machined a small silicone print at sub-millimeter resolution in a portable resin printer Declan, in his entirely calm way, had produced from one of the tactical bags upon her request.

The small silicone print was, at this moment, in a sealed plastic envelope in her hand.

She affixed it to her own right index finger with a small dab of skin-adhesive medical glue.

She pressed her finger to the biometric reader.

The biometric reader thought about it for perhaps four seconds.

The biometric reader, in a green LED chirp, said yes.

The magnetic stripe, the PIN pad, and the door's electronic lock all disengaged in a coordinated chorus.

The door, weighing perhaps four hundred pounds, swung open six inches with a soft pneumatic hiss.

Sophia, in Lana's ear, said, quietly, "You have been holding out on me, kid sister."

"I am extremely good at my job, Sophia."

"I am beginning to understand that."

They went inside.

The interior of Stanton's service entry was a long, low, stone-walled corridor lit by recessed amber sconces, with a sloping floor that descended, by the Defender Lana's tablet was now displaying, into the lower level of the villa proper. The corridor was empty.

Above their heads, somewhere in the building, Lana could hear the very faint, very distant sound of recorded classical music. Brahms, maybe. Old Stanton money.

Sophia signaled forward.

The team moved.

Up ahead, behind a heavy walnut door, in a wood-paneled office on the second floor of the villa, a man named Marcus Stanton was, at this exact moment, pouring himself a glass of single-malt, considering his dinner invitation for the following evening, and beginning, in the small slow back of his mind, to wonder why he had not, in the last forty minutes, heard from his perimeter guards.

He did not yet know that, on the floor below him, four people had just walked through his service door.

He did not yet know that one of them was looking, on her tablet, at the floor plan of his office, which had been mapped in 1923 by an Austrian architectural firm whose records had, after careful searching, surrendered to a tablet on a flight over the Atlantic.

He did not yet know that the man who had been, for twelve years, his most trusted lieutenant, Henrik Vanek, was at this moment in the dining room two floors below, calmly pouring himself a glass of the same single malt, *waiting.*

Henrik, in the dining room, lifted his glass.

He looked, with great fondness, at the antique grandfather clock in the corner, which read, in the warm yellow glow of its dial, seven thirty-eight in the evening.

He took a small, sip.

He waited.

Chapter 10: *Cascade*

The lower level of the villa was a long, low-ceilinged corridor of polished local stone, lit by amber sconces at intervals, with antique wooden doors set into the walls every twenty paces. Wine cellars on the right side. Mechanical and storage on the left. The corridor ran the full hundred-and-forty-foot length of the villa's footprint, and at the far end, in the dimness, the team could see the bottom of a wide stone staircase that climbed, in a shallow turn, up to the ground floor.

Sophia took point.

Declan, with the rifle, took rear-guard.

Lana, in the middle, with the tablet, watched the building's heat signature in real time on Lucas's feed and walked, with the, slightly-too-aware footsteps of a person who had been told that the floor she was on was approximately a thousand years old and who did not want to be the person who scuffed it.

In her ear, Lucas, low and steady: "You have the corridor. No movement. Top of the stairs, you'll come up under a small reception alcove. Beyond that, the kitchen. Beyond the kitchen, the dining room. Stanton's office is at the top of the next staircase, southwest corner of the second floor. He has, I am confirming, three personal staff in the building. One in the kitchen, one in the upstairs library, one with him in the office. None of them are the kind of staff who would have, on their resume, the words *butler* or *housekeeper.* They are armed."

"Copy."

"Henrik Vanek is in the dining room."

Sophia did not break stride.

"Confirmed?"

"Confirmed," Lucas said. "The thermal feed shows one human heat signature, seated, in the dining room. He has been seated for forty minutes. He has not moved. He is, I am pretty sure, drinking."

"...drinking."

"He has a glass at the table beside him. He picks it up every nine minutes. The temperature of the glass cycles between eighteen Celsius and the low ambient of the room. It is consistent with a fifty-year-old single malt being slowly nursed. I cannot, on a thermal scan, confirm the brand. But I note he is in a wine cellar full of single malts that older than I am, so."

Sophia, very softly, said, "He's waiting for Marcus to come down for dinner."

Lana, in the corridor, paused.

"Sophia."

"What."

"Marcus has not, by the way Lucas just described it, been *invited* to dinner with Henrik tonight. Marcus has been invited to dinner with the man in the leather chair, *tomorrow* night. Henrik is here a day early. Henrik is here when Marcus does not know he is here. Why."

A pause.

Sophia, in front of her, was looking at a closed door on the corridor's left side. The door was a heavy oak service door. It was, on the floor plan, a stairwell that led directly up to the second-floor service corridor outside Marcus's office.

Sophia said, very quietly, "Henrik is here to escort Marcus to dinner tomorrow. He is also here, tonight, in case Marcus has any second thoughts."

"...meaning."

"Meaning Henrik is here to make sure Marcus, in the next sixteen hours, does not do anything inconvenient. Which means Henrik has, this entire time, been waiting in Marcus's own dining room, drinking Marcus's own scotch, planning to escort Marcus to a dinner Marcus does not, yet, fully understand. Marcus has been, since approximately ten this morning, a man being walked to his execution who has not yet, in any meaningful way, registered that he is the dish."

Lana absorbed this.

"...that's bleak."

"It is bleak."

"He doesn't know."

"He has not allowed himself to know. He is consoling himself with a single malt and the comforting fiction that his employer, who is, his executioner, is sympathetic. He is, by every measure I can guess, not having a good evening. We are, in some uncomfortable sense, going to be doing him a favor."

"By kidnapping him."

"By kidnapping him, yes."

"Sophia, we are absolutely going to do this whole thing wrong if I think about it too long."

"Then don't."

The team went up the service stairs.

The service stairs were narrow, dimly lit, and uncarpeted, the kind of staircase that had been built in 1923 to allow staff to move through the building without bothering the people whose presence the building was designed to celebrate. Sophia, in the lead, climbed it the way she did everything else, which was without sound.

Lana, behind her, did her best.

Declan, behind Lana, made no more sound than Sophia.

At the top of the stairs, behind a service door, the team paused.

In Lana's ear, Lucas, very quiet now: "Two of Stanton's personal staff are crossing the second-floor hallway right now. Heading from the library to the office. They are going to walk into the office in approximately twenty seconds. Do you wait?"

Sophia, after a half-beat: "We wait."

Twenty seconds later, two doors opened and closed, in sequence. Footsteps on hardwood. Voices, indistinct, behind walnut paneling. Then nothing.

Lucas: "Both staff are now in the office with Stanton. The third staff is still in the kitchen on the ground floor. The dining room, also still on the ground floor, is still occupied by exactly one person, who has, in the last forty seconds, picked up his glass twice. I do not, in any way, like that he picked up the glass twice. I think he heard you."

Sophia: "Lucas, are you seeing him move."

"He is not moving."

"Then he didn't hear us. He is enjoying his evening."

"...copy."

Sophia opened the service door.

The hallway beyond was carpeted in deep red, lit by Tiffany sconces, hung with framed antique maps of the Tyrolean Alps in various centuries. At the far end of the hallway, a heavy walnut door. The door was closed. From behind the door came the faint murmur of voices and, very faintly, the recorded Brahms.

Sophia gestured. Declan moved to the right of the door. Lana moved to the left.

Sophia took the center.

She did not knock.

She put her shoulder against the door, slid the latch up with one practiced motion of her gloved hand, and went through the door already moving, already low, already inside the room before the door had finished swinging open.

What followed took six seconds.

The first staff member was at the desk, with his back to the door, leaning over Marcus Stanton's shoulder. He turned at the sound of the latch, with his hand reaching for the holster at his hip. He did not, in any meaningful sense, complete the motion. Sophia, crossing the room in three long strides, put her shoulder into his ribs and her left elbow into the side of his neck and he went down across the desk in the unhurried fold of a man who had been firmly redirected.

The second staff member was at the side bar, pouring a fresh single malt for his employer. He turned more quickly than the first one. He had drawn his weapon by the time Declan came through the door.

Declan shot him in the shoulder.

The shot was, by Declan's standards, surgical. The round took the man at the joint of his collarbone and his deltoid, in a way that, even an inch in any direction, would have been a much messier wound. The man's pistol slid out of his hand and clattered onto the parquet floor. The man, in shock, sat down very hard against the side bar, knocking over a decanter.

The single malt poured itself across the floor in a small rich amber river.

Marcus Stanton, behind his desk, did not move.

Marcus Stanton was a tall, slim, silver-haired man in his middle fifties, in a charcoal three-piece suit, in the exact posture of a man who had spent his entire career cultivating the kind of composure that did not, in any way, deserve to be on the same page as the chaos that had just bloomed in his office. His glass, in his hand, was halfway to his mouth. His mouth was slightly open. His eyes, very large, very pale, were fixed on Sophia.

Then his eyes, with a small visible mechanical effort, slid sideways, and fixed on Lana.

His eyes did the thing eyes did.

He saw Sophia. He saw Lana. He saw, in his office, two women with the same face, and his brain, for the first time in his life, did the thing brains did when they were given a piece of information they had not previously believed could exist.

"...oh," said Marcus Stanton. "Oh. Oh, you have got to be *kidding* me."

Sophia, behind the desk now, took the glass out of his hand and set it on the desk. She did not, by any sign, particularly care that he had said anything. She placed her free hand on his shoulder, with the slightly intimate weight of a woman who had been practicing, in her head, for a long time, what it felt like to put a hand on this particular shoulder.

"Marcus," she said.

"...you're *twins.*"

"Yes."

"Henrik did not, at any point, mention that Sophia had a twin."

"Henrik has known for forty hours. Henrik has been telling you the parts of the truth that suit him. It is a habit you should have noticed sooner."

Marcus, in the chair, closed his eyes.

He opened them.

He looked, with a kind of distant academic interest, at Lana.

"You," he said, "are the one who took my regional."

"Yes."

"...that was extraordinary work."

"Thank you."

"You realize you have killed me. By tomorrow afternoon. With the grace of a friend."

"Yes," Sophia said, gently. "That has been the situation since approximately ten this morning. We are here to offer you a different option."

Marcus Stanton looked at her.

"...explain," he said, slowly.

Sophia said, "You are about to make a choice. You are going to give us your tier-two credential, and you are going to put your hand on the biometric reader behind the panel in your wall, and you are going to do this within the next three minutes, because you are going to work out, in approximately forty seconds, that the alternative is dinner tomorrow with Henrik's principal, and that dinner does not, despite the menu, end with you driving home in the morning. We will, in exchange, take you out of this building tonight. You will be in the custody of an Austrian federal officer by morning. You will, by tomorrow afternoon, be giving testimony to a sealed grand jury in the Southern District of New York. You will be in protective custody for the rest of your natural life. You will, however, *have* a natural life. Henrik's principal will not. We are going to use your credential to remove him from the equation. After that, the math is much simpler for everyone. Yourself included."

Marcus Stanton, in his chair, was quiet for a long time.

He was a very intelligent man. He had built, with his own hands and his own twenty-two years of careful work, the most successful privately-held criminal logistics enterprise of the early twenty-first century. He had not, in the previous forty-eight hours, expected to find himself sitting in his own office across from two women with the same face being told, in extremely civil language, what the rest of his life was going to look like.

He thought about it.

Then he reached, slowly, into the inside pocket of his suit jacket.

He produced a small black smart card, on a thin chain.

He set it on the desk, in front of Sophia.

He said, "...I want a deal in writing before I press my finger to anything."

"You will get one in the morning," Sophia said. "In writing, on letterhead, signed by the Acting Assistant U.S. Attorney for the Southern District of New York, who I have been on the phone with twice in the last seven hours. Tonight, you will get my word."

"Your word."

"Yes."

"And you are."

"I am Helena Harper's daughter."

Marcus Stanton, in his chair, did the small involuntary thing eyes did when a man heard a name he had been avoiding hearing for twenty-three years.

His face did not change.

His shoulders, very slightly, dropped half an inch.

He said, in a voice that was almost, but not quite, conversational, "Helena. Of course. I had wondered."

Sophia said, "You had more than wondered, Marcus."

"...fair."

"Press the panel."

He pressed the panel.

The wall, three feet to his right, behind a small antique tapestry depicting the surrender of the city of Vienna, accepted his fingerprint, then his retinal scan, then the smart card he held up to a reader concealed in the molding, and then, with a small mechanical *thunk,* it slid open four inches and revealed a small server cabinet, bristling with cabling, with a single fiber jack labeled CORE-01, and a single keyboard, and a single screen, and an angry red display in the upper right corner that had been counting down, since the moment the panel slid open, from a starting value of ten minutes.

Lana looked at the countdown.

Lana said, "Marcus."

Marcus, who had folded his hands in his lap, said, "I did not press the self-destruct."

"I am aware that you did not press the self-destruct. The panel pressed it. The panel pressed it because the panel was rigged to press it the moment any unauthorized person was in the room with you when it opened. That is, in fact, very smart of you."

"Thank you."

"It is also, however, deeply inconvenient."

"I am sorry," Marcus said, mildly, "about the inconvenience."

Lana turned to her sister.

"Sophia," she said, "the upload takes three minutes. The countdown is ten. I have, in theory, plenty of time. In practice, the countdown also wipes the server stack the moment it hits zero. If the wipe runs while my upload is still propagating, the upload may corrupt, or may abort, or may, in the worst case, deploy as garbage and burn our payload without any of the cascade going through. I need either six more minutes than the countdown, or I need to stop the countdown."

Sophia, calm: "Stop the countdown."

"It is, in this kind of system, an electrically physical mechanism. I cannot, by software, override it. Somebody has to physically pull a lever. The lever, by the documentation I am, *as we speak,* extracting from Marcus's own filing system, is in a maintenance conduit two rooms over. It is connected to the core power loop of the server. Pulling it stops the destruct sequence. It also, while pulled, is an electrical hazard of a kind that, if you do it wrong, will electrocute you."

"Of course it will," Sophia said.

"Declan."

"Yeah," Declan said. "I'll do it."

"...Declan."

"Sophia. I'll do it."

He was already moving, the rifle slung across his back, his pace unhurried, the way Declan moved through any room he had decided to take responsibility for. He paused at the doorway, looked back at Sophia, gave her a small salute, and stepped through.

Lana sat down at the keyboard.

She slotted Marcus's smart card.

The system, after a brief consideration, accepted the credential.

The kill switch began to load.

In the corner of the screen, the countdown ticked over to nine minutes thirty seconds.

In the dining room, two floors below, Henrik Vanek set his glass of single malt down on the table and stood up.

He, like Lana, had begun to listen to the building.

He had always been very good at listening to buildings.

* * *

He came up the main staircase the way he did everything else, which was and observant and almost completely silent. He did not draw a weapon. He did not, by any visible sign, intend to do so. He carried his glass in his left hand and a small black flip phone, identical to the one he had given Lana in the bar three nights earlier, in his right.

He paused on the landing of the second floor.

He considered the spilled decanter outside the door of Marcus Stanton's office. He considered the trail of single malt that ran across the parquet floor in a small rich amber river. He considered the body of one of Marcus's personal staff, slumped against the side bar with a hand pressed to his shoulder, breathing.

He did not enter the office.

He stepped into the office.

He stepped into the office in the way a man entered a room he had been planning to enter, on his own schedule, with no particular intention of being a surprise to anyone in it.

Sophia, at the desk beside Lana, was the first to see him.

Sophia did not move.

Sophia did not, by any sign, react.

Sophia simply watched him cross the threshold and noted, as he came in, that the small black flip phone in his right hand had a single line of text on its screen, which was glowing faintly in the dim office light.

The text read, *NEW MESSAGE.*

The text read, in smaller script underneath, *FROM: PRINCIPAL.*

Henrik Vanek closed the office door behind him with the quiet precision of a man who had during his life closed many doors.

He looked at Marcus.

He said, in a tone of mild, almost paternal disappointment, "Marcus. You are not going to like this. Truly, I am sorry. The principal has heard about your cooperation. He has chosen not to wait. He has chosen, in light of recent developments, to handle the dinner this evening."

Marcus Stanton, in his chair, with his hands folded in his lap and the smart card already slotted into his own keyboard, did not look surprised. He did not, in any way, look heartbroken. He looked, in the slack way a man looked when his lifelong concentration finally cracked, *tired.*

"...thank you, Henrik," he said. "Truly. For the courtesy."

"Of course, Marcus."

"Will you give me a moment?"

"I am sorry, Marcus. I cannot."

Henrik raised the small black flip phone, and pressed a single key, and then he set the phone down on the corner of Marcus Stanton's desk, in a careful, polite gesture.

The flip phone, on the desk, made a small electronic chime.

Then, in a quiet, terminal way, Marcus Stanton's body, in his chair, stiffened. His mouth opened, very slightly, in a small surprised round shape that Lana had not previously seen a face make. A single bright drop of blood beaded at the corner of his left nostril. His eyes, very pale, fixed on a point on the wall above his desk, and they remained fixed on that point.

He did not, by any visible sign, suffer.

He simply, after the brief pause of his body deciding what it was going to do, slumped, with great composure, sideways in his chair.

The principal's flip phone, on the desk, made another small chime, and the screen displayed a new line of text.

OBJECTIVE: COMPLETE.

Henrik Vanek looked, for a single second, at Marcus Stanton's body.

Then he looked, with the same gentleness, at Sophia and Lana.

He said, "Hello again, ladies."

"...what," Lana said, "did you just *do*."

"Marcus had," Henrik said, "a small subdermal device installed in his neck approximately eleven years ago. He believed it was a cardiac monitor. It was not. It was a kill device. It is the principal's standard contract with his Council members. None of them are aware of it. They all believe, on the contrary, that it is a perk."

"You just murdered your own boss."

"I did," Henrik said, mildly, "as the principal asked. Yes."

He set the flip phone down on the desk, beside the body of Marcus Stanton, and he turned his attention, fully, to Sophia.

He said, "Sophia. I have been wanting to meet you, properly, for a very long time. I have, in the last week, watched you do excellent work. Truly excellent. The Council, going forward, is going to need to staff itself with people of your caliber. The principal, who is, I will tell you frankly, a more sentimental man than his reputation, would like to extend to you a personal invitation to dinner. There is a great deal we could offer you. There is a place that we have been holding for you for a number of years."

Sophia, quietly, said, "...you have been holding a place."

"For Helena's daughter, yes. I want you to understand. The principal admired your mother. He did not want her killed. The man who killed your mother was not him. The man who killed your mother was a small, paranoid man named Albert Goss, who has been dead for fifteen years for, I am afraid, exactly that reason. The principal had your mother killed in 2002, but it was not his idea. It was a tactical necessity. He has, in the years since, regretted it. He would like, in his way, to make it up to her, and to her daughters."

Sophia did not, by any sign, react.

Lana, at the keyboard, with the kill switch loading underneath her hands, did the thing she did when she was reaching, while not appearing to reach, for a weapon.

Henrik noticed.

He did not stop her.

He turned, slightly, to her instead.

"Lana," he said, with great warmth. "I know, by now, that you are not your sister. I admit, I was charmed by my own mistake. I have come to feel, in the last seventy-two hours, that the mistake was, in its own way, the most fortunate one of my career. The principal has been particularly impressed by you. He has, on his own initiative, suggested that perhaps the offer should not be solely for Sophia. He has, in fact, suggested that perhaps the offer should be for both of you. There is a considerable amount of work the Council has been needing done that you, individually, would be uniquely well-suited to. The compensation would, of course, reflect that. Your father, who has been living in extremely modest circumstances in the Bitterroots for the last fifteen years, could be made comfortable in a way that, I imagine, would deeply please him."

The silence in the office was, in that moment, very thick.

Lana's hand was, by the time Henrik finished speaking, all the way down at her hip.

She had been very slow about it.

He had been very polite about not noticing.

The kill switch deployment, on the screen, was at thirty-one percent.

Lana said, "Henrik."

"Lana."

"...you killed my mother."

"I did not kill your mother. The principal did. I, at the time, was a different man. I did not become his man until 2003. I was, in 2002, a contractor in another principal's organization, working in another part of the world. I learned about Helena's death from a Reuters wire."

"You knew her."

"I knew of her. I had heard her name in rooms. I had heard your mother described, by people I respected, as the most dangerous intelligence officer of her generation. I was, when I learned she had died, deeply disappointed, both as a professional admirer of her work, and as a man who had, in his own way, hoped to one day meet her."

"You are now," Lana said, "in this room, asking me to come work for the man who killed her."

"I am asking you to come work for the man who has, in the years since, wished he had not had her killed. There is a difference."

"Henrik."

"Yes."

"There is, in this case, no difference."

She drew the pistol.

She was not fast about it. She did not have any of Sophia's quick draw, or Declan's economy of motion. She drew the way an IT consultant drew, which was with a slightly fumbling resolution, and the muzzle came up at Henrik's center mass with the careful, two-handed grip of a woman whose Taekwondo instructor had also, four years ago, given her one (1) afternoon's lesson on the operation of a 9mm sidearm in case she ever, in his words, *needed to settle a parking dispute the old-fashioned way.*

Henrik, observing the pistol, did not move.

Henrik's face did not change.

Henrik's right hand, which had been at his side, slid, with the elegance of a man for whom this was a very practiced motion, into the breast pocket of his suit jacket. From the breast pocket, with the same elegance, he produced a small, unsuppressed automatic, of the kind a man carried when he expected, at most, to use it twice in his career.

He pointed it at Sophia.

He said, "I would prefer that you put down your weapon, Lana."

Sophia, beside Lana, calmly, said, "Lana. Pull the trigger."

"...Sophia."

"Pull the trigger. Lana. Now."

Henrik smiled, very faintly. "Lana. I assure you. If you fire that weapon, I will fire mine in the same instant. I will not miss. Sophia is, in this moment, in my line of fire. Your sister will die. You will, in the resulting chaos, also probably die. We will all of us, in this room, die. The principal will be very disappointed, but he will, in the morning, have several other excellent contractors. Whereas the two of you.."

He never finished the sentence.

The window of Marcus Stanton's office, behind Henrik's left shoulder, was a tall arched casement of leaded glass that had been installed in 1923 and which had not, until that exact moment, been disturbed by any object more violent than a winter wind.

The window, in three quick succession, made the hard, percussive *crack-crack-crack* of three high-velocity rifle rounds passing through it from the outside.

The first round took Henrik Vanek high in the right shoulder, in the joint of the deltoid. The second took him in the upper thigh. The third, by the mathematics of distance and ballistic drift over several hundred meters, missed him entirely and lodged in the wall behind Marcus Stanton's body.

Henrik's right arm, by the destruction of the joint that connected it to the rest of him, went numb.

His automatic, in his right hand, dropped, with the same unhurried elegance with which he had drawn it, onto the parquet floor of the office.

In Lana's earpiece, Lucas, sounding deeply unsettled by his own initiative, said, "Sorry. Sorry. I had a clean line. I, uh, I had a clean line, and he was about to kill her, and I just, I just.."

"Lucas," Sophia said, in a voice of extraordinary, soft warmth, "you just saved both our lives. Take a breath."

"...copy."

Henrik, on one knee now, with his left hand pressed to his shoulder, looked up at Sophia and Lana.

The smile, very faintly, was still on his face.

"...well," he said, "that was unexpected."

Sophia drew her own pistol, slowly, and stepped, slowly, around the desk.

She stopped three feet from him.

She did not, immediately, raise the pistol.

She said, "Henrik."

"Sophia."

"You knew her."

"I knew of her. I told you the truth. I never met her in life."

"Why," Sophia said, "are you smiling."

Henrik, on one knee, with blood beginning to seep through his immaculate dark suit at two separate points, looked, for a long moment, at her face. Then he looked at Lana's face. Then he looked back at Sophia.

He said, "Because I never thought I would see what Helena's daughters would look like, when they came for him. I have been waiting for this exact moment for twenty-three years. I am, with respect, only sad I will not see how it ends."

Sophia, softly, said, "Henrik. You worked for him."

"I worked for him," Henrik said. "Yes. I am a small, professional man. I have been, for a long time, his hand. I have done, in his name, things that I will not, over the next thirty seconds, attempt to itemize. I will say only this."

He looked at Lana.

His pale eyes, very tired now, and very gentle, settled on her face.

He said, "Helena would be proud of you. Both of you. She used to say, in the rooms I heard about her, that it would come down to her daughters in the end. She believed in you before either of you was old enough to be believed in. She had a small saying about you, in particular, Lana. She used to say, 'My little one, when she grows up, will run rings around all of us. She doesn't know it yet. But she will.' She was, in my professional assessment, absolutely correct."

Lana, with the pistol still in her hand, did not, for several seconds, breathe.

Henrik, after a moment, with some difficulty, turned his head and looked at the small black flip phone on Marcus Stanton's desk.

He said, "There is one more thing I would like, before we end this."

Sophia, very still, said, "What."

"I would like to use that phone. Just one short call. To the principal. I would like to tell him, on a recorded line, the names of the two Council members he has been hiding from his own organization for the last six years. He has been keeping them off the books. I have, as you know, an excellent memory. The names will be very useful to you. I have not, in twenty-three years, given them to anyone. I would like to give them, now, to you."

"...why," Sophia said.

Henrik, very softly, smiled.

"Because," he said, "my mother, also, was a Helena. It was a popular name in the Carpathians. I have been thinking, lately, about my own mother, more than I did ten years ago. I find, on reflection, that I am tired."

Sophia did not say anything.

Sophia, after a long moment, lowered her pistol.

Sophia gestured, with her free hand, at the flip phone on the desk.

Henrik, with his left hand, with great difficulty, picked up the flip phone, and dialed a number from memory, and held the phone to his ear.

He waited two rings.

Then he said, in a voice of perfectly composed clarity, "Principal. It is Henrik. I am, I am sorry to tell you, no longer your asset. I would like, before this conversation ends, to enter into the record the names of two Council members whose existence you have, in my opinion, unfairly concealed from the rest of your organization. The names are: James Rourke. Julian Braxton. Both of them are operating, as of this moment, in plain sight under aliases I will now also enter into the record. Rourke is, in the Geneva accounts, listed as Stillman. Braxton is, in his Connecticut country club, listed under the name Whitcombe."

Henrik paused, on the line, for a small, civilized moment.

Then he said, "Goodbye, Victor."

He hung up.

He set the flip phone down on the desk, beside Marcus Stanton's body.

Then he looked at Sophia, with the same gentle exhausted face, and he said, "His name is Victor Markov. He is in St. Petersburg this evening. He has, in the next forty-eight hours, a board meeting. The full board will assemble in person for it. You should plan accordingly."

Sophia raised the pistol again.

Sophia said, very quietly, "Thank you, Henrik."

Henrik smiled.

He said, "Tell Helena, when you next see her in your dreams, that I was sorry."

Sophia pulled the trigger.

It was, in the warm, wood-paneled office of Marcus Stanton's villa in the Hohe Tauern, the only mercy any of them, in that moment, had left to give.

* * *

The cascade completed at four minutes and eleven seconds.

Lana, at the keyboard, with her hands no longer entirely steady, watched the propagation log climb past the boundary that had, three days earlier at the dockyard, been the wall the kill switch could not climb. The wall, now, with Marcus's tier-two credential, simply was not there. The kill switch climbed past Stanton Industries. It climbed into the Council's broader trust network. It found the second tier of authentication. It cleared the second tier. It found the third tier. It cleared the third tier. It propagated, in a clean cascading sweep, into the regional financial networks of fourteen Council subsidiaries on four continents, and it began, with the patient irreversibility of a virus designed by professionals, to destroy them all.

The countdown, in the upper corner of the screen, hit one minute fifty-two seconds.

Then it stopped.

It stopped because Declan, two rooms away, in a maintenance conduit of the villa, with his teeth gritted and a thick rubber-soled boot against the floor for grounding, had pulled a heavy metal lever and was holding it in the *off* position with both hands, ignoring the small electrical burn that was running up his right wrist.

The countdown froze at one minute fifty-two seconds.

The cascade continued.

The cascade hit one hundred percent at six minutes thirty-eight seconds.

GLOBAL PROPAGATION: COMPLETE. COUNCIL TRUST RELATIONSHIPS: SEVERED.

Lana, at the keyboard, sat back. She closed her eyes.

She did not, in any meaningful sense, feel like celebrating.

She felt, instead, a clean crack opening up at the base of her sternum, the kind of crack a person felt when they had spent a great deal of energy on something and the something was, in the unfair way of accomplished things, suddenly *over.*

In the maintenance conduit, Declan, with great care, released the lever, which sprang back into its upright position. The countdown on the screen, which had been frozen, flickered briefly, displayed *DESTRUCT SEQUENCE OVERRIDDEN, MANUAL,* and then went dark.

The wall panel slid closed.

In Lana's earpiece, Lucas, in a voice that sounded very much as though it had been crying for the last several minutes: "...you got it."

"We got it," Sophia said.

"...I shot him."

"You did, Lucas."

"I have, by way of context, never shot anyone before."

"I know."

"I am, I think, going to be processing that for a while."

"Lucas. Take the time you need. We are leaving the building. Pack the cave."

"...copy."

* * *

Six minutes later, Sophia, Lana, and Declan, with a captured Henrik Vanek's body wrapped in a tarp from Marcus's gardening shed and Marcus's own body still slumped composedly in his chair, exited the villa through the courtyard door.

They did not, on the way out, encounter resistance.

The third member of Marcus's personal staff, the woman in the kitchen, had, by the time the team came down the main staircase, already exited the building through the kitchen's back door, having apparently made her own private calculation about the evening's developments. The rest of the villa was, as far as the team could determine, empty.

In the courtyard, in the cold thin Alpine air, two figures stood waiting.

The first was a man in a heavy parka with the patch of the Austrian Bundeskriminalamt on the shoulder. He was middle-aged, severe, professional. He nodded, once, to Sophia, with the clipped efficiency of a man who had been on the phone with her for the last three hours and who was unwilling, even now, to ask any more questions than were strictly required.

The second, beside him, was an American.

He was a tall Black man in his late fifties, in a dark suit under a long wool coat that did not quite suit the climate, with greying temples and tired, kind eyes, and the slightly stooped posture of a man who had been waiting, for the last fifteen years, for a phone call.

Sophia, in the courtyard, with the wind moving the loose ends of her hair, looked at him for a long moment.

The man, in the courtyard, looked at her for a long moment.

Then he said, in a voice that had a light Atlanta drawl underneath it, "Helena's girl."

Sophia, in a voice that was almost, but not quite, steady, said, "...Agent Reed."

"You found him."

"We found him."

"...and Henrik Vanek."

"And Henrik Vanek."

The man closed his eyes for one second.

When he opened them, he said, in the kind of slow, measured tone of a man who had learned, a long time ago, how to use the act of speaking carefully as a way of holding himself together, "...your mother promised me, in the spring of 2001, that we would, one day, have this conversation. I have, frankly, never quite believed it. I am, sweetheart, so very glad to be wrong."

Sophia did not, immediately, answer.

Sophia, after a small moment, did the thing she had been doing only twice in this entire book: she lifted her hand to her mouth, and she pressed it there, and she looked, briefly, at the snow.

When she dropped her hand, her face was the iron face again.

"Agent Reed," she said. "I am pleased to formally introduce my sister Lana, and my colleague Declan. We have here for you, under the tarp, the body of Henrik Vanek. We have, in the office on the second floor, the body of Marcus Stanton, who was killed at the order of his employer, a man we now know to be named Victor Markov, of the Russian Federation, currently in St. Petersburg. We have, in our possession, the names of the remaining members of the Council. We have, on this server stack, evidence sufficient to pursue all of them. And we have, in the next sixteen hours, an extremely tight window before Markov assembles his board for an emergency meeting and reorganizes around our cascade."

Agent Reed, after a long moment, smiled.

It was, Lana noted in the small clean part of her brain that was still keeping records, the smile of a man who had been holding a piece of grief for fifteen years and had, in the last thirty seconds, been told that the grief had finally, in some small way, been useful.

"Sweetheart," Reed said. "You take a breath. You hand me the file. I am going to be the most awake I have ever been for the next sixteen hours, and so are about three hundred federal agents I have on the phone right now. We will move on Rourke and Braxton at dawn. We will, in the next sixteen hours, get you a meeting with the Acting AAG. You will want, by then, to have a list of conditions."

"I will, by then, have a list."

"Of course you will."

The Austrian officer behind Reed coughed, politely, with the impatient cough of a man who had a body in a tarp to process and a great deal of paperwork to do before dawn. Sophia, with the civil incline of a head, gestured the team forward.

As Lana walked past Reed, the older man caught her eye, briefly.

He did not, by any visible sign, single her out. He simply, in passing, said, "Your mother used to talk about you."

Lana, who had been told this several times in the last forty hours, and who was getting, in spite of herself, used to it, said, "She did?"

"She did. She said, *Lana is going to be the smart one.* I want you to know, Lana, that we, on the federal side, have been waiting for the smart one to grow up for fifteen years. We have not, until this evening, been disappointed."

He inclined his head, gently.

He stepped back.

The team walked across the cold snowy courtyard to the waiting vehicles, and the Austrian officer's people moved past them, into the villa, and somewhere in the long thin cold air a helicopter's distant whup-whup-whup signalled the arrival of several more law-enforcement professionals than this small mountain valley had heard at one time in some years, and the operation, in any meaningful sense, was over.

* * *

The drive down out of the mountains, in a black Mercedes-Benz that Reed's people had arranged, was, for the first hour, almost entirely silent.

Lana sat in the back seat, beside Sophia. Sophia's eyes were closed. Sophia's bandaged forearm, which had reopened, again, during the office, was wrapped fresh in a clean white compress that one of Reed's medics had pressed into place before they had pulled out of the courtyard. Sophia's hand, at her side, was loose. The hand was not, anymore, holding a weapon. It was resting on the leather of the Mercedes seat, palm up, with the unconscious posture of a person who had not, in a very long time, allowed her hands to simply rest on a thing.

Lucas and Declan were in the front seats. Declan was driving. Lucas, in the passenger seat, was looking out the window at the long dark mountain landscape going past, and his face, in the dim dashboard glow, had the slack, slightly-vacant expression of a man whose first kill was sitting on him in a way he had not, in any of his previous life, had to think about.

Nobody, in the car, asked Lucas if he was okay.

Asking, Lana had come to understand, was for later.

She turned her head, slowly, and looked at her sister.

Sophia, without opening her eyes, said, softly, "Don't say anything yet."

"Okay."

"I am, at the moment, holding a great many things in a very specific order, and I would like to keep holding them in that order until we get to Innsbruck."

"Okay."

A long pause.

Lana, after a while, said, "Sophia."

"What."

"He said the principal had her killed. He said it was tactical necessity. He said the man who actually did it was named Albert Goss."

Sophia, eyes still closed, said, "I know."

"He said the principal regretted it."

"He did say that, Lana."

"Was he telling the truth?"

Sophia opened her eyes.

She looked at the ceiling of the Mercedes for a moment, with the dim track lighting of the cabin. Her face, for a moment, was the iron face. Then it cracked, just a little, around the eyes, the way her face had been, very gradually, learning to crack again.

"He was telling the truth," Sophia said, "about what he believed. Henrik was not, in his own mind, a liar. He was, in his own mind, a very precise professional. He believed, when he said it, that the principal regretted having Helena killed. The principal does not, however regret it. Markov is a sociopath in the strict clinical sense of the word. He does not regret things. He builds, around himself, the appearance of regret, because regret is a useful currency in the kind of work he does. Henrik mistook, for many years, his employer's performance of feeling for actual feeling. Henrik was a kind man, in his way. He was the kind of man who, when given a chance to believe a story, believed it. That was, in the end, his weakness."

"But there was an Albert Goss."

"There was. Helena's old colleague, in 2002. Goss was a U.S. asset who had been turned and was working for Markov. Goss was the one in the room when our mother died. Goss was, by Henrik's account, killed in 2009. By, presumably, Markov. For knowing too much."

"...how did our mother die."

The Mercedes was quiet.

Sophia, for a long time, did not answer.

Then she said, "I will tell you tomorrow."

"...Sophia."

"Tomorrow, Lana. I promise. Tomorrow morning. We are at a hotel in twenty minutes. You are going to take a hot shower. You are going to eat real food. You are going to sleep in a clean bed. In the morning, after coffee, I will tell you everything."

"You promise."

"I promise."

"...Sophia."

"What."

"He said *my little one will run rings around all of us.* That, too. Was that real?"

Sophia, in the dark of the Mercedes, with the long alpine road unspooling in the headlights ahead of them, said, very softly, "Yes, Lana. That, too. That was real."

The car kept going.

Somewhere on a quiet street in St. Petersburg, in a building Lana would never enter, a man in a leather chair set down a small black flip phone and stared, for a long, unmoving minute, at nothing in particular.

Then he reached, with one hand, for the small antique brass bell on the corner of his desk, and he rang it, twice.

A woman, in dark tactical clothing, with a hard, clean, professional face that Lana had not yet seen and which would, in eight days, walk into a corridor in a black site in Moldova and try to kill her sister, stepped out of the shadow of a doorway and inclined her head.

The man in the leather chair did not raise his voice.

He said, in flawless, unaccented English, "Begin the contingencies. All of them. Bring me Helena's daughters."

The woman in the dark tactical clothing inclined her head.

She did not say anything.

She turned, and she walked, soundlessly, out of the room, and the door, behind her, closed.

Chapter 11: *All Is Lost*

The hotel was a small family-run inn in the old town of Innsbruck, four floors of whitewashed stucco and dark timber under a tile roof, on a street so narrow that the morning light, even at nine o'clock, was just beginning to touch the upper windows.

Lana came out of the bathroom in a borrowed flannel robe, with her hair wet, with her skin pink from the kind of shower that had been, by the standards of her recent life, near-religious in its therapeutic value, and she found Sophia on the small balcony of their suite with two cups of coffee and a basket of pastries from the bakery on the ground floor.

The basket contained a single croissant, two small kipferl, a slice of buchteln with apricot jam, and a small chocolate bun that, Lana noted as she sat down across the small wrought-iron table from her sister, had no raisins in it.

Sophia, in a black tank top and jeans, with her hair, for the first time in seventy-two hours, undamp and slightly mussed, said, "I asked for that one specifically."

"...the chocolate one."

"Yes."

"...thank you, Sophia."

"You're welcome, Lana."

They ate.

They ate in the small, careful, wordless way two sisters ate when they had not, in twenty-three years, been able to eat breakfast across from each other, and when both of them, in their separate ways, were aware that the morning was, despite the pastry, the morning Sophia had promised.

The chocolate bun was, very good.

After a while, Sophia set her empty cup down. She looked, for a long moment, at the timbered façade of the building across the alley. Her face was the iron face. Her eyes, very tired, had the small pre-grief stillness of a person preparing to say something they had been preparing to say, in some form, since they were twelve.

She said, "Are you ready."

Lana, softly, said, "Yes."

* * *

"It was a Saturday in July," Sophia said. "Twenty-three years ago. The eleventh. I remember because it was your birthday in three days. Mom was already plotting the cake. You wanted, that year, a unicorn cake. She had been, the previous evening, on the phone with the bakery in Wilmette where she always ordered our cakes, asking the man who ran the bakery if it was possible to make the unicorn's horn out of sugar glass. The bakery man, by Mom's report, was deeply skeptical."

"...I don't remember the cake."

"The cake never happened, Lana. We got to the part of the morning where you had a unicorn. We did not get to the part of the morning where you had a cake."

"...oh."

Sophia, after a moment, continued.

"Dad," she said, "was at the shop. He was working a Saturday because he had taken the previous Tuesday off for an errand. Mom packed us a picnic. She had a paperback in the bag, and a small thermos of iced tea, and a Tupperware container of apple slices, and a single very large slice of cold meatloaf wrapped in waxed paper that Dad had sent us with as a peace offering for not being there. We drove to a park about twenty minutes from the house. It was a small park. There was a creek. There were oak trees. It was, by every measure, a very ordinary July Saturday. The sun was high. There was a barbecue going somewhere downwind. The air smelled of cut grass and charcoal and the very thin sweet edge of honeysuckle from the chain-link fence at the back of the park."

"I remember the honeysuckle," Lana said, slowly. "I remember... something like the honeysuckle. I remember the dream."

"You dreamed it. Yes. Many times."

"Yes."

"It was real, Lana. It was a real day. I have, since then, been to that park exactly once. I went, in 2008, on what would have been your seventeenth birthday. The honeysuckle was still on the fence. The barbecue was no longer going. The oak trees were exactly the same. They are very long-lived, oak trees."

Lana, with her hands wrapped around her coffee cup, did not, for a moment, breathe.

Sophia, in a voice that was almost conversational, said, "You ran across the grass. You did the thing you used to do where you would, halfway through running, look back over your shoulder to make sure I was still there. You did this once, twice, a third time. You wanted me to chase you. You yelled, Bet you can't catch me, Lana, which was, in a sense, a thing you yelled because the shape of your sentences when you were six was a little weird. You meant, of course, *bet I can't catch you, Lana,* but you said it backward, with my name on the wrong end of it, because your six-year-old grammar was your six-year-old grammar. You used to do this often. You called yourself *Lana* in your own dialogue. Mom and I thought it was the funniest thing on earth. Dad was a little worried about it. The pediatrician told him to relax. You grew out of it by the time you were seven."

Lana, in the small sunny chill of the Innsbruck morning, with the steam from her coffee rising in the still air, made a single small wet sound that did not, properly, have a name.

"And then," Sophia said, gently, "Mom's phone rang."

* * *

"It was a flip phone," Sophia said. "A small grey Motorola. Mom had carried it for six years. She did not, on that particular morning, look at it for nearly long enough before she answered it. She had been distracted by the meatloaf, which was, in her view, going to give her a stomachache, and which she had been stalling on. She picked up the phone. She said, *Hello.* She listened. Her mouth, in the next half-second, did the thing it did when she was hearing something she did not believe. Then she said, in her work voice, *Yes. Yes, I understand. I'll be there in twenty.*"

Sophia paused.

"The work voice was, for me, a tell. I had, by twelve, learned to recognize it. The work voice came out when she was on the phone with the people she had not, in any meaningful way, told us about. She had a job that, in our house, we were not supposed to ask about. We did not ask. We were good kids."

"...what did she say to us."

"She said, *I have to go, sweet pea. I'll be back. Just an hour. Promise.* She had been calling you sweet pea since you were one. She kissed your forehead. She kissed the top of my head, with her hand cupped around the back of my skull, and she held me there for a beat longer than she usually did. I have, since, decided that this was a tell. She was not, I think, sure she was coming back. She had, I think, the small bone-deep instinct of a woman whose work had taught her to take phone calls seriously, and she was, in the brief moment of the kiss, telling me, in the only language she had available, to look after you. She had never, in twelve years, held the kiss on me that long. She has never held it that long since."

Lana, quietly, said, "...I felt that. I felt that, in the dream. That she held you longer."

"You felt it because it happened. You were, even at six, very observant. Mom used to say, *Lana sees everything. She just doesn't have the words yet to tell anyone what she sees.* I am, with respect, not surprised that some of what you saw, that morning, you have remembered."

"...what was the call about."

"I will tell you what I think it was about," Sophia said. "I have spent twenty-three years working it out. I cannot, in any final sense, prove it. But this is what I believe. The call was from her colleague, Albert Goss. Goss was a senior intelligence analyst, like Mom. They had worked together at a federal joint task force for the previous five years. He had been, throughout that time, slowly compromised by a man named Victor Markov, who had been paying him to feed information out of the task force into Markov's network. Goss had become aware, over the past several days, that Mom was building a case against Markov. He had become aware that the case was nearly complete. He had become, more recently, aware that Mom had told her handler, in confidence, that she intended to take her family and go into protective custody as soon as she had finished writing it up. Mom had, by my best estimate, twenty-four hours of writing left. Goss had two choices. He could let Mom finish, and watch his own life end in a federal courtroom. Or he could call her, that morning, and find a way to bring her into a room where someone could end her instead."

"He brought her home."

"He brought her home. He told her, on the phone, that something had happened to Dad. He said there had been an emergency call from the shop. He said he had been the closest authority to the area and was meeting her at the house. He said Dad was alive but that there was a situation, and that he, Goss, would explain when she got there."

"...and Dad was."

"Dad was completely fine, at the shop, working on a 1987 Bronco, eating a tuna sandwich, with no idea that anything was happening. Dad did not know our mother had been killed for nearly an hour and a half after the fire department got there."

Lana closed her eyes.

She did not, at any point, lift her hand to her face. She allowed the tears, when they came, to come. There were not many. They had, in the last seventy-two hours, become a thing her body knew how to do without her supervision.

Sophia, after a moment, said, "I am going to skip the next two hours. You don't need them. I am going to tell you only what you need."

"Okay."

"Mom went home. She arrived about fifteen minutes before Goss did. We do not know what she did, in those fifteen minutes, because we have only the physical evidence. The physical evidence is that she went straight to the basement. Mom had, behind the workbench down there, a hidden cavity in the floor, and inside the cavity she had a fireproof briefcase. The briefcase contained a backup of her case, on a digital drive, plus paper notes, plus a small handwritten letter to me and to you that she had updated, by my count, three times over the past year. She kept that letter in the briefcase. She had, in the fifteen minutes before Goss got there, retrieved the briefcase, and carried it upstairs to the kitchen, and started, by the marks I found later in the wood, to take the back off the kitchen pantry to hide the briefcase in the wall cavity behind it. She had not, by the time he arrived, finished. The briefcase was, when he came in, on the kitchen floor. She had a hammer in her hand."

Lana made a choked sound.

"She knew."

"She knew, by then, what was happening. Yes. She had not, when she answered the phone, known. She had hoped, when she walked into the house, that she was wrong. She had, by the time she got the briefcase up to the kitchen, been certain. She was, in the fifteen minutes, doing the only thing she knew how to do, which was preserving the work for somebody else to find."

"...the somebody else was you."

"The somebody else was me. Yes. She did not know, at the time, that the somebody else was me. She had, in her notes, intended that, in the worst-case scenario, the somebody else would be Reed. She had not anticipated me. She had, however, raised me to find her work in basements. She had been teaching me, in her quiet way, to do exactly the kind of search I would, in fact, do, two weeks later."

"...what happened to her."

"Goss came in. Through the back door. He had, by his own preparation, brought a small leak-source kit and a delayed igniter. He had, in the small ugly economy of men in his line of work, planned the home accident before he had walked into the house. He intended to render her unconscious and stage the rest. He did not, by his own briefing, intend for it to look like a struggle. The official record was supposed to read as a faulty gas line and a tragic aspiration of fumes."

Sophia paused.

She closed her eyes for one second.

"It did not, by what the fire investigators later were able to read, go cleanly. Mom hit him in the face with the hammer. He did not kill her without effort. She fought him. She made him work for it. She did not, in the end, win the fight. She had, however, by the time he killed her, done a great deal of damage to the back of his right hand and a piece of his face that he carried for the rest of his life. Goss died in 2009. Mom is the reason he had the limp he had, in 2009, and the slight tremor in his right index finger that the obituary photo did not, quite, hide."

Lana opened her eyes.

She looked, for a long time, at her sister.

She said, very softly, "She fought him."

"She fought him."

"...I remember. I remember, now, the dream. I remember the silence at the end. I always thought the silence was the silence of nothing happening. But the silence was the silence of her, somewhere, being done."

"Yes," Sophia said. "That, too, was real."

* * *

"I went home with Margit," Sophia said, quietly, after a long time. "She had, by chance, been the person Mom had asked to swing by the park to pick us up if she did not come back in an hour. Margit was, in 2002, three hours away in Iowa. She did not, technically, swing by. She drove like a woman who already knew. By the time she got to us, in the late afternoon, the fire department had been at the house for two hours. The neighbors had taken us in. You did not know, yet, that Mom was dead. I knew. I had not been told. I knew. Margit, when she arrived at the neighbors' house, did not have to tell me. I had been waiting for her. She walked in. She put her hands on my shoulders. She looked me in the face. She said, in Hungarian, *I am sorry, ducky.* And I said, in Hungarian, *I knew.*"

"...you spoke Hungarian."

"I had been speaking Hungarian since I was three. Mom had taught me. Mom had been teaching me a great many things since I was three. You were too young, by the time she died, for that part of the curriculum. I have, in the years since, been a little jealous of you, that you got the part of her where she was a mom, and I got the part of her where she was, in the way of women in her work, slowly preparing me to take her place."

Lana, in the morning light of the Innsbruck balcony, with the steam from her coffee long gone cold, did not, for a long time, speak.

When she did, she said, "Sophia."

"What."

"I was the one who got the better deal."

Sophia, for the first time in the entire conversation, smiled.

It was a small smile. It was not a healing smile. It was the smile of a woman who had, in the long quiet labor of fifteen years, been waiting for someone to say, in those words, that exact thing.

"Yes, Lana," Sophia said. "You did."

* * *

"Two weeks after the funeral," Sophia said, "I went down to the basement. I knew, by then, that there was something to find. Mom had, six months earlier, taken me down there to show me the workbench and the floor. She had made me memorize the tile pattern. She had said, with care she had said many things, *If anything ever happens to me, this is where to look.* She had been very specific about the tile pattern. I had, until two weeks after the funeral, not allowed myself to remember her telling me. After the funeral, I let myself remember. I went down. I lifted the tile. I found the briefcase."

"...in the kitchen."

"No. In the basement. Mom had had two."

"...of course she had."

"She had a primary in the basement, which was where her main backup lived. She had a secondary in the kitchen, which she had been moving on the day she died. The primary was undisturbed when I found it. Goss had not, in any of his preparation, known there was a primary. He had only known about the secondary, which he had retrieved after he killed her, and which had, by the time the fire ate the kitchen, been, in his own pocket, removed from the building."

"What was in the basement briefcase."

"Everything Mom had ever written. A complete digital backup of her case on a small drive. A handwritten thirty-page letter to me. A handwritten ten-page letter to you, sealed, marked *Lana, when she is twenty-five.* A small leather notebook of training notes she had prepared for me, in case anything should ever happen, on the protocols of basic countersurveillance, the people in her network it would be safe to find, and a single name in Hungary that would, if I gave my own name correctly, take me in."

"...Mariakos."

"Janos Mariakos. He was Mom's first instructor when she was twenty. He had retired in 1998. He was living, in 2002, in a village three hundred kilometers from Budapest, with his wife, raising goats. He was, by the time I got to him at thirteen, sixty-eight years old, deeply tired of war, and convinced that he was going to die in the village. Mom's letter, to him, asked him for one favor. He gave it. He spent the next nine years of his life teaching me the work. He died, of a heart attack, in 2017. His wife, Erzsébet, is alive. I see her, when I can. She is a complicated person. I love her very much."

Lana, in the morning light, said, very quietly, "...I have a letter."

"You have a letter."

"I have not opened it."

"You have not. The letter is, as I said, marked *Lana, when she is twenty-five.* You are twenty-nine. The letter is, in any reasonable reading, overdue. I have, in my possession, since 2002, kept it in a sealed waterproof envelope. The envelope is, at this moment, in a safe-deposit box in a Swiss bank in Zurich, two and a half hours from where we are sitting. After this is done, when you and I are on the same continent again, we will go and we will retrieve the letter. We will sit in a café, somewhere quiet. You will read it. I will, in your presence, read mine, again, for the first time in fifteen years. We will, after, drink an enormous amount of wine."

"...what does mine say. Sophia. Tell me. Just one thing."

Sophia, after a long moment, said, "I do not know what yours says, Lana. I have never read it."

"Sophia."

"I have not. It was not addressed to me. I have, in twenty-three years, never opened the seal. I will not be the one who does."

Lana, in the morning light, on the small wrought-iron balcony of an Innsbruck inn, with her sister across from her in a black tank top and jeans, with the smell of coffee and apricot jam and the very faint thin alpine air all around them, did the thing she had been doing, in small careful pieces, since the parking garage in Chicago.

She let, in a small clean way, her shoulders drop.

She let the dream go.

She had, in twenty-three years, been unable to name the silence at the end of the dream. The silence had, in those twenty-three years, been the central unfinished sentence of her own interior life. The silence, this morning, in the Innsbruck light, had a shape to it. The shape was a kitchen and a hammer and a woman fighting for time, and a basement under it with two letters in a fireproof briefcase, and an oak tree in a park whose honeysuckle was still on the chain-link fence, and a man named Janos Mariakos, in a small Hungarian village, who had, on receiving a letter, said yes.

The silence, in the morning, was not silent anymore.

The silence was, in the words of a woman she had not been old enough to remember, *full.*

Lana, after a long moment, said, "I would like to drink that wine. Sophia."

Sophia, quietly, said, "We will, Lana. We will."

* * *

The phone rang at twenty past nine.

It was the room phone, on the small wooden desk by the window of the suite, and its ring, in the morning quiet, was small and delicate and somehow far more disruptive than a cell phone's ring would have been.

Sophia got up.

She crossed the room.

She picked up the phone.

She listened.

Her face did not change.

After a long time, she said, "...how many."

She listened again.

She said, "Names."

She listened.

She wrote, on a small pad of inn-issued stationery, with a stub pencil, in her sharp clean hand, a list of names. She did not, on any of the names, pause. She did not, on any of the names, close her eyes.

When she was done, she said, "Reed. We will be in your office in two hours. Have the maps."

She hung up.

Lana, on the balcony, who had been listening, said, "...how bad."

Sophia, with her hand still on the phone, did not, immediately, turn around.

She said, "Markov triggered the cascade contingencies eleven minutes after our cascade hit a hundred percent last night. He has a list. We have not been on the list. Reed has been on the list. The list is, in totality, sixty-three names, in eleven countries. By the time Reed got off the airplane in Vienna this morning, twelve of them were dead. By the time Reed called me, twenty minutes ago, there were eighteen. By the time you and I get to his office in Vienna, the count will be higher."

Lana stared.

"...Reed himself."

"Reed is alive. Reed is the central node Markov can't, by federal protection, immediately reach. But Reed's people, his old contacts, the witnesses he has been protecting for fifteen years, the analysts at the joint task force who were, even before our cascade, the people who would have brought this prosecution to court, every single one of them is now, in the next forty-eight hours, going to be either dead or in deep custody. Markov is shedding, in real time, the entire human infrastructure of any case the federal government can build against him. He is, even now, watching us, and he is reading us correctly, and he is making, as he always does, the decision to take, from us, the only thing we did not, until now, fully understand we needed."

Lana sat down on the edge of the bed.

She did not, for a moment, say anything.

The pastries on the balcony, in the mid-morning sun, were getting warm.

Sophia, after a moment, walked back to the balcony. She sat down across from Lana again. She picked up her cold coffee.

She said, very quietly, "This is the moment, Lana."

"...the moment of what."

"The moment when somebody says, *we cannot win this,* and everybody who is going to quit, quits."

Lana looked at her sister.

She said, "...am I supposed to quit."

"You are supposed to consider it. You have a life, Lana. You have a father. You have a cat. You have, somewhere in Chicago, an apartment over a Thai restaurant that you have been paying rent on for four years. We have, in the last hour, secured for you the cleanest exit any human in your position has ever been offered. Reed will, as of this morning, formally bring you in as a federal witness. You will be in protective custody by tomorrow night. You will have a new name. You will, in three months, have a new address. You will, in a year, have a small house with a yard, and a job at a software company we will pick out for you, and a quiet dignified life that nobody, in this organization, will ever find. Dad, by then, will be living with you, in an arrangement Reed and I will work out by the end of the week. Pixel will, on the same arrangement, be there too. You will have, in essence, the rest of your life, in a clean and protected version of your former life, starting tomorrow. You can take that. I will not, in any way, blame you. I will not judge you. You did not sign up for this. I did. This is my work. I have been doing it since I was thirteen. It is not yours to inherit."

Lana, on the edge of the bed, looked at her hands.

She thought about the unicorn cake.

She thought about the line of eleven raisins on the dashboard of a Lincoln Town Car.

She thought about her father, in a cabin in the Bitterroots, with a small dog, fishing on a Saturday morning, who had been waiting for her phone call for fifteen years.

She thought about Henrik Vanek, who had been *tired,* and who had said, in his last sixty seconds, that her mother had used to talk about her in the rooms where assassins gathered, with great patient confidence in the woman she would, if given the time, become.

She thought about the small shape of her own hand, six years old, in the larger hand of a sister she had let go of in a long summer afternoon.

She thought about the math.

The math, sweetheart, said her father, was the math.

She looked up.

She said, "Sophia."

"Yes."

"I am not going to quit."

Sophia, watching her, did not, immediately, react.

"...you don't have to," Sophia said. "Lana. You don't have to."

"I know."

"You can. You should think about it, for at least.."

"Sophia. I have. I just did. I am twenty-nine years old. I have spent twenty-three of those years not knowing what happened in a kitchen in Wilmette in July of 2002. I now know. I know, also, who did it. He is sitting in a leather chair in a building in St. Petersburg. He has, in the last sixty hours, killed eighteen people. He is, in the next forty-eight hours, going to assemble a board of his peers in the same building. We have, by the grace of a man named Henrik who chose, at the end of his life, to do one good thing, the names of two of those peers, and the floor plan of the building they will be in, and the keys, in a digital sense, to his entire infrastructure. We have a sixteen-month-pregnant tactical window. I have, by what feels like the confluence of unreasonable miracles, the woman who taught me the back of the knee kick when I was eleven sitting across from me on a balcony in Innsbruck, drinking cold coffee, asking me if I am ready to go finish the conversation our mother started. I am ready. Of course I am ready. I have, in my entire career, never been more ready for anything."

Sophia, after a long moment, said, "...Lana."

"Yes."

"That," Sophia said, softly, "was the most you have ever sounded like Mom."

Lana, despite everything, smiled.

It was a small, sharp, slightly wet smile, and it carried in it, in a clean way of inheritances, every single thing she had not, until that morning, allowed herself to know about who, in fact, she came from.

She said, "Tell me where to start."

* * *

The call to Dad, at the inn's hardline phone, lasted seven minutes.

She did not, at any point in the call, tell him what she now knew.

She told him she loved him. She told him she was safe. She told him she had been, in the last day, given a piece of news about her mother that she would, in the next month, want to talk to him about, and that she wanted to do it in person. She told him she had heard Mom's name said out loud for the first time in her life, by people who had loved her. She told him she would, when she came home, want to hear him say the name too, finally, after all the years.

He cried, on the line, for thirty seconds.

He did not apologize for it.

He said, "I'll say it, kiddo. I'll say it as many times as you need to hear it."

He said, "You go finish what you have to finish. You come home. You hear me?"

She said, "I hear you, Dad."

She hung up.

She sat in the small wood-paneled study at the inn for a moment longer.

Then she stood up.

She walked back into the suite.

Sophia, Declan, and Lucas were at the small dining table, with Sophia's pad of inn stationery laid open on it, with Reed's list of names beside it, with the rough hand-drawn outline of a building Lana had not, until that morning, ever seen on top of all of it, and they were, as Lana came in, pointing at things.

The building was on the Petrograd embankment, in St. Petersburg, three blocks from the Winter Palace.

The building was, by the floor plan Sophia and Reed had managed to assemble in the past hour, six stories. It had a private boardroom on the fifth floor. It had a private elevator from the basement parking garage to the boardroom that did not, on any blueprint, appear.

Markov's board meeting was scheduled, by Henrik's last input to his employer, for thirty-eight hours from now.

Rourke was in Geneva. Braxton was in Connecticut. The remaining three named members of the Council were scattered across two continents.

The team had thirty-eight hours.

The team had, in those thirty-eight hours, to decapitate the Council.

Lana, walking up to the table, looked at her sister, and her sister looked back at her, and Lana said, "Where do you want me to start."

Sophia, smiling, with the iron just beginning, somewhere underneath, to remember how to be soft, said, "Sit down, Lana. Let's go to work."

Chapter 12: The Architect

Stillman Asset Management occupied the third floor of a six-story limestone building on the rue du Mont-Blanc, half a block off the Quai des Bergues, with a view, from its conference rooms, of the Jet d'Eau and a small sliver of Lake Geneva that the firm's brochure had, for nineteen years, photographed from a slightly more flattering angle.

The firm had thirty-one employees, fourteen high-net-worth clients, and a single named partner, James Stillman, who was, by his official biography, a former American banker who had moved to Geneva in 2008 and who had, in the years since, built a small, deeply respected private wealth management firm specializing in *bespoke portfolio architecture for ultra-high-net-worth families.*

James Stillman did not, in any of his publicly available photographs, look like a man named James Rourke who had, until 2008, been the chief financial officer of Stanton Industries, and who had, in the year of his Geneva relocation, been formally pronounced dead in a private boating accident on Lake Michigan whose body had never, by what the

Coast Guard had described as *unfortunate hydrological conditions,* been recovered.

He did not look like that man because he had, by Lana's analysis of his current biometric records, undergone, over the course of three years between 2008 and 2011, approximately one hundred and forty thousand Swiss francs of cosmetic adjustment in a clinic outside Lausanne. The adjustments had altered, primarily, his nose, his jawline, and the shape of his ears.

The adjustments had not altered his teeth.

Lana, sitting in the back of a parked black VW Passat across from the rue du Mont-Blanc at a quarter past nine in the morning, watching the firm's third-floor windows on her tablet, had pulled, in the past two hours, a cached high-resolution dental X-ray from a Cook County tax fraud investigation in 1998 in which James Rourke, then a junior controller at Stanton Industries' parent holding company, had been deposed for a piece of testimony that had not, in the end, been needed.

She had then pulled, from the public-facing portion of a Geneva insurance database, the dental X-ray of one James Stillman, taken in 2014 for an entirely routine claim related to a small chipped molar.

The two X-rays were, except for the molar, the same X-ray.

People changed, Lana had learned in the course of her career, an enormous number of things about themselves when they wanted to disappear. They almost never thought about their teeth. The teeth, in a clean way that biometric data had, were the most stable signature most people carried, and they were, almost universally, ignored.

The radiograph match was at ninety-eight point four percent confidence.

The radiograph match was, by any standard a federal court would care about, conclusive.

Lana had, by ten in the morning, sent the comparison to Reed in Vienna, who had, by ten-fifteen, secured a sealed federal warrant authorizing the cooperation of the Swiss federal police, who had, by eleven, agreed to keep their distance from the rue du Mont-Blanc until further notice from the U.S. side.

The Swiss federal police, in Lana's experience of the last hour, were extremely good at keeping their distance from things until further notice.

"How much," Lucas asked, from the driver's seat of the Passat, where he had been quietly nursing a coffee for forty minutes, "do you think a Geneva banker pays in office rent."

"Lucas."

"I am trying," Lucas said, "to make small talk. I am very stressed, Lana, and small talk is calming."

"You have killed one man and are currently helping me catch another."

"...that is exactly why I am stressed, Lana."

She patted his shoulder.

In her ear, Sophia, very calm: "Two minutes."

Lana looked, again, at the third-floor window.

The window was, on the firm's interior layout, the corner office of James Stillman, who was, even now, on the phone with what Lana had identified as a private banker in Singapore, attempting to wire several million U.S. dollars out of a Swiss account into a Singaporean account before a federal seizure order Stillman had been alerted to fifteen minutes earlier could be processed.

The federal seizure order had not, in any practical sense, been processed.

The federal seizure order wasa small piece of staged email Lana had built that morning, sent, with great care, to Stillman's panic alert system, in order to get him to do exactly what he was, at this moment, doing.

Stillman, for the duration of his wire transfer, would be at his desk.

Stillman, for the duration of his wire transfer, would have his hands occupied.

Stillman, for the duration of his wire transfer, would be sitting on the only piece of evidence the federal prosecutor in the Southern District of New York actually needed to obtain a sealed indictment against him, which was, by the kind of clean structural irony that Helena, in another life, would have appreciated, the wire transfer itself.

In Lana's ear, Sophia: "On the floor."

"Copy."

The lobby of Stillman Asset Management was, by Geneva private banking standards, restrained: a small marble vestibule with a single security desk, a discreet brass plate, a Mondrian print, and a single soft-spoken receptionist named Adèle who had, on the morning of her interview in 2019, indicated to her future employer that she preferred not to handle any guests who had not, in advance, made an appointment.

Sophia walked into the lobby carrying a small leather attaché case and wearing a charcoal pinstriped suit, low heels, and the kind of tortoiseshell glasses no one in fact wore except as a tell that they were, in their professional self-presentation, performing *Geneva private banker.* She set the attaché case on the security desk. She produced, from an inner pocket, a discreet black business card.

The card identified her as one Mlle. Solange Briand, of an obscure Luxembourg compliance firm, who had, by previous email, been scheduled to confer with Mr. Stillman that morning regarding a routine cross-border data residency review.

Adèle, who was on the morning shift, did not, on first inspection of the card, recognize the name of the firm.

This was unsurprising, because the firm did not exist.

The firm had, however, been the subject, in the previous forty-eight hours, of a very small but extremely well-placed series of digital footprints that Lana had built across three Luxembourg corporate registries, two industry directories, and one minor Swiss banking association website, all of which Adèle, at her desk, on her PC, had now, by Lana's quiet remote prompting, just looked at.

Adèle, satisfied, picked up her phone. She murmured, in elegant Swiss French, that Mr. Stillman's ten o'clock had arrived. She listened. She set the phone down. She gave Sophia a small, professional smile.

"Mr. Stillman will be ready for you in seven minutes, Mademoiselle. Would you like a coffee?"

"That is very kind. A small espresso, please."

"Of course."

Sophia, in a tortoiseshell-glasses way that was, Lana had to admit on the surveillance feed, *deeply convincing,* sat down on the small velvet bench by the window.

Declan came in approximately ninety seconds later, carrying a small black tool bag, in coveralls with the embroidered patch of a fictitious telecommunications company on the chest, and presented himself to Adèle as a contractor from Swisscom, here for a scheduled service call on the building's third-floor data line. He had paperwork. The paperwork was, on inspection, both forged and impeccable. Adèle, with mild apology, asked him to wait, which Declan did, with the patience of a man who had, in his career, waited in many lobbies.

The third member of the team, Lucas's voice in Lana's ear confirmed, had already entered the building through the loading bay, in the brief seven-minute window during which the building's security feed was cycling through its hourly recompilation.

The third member of the team was Sophia's contact from Vienna, who Reed had, on Sophia's recommendation, briefed in at four that morning, and who was, at this moment, in the building's small, private third-floor server closet with a laptop, a fiber tap, and the patient calm of a federal cyber forensic specialist who had, Lana suspected, been waiting most of his career for exactly this kind of morning.

His name was Alexei. He was thirty-six. He was, by Sophia's brief, fluent in five languages, deeply discreet, and, once a year, the only person in the world Sophia trusted to cut her hair.

Lana, in the back of the Passat, had decided not to ask follow-up questions.

At nine fifty-eight, Adèle's phone chimed.

Adèle looked up.

She said, with her professional smile, "Mademoiselle, Mr. Stillman will see you now. The elevator is just there. Third floor, please. The receptionist on the third floor will direct you."

Sophia stood up, smiled, picked up her attaché case, and got into the elevator.

The elevator doors closed.

The doors did not open on the third floor.

The doors opened, by the electrical assistance Alexei provided from the server closet at five minutes past ten, on the second floor. Sophia stepped out into a quiet wood-paneled corridor that was, on the building's official map, simply *Storage,* and which contained, at the end of it, a door marked, in small brass letters, *COMPLIANCE, RESTRICTED.*

The door was a fire door with an electronic lock.

Sophia opened it with a magnetic stripe Alexei had, six minutes earlier, copied from the access record of a junior compliance officer who had taken the previous Friday off for a wedding in Bern.

Beyond the door was a small unmarked stairwell.

The stairwell led, two flights up, to an unobtrusive maintenance door on the third floor.

The maintenance door opened, on the inside, into the private kitchenette directly beside James Stillman's office.

In Lana's ear, Sophia, very softly: "At the door."

"He's still on the phone," Lana said. "He has, by my read of his transfer queue, about ninety seconds left to commit the wire."

"Wait for the wire."

"...copy."

She watched her tablet.

The wire transfer, on Stillman's terminal, completed at ten-oh-six and twelve seconds.

The transfer, by the time it cleared Stillman's outgoing screen, had also, simultaneously, cleared Lana's monitoring side-channel, where the entire transmission had been mirrored to Reed's federal investigators in Vienna and to a sealed evidence locker at the Southern District of New York. The

U.S. attorney's office, by ten-oh-six and fourteen seconds, had a full record of James Rourke, alias James Stillman, willfully wiring three million two hundred thousand U.S. dollars of laundered Council funds out of one bank and into another in active anticipation of a federal seizure he had been led to believe was imminent.

He was, on the legal record, now indictable.

He was, on a more practical level, sitting at his desk, looking at the screen, with the slack expression of a man who had, in the last fifteen seconds, just finished doing something he believed had saved him.

"Now," Lana said.

The kitchenette door opened, quietly, behind James Rourke's left shoulder.

Sophia stepped into the office.

She did not, on her first step, say anything.

James Rourke turned around in his ergonomic chair, with the slightly distracted half-smile of a man expecting a colleague.

He saw Sophia.

He saw her face.

Lana, on the surveillance feed, watched the man's entire constructed life, in the course of one second, fall over.

"...Helena," James Rourke whispered.

"Not Helena," Sophia said. "Helena's daughter."

His hand moved, a fraction of an inch, toward the panic alarm under the lip of his desk.

Sophia, very mildly, said, "James. The alarm is disabled. The Swiss federal police are downstairs. The U.S. federal warrant for your arrest has, as of approximately ninety seconds ago, formally cleared the Acting AAG. Adèle, downstairs, has been, in the last four minutes, served with notice that she is no longer to receive visitors. Your phones have, in the last fifty seconds, all been routed through a federal listening post in Bern. You have, James, completed your last wire transfer. We can do this in a way that involves you cooperating with us for the next six hours, or we can do this in a way that involves you cooperating with the Swiss authorities for the next six hours, by which point Markov, in St. Petersburg, will have been alerted that you are in custody, and will have made you, on his standard protocol, the same offer he made Marcus Stanton last night. The deciding factor between those two options is what, exactly, comes out of your mouth in the next ninety seconds. Choose wisely."

James Rourke, in his ergonomic chair, in his Geneva office, with the Jet d'Eau visible through his window, lifted his hand off the panic alarm.

He set it, very carefully, on the surface of his desk.

He said, in a quiet, almost academic voice, "...what, specifically, do you want."

* * *

What James Rourke gave them, over the course of the next forty minutes, in the small wood-paneled office of Stillman Asset Management, with Sophia in the second client chair and Declan in the doorway and Lana, three blocks away, listening through Sophia's earpiece while typing furiously on her own laptop, was, by any measure, the largest single intelligence transfer of his eleven-year second career.

He had been Markov's chief financial officer in everything but title since 2014.

He had personally engineered, over those eleven years, the financial architecture of every active Council operation in eight countries.

He had three full sets of credentials to Markov's St. Petersburg infrastructure, including the credential that would, by the protocols Lana was now decoding in real time, allow her to remotely render Markov's personal assets, in the course of approximately six minutes of work, *publicly visible.*

He had, in his memory, the names of the four remaining Council members Henrik had not, the previous evening, named.

He gave them the names.

He gave them the bank account numbers.

He gave them the deep-fake protocols Markov had been using to confirm transactions remotely.

He gave them, with a small hesitation that Sophia, in the second client chair, did not, in any way, push, the name and current operational alias of the woman Sophia and Lana had encountered, briefly, in the smoke of a print shop in Bridgeport on the night they had broken Marcus Stanton's regional cascade.

The woman's working name was *Wren.*

Wren, by Rourke's account, was Markov's longest-serving personal asset. She had been in his organization since 2007. She was, by reputation, the only operative Markov had ever met whom he genuinely respected. He had, in 2009, sent her to Hungary, to a small village three hundred kilometers from Budapest, where she had, by Markov's specific request, spent two years training under a man named Janos Mariakos.

Sophia, in the second client chair, did not, by any visible sign, react.

Declan, in the doorway, did.

His face, very briefly, did the thing that, for Declan, was the closest analog to a man absorbing a piece of bad news.

Lana, in the back of the Passat, with her hand on her tablet, said, on the secure channel, "Sophia."

Sophia: "I heard."

"...she trained with.."

"I know. Lana. I know. Continue."

Rourke continued.

Wren had been with Mariakos for two years. She had not, during those two years, been told that the old man's other current student was a young woman named Sophia Harper. She had, by Markov's design, been kept on a separate part of his property and trained on a separate schedule. Wren had, however, in the course of those two years, found, in the old man's filing cabinet, a single photograph of a young woman she had not recognized, and she had asked Mariakos, one evening, who the woman was.

Mariakos, by Rourke's account of what Wren had later, much later, told Markov, had said simply: "Someone you may, one day, meet."

Mariakos had then closed the filing cabinet, and the two of them had not, in the remaining year of Wren's training, spoken of it again.

Wren had, by Rourke's read, never forgotten the photograph.

Wren had, spent the last sixteen years quietly, patiently, professionally waiting to meet the woman in the photograph.

Sophia, in the chair, said, softly, "...of course she has."

Rourke, who had been observing Sophia's face with the careful interest of a man whose own life was, at this moment, being weighed, said, "I am sorry, Ms. Harper. I do not know her real name. Markov has, even from me, kept it. I can tell you that she is, by the only psychological assessment I have ever seen her undergo, what the Council's resident psychologist described as *a person of unusually focused interior life.* I can tell you that she has, in the last six years, completed thirty-one operations for the Council, of which thirty have been terminal, and that the one which was not terminal was, by what little record I have, an operation she chose, on her own initiative, to abort. The target of that aborted operation was, by my best read, a young woman in Vienna whom Wren had, on first observation, decided was, in some quality I cannot describe more precisely, *worth keeping.*"

"...what was the woman in Vienna's name."

"I do not know, Ms. Harper. The file was deleted at Wren's request, with Markov's permission. The woman in Vienna is, somewhere, alive, and is, somewhere, by Wren's intervention, the only person in the world Wren has ever spared. I find that detail interesting. I offer it, for what it is worth, as a piece of information about a woman who, in the next twenty-four hours, is going to attempt to kill you."

Sophia, in the chair, did not, for a long moment, respond.

When she did, she said, "James. Thank you."

He inclined his head.

He looked down at his hands for a moment.

Then he said, quietly, "I would like, when I am formally in Reed's custody, to provide a full deposition. I would like to be processed under whatever protective protocol the Acting AAG has available. I would like, in particular, to spend my retirement in a small house somewhere quiet that is not, in any way, on the European continent. I have, in the last sixteen years, never not been afraid. I would like, before I die, to have a year in which I am, in the small way of human beings, *not afraid.*"

Sophia, after a moment, said, "You will have it, James."

He nodded.

He stood up, slowly, from his chair.

He said, "Then I think, ladies, I am ready to meet the Swiss federal police."

* * *

Outside on the rue du Mont-Blanc, twenty minutes later, James Rourke was loaded, with great Swiss courtesy, into the back of an unmarked grey sedan by two men in plain dark overcoats, neither of whom spoke. The sedan, with no fanfare, pulled, slowly, into traffic and merged into the unhurried morning flow of bankers and tourists along the Quai des Bergues.

The Swiss federal police, even as they did this, had not, by any visible action, drawn attention to themselves.

By the small mercy of Geneva, the entire arrest had taken less than four minutes.

Lucas, in the Passat, watched the sedan drive off with his coffee gone cold in his hand.

Sophia, joining Lana in the back seat, slid into the leather and, for the first time since the kitchenette, let her shoulders, by half an inch, drop.

Declan, getting in beside Lucas, said, "Reed?"

"He's already at the federal building," Lucas said. "He has eight investigators on the receiving end, three of them speaking French. Rourke is, by the time he gets to that conference room, going to find a federal stenographer and his very first lawyer in fifteen years."

"...that may be the kindest thing James Rourke has done in fifteen years," Declan said.

"I think," Lucas said, "he agrees."

Sophia leaned her head against the headrest.

She closed her eyes.

She said, "Lana."

"Yes."

"Tell me Connecticut."

Lana, who had, in her ear, been listening to a parallel comm channel for the last eighty minutes, said, "Reed's tactical coordinator hit the Whitcombe estate at exactly the same minute we entered Stillman. Braxton was at his country club, at a private dinner with three sitting senators and a federal judge, all of whom are now, by federal warrant, also being detained for questioning. Braxton himself was apprehended at the door of his office at seven thirty-six p.m. local time. He is, currently, on his way to the federal courthouse in Hartford in handcuffs. By tomorrow morning, when *The Hartford Courant* gets the story, the entire Connecticut political class is going to have a very bad week."

"...Markov."

"Markov has, in the last twenty minutes, been informed of all of this. Reed's intercepts on his communications channels have caught two pieces of traffic in real time. The first was a message to his board telling them the meeting has been moved up. The second was a message to a contact code-named *HOUSEHOLD.* The contact code-named *HOUSEHOLD* is, by everything we have so far, Wren."

Sophia opened her eyes.

She said, "What did the message to Wren say."

"It said," Lana said, slowly, "and I am translating from the Russian, *Begin the contingencies. All of them. Bring me Helena's daughters.*"

The Passat, for a long moment, was silent.

Outside the window, a tram glided past, full of midmorning commuters with their faces turned, briefly, toward the lake.

Lucas, in the driver's seat, said, "...how soon."

Lana, looking at her tablet, said, "The board meeting has been moved to fifteen hundred Moscow time tomorrow. That gives us, Lucas, twenty-eight hours and forty minutes. I have a flight to St. Petersburg leaving Geneva-Cointrin in three hours and ten minutes. I have, on the flight, a window seat. I have, in the row behind me, three other window seats."

Declan, after a moment, said, "...three?"

"I assumed," Lana said, "you were coming with us."

"...you assumed correctly."

Sophia, in the back seat, finally opened her eyes properly, and looked at her sister.

She said, very softly, "Lana."

"Yes."

"You booked the flight."

"I booked the flight."

"...when."

"While Rourke was talking. I had a free hand. I felt, given the schedule, that we were going to need it."

Sophia, looking at her sister with an expression that had, for the first time in twenty-three years, something in it that was almost like maternal pride, said, "...you are *exactly* like Mom."

Lana, with the kind of small dry smile that she had, in the last thirty-six hours, been practicing, said, "Yes, Sophia. I suspected."

The Passat, after a moment, pulled away from the curb and began the slow turn toward the airport, and somewhere in the middle distance the Jet d'Eau threw its enormous white plume up into the cold Genevan morning, and somewhere very far away in a glass-walled office above the Petrograd embankment, a woman who had been waiting, for sixteen years, to meet a face from a photograph, picked up a small black valise and began, methodically, to pack.

Chapter 13: The Petrograd Embankment

The flight from Geneva to Helsinki was three hours and twenty minutes long, and for the first thirty of those minutes, the team was quiet.

Lana, in the window seat of row twelve of a half-empty Finnair A320, watched the high white cloud cover slide past beneath the wing and thought, in the way her brain had begun to do when nothing else was demanding her attention, about the geography of the next twenty-four hours.

Geneva to Helsinki was easy. Helsinki was a friendly country with a sane border, a working federal apparatus, and an airport that, in 2025, accepted U.S. passports with the civic enthusiasm that small Nordic democracies brought to the act of accepting U.S. passports.

Helsinki to St. Petersburg, in any other decade, would also have been easy. There was, in any other decade, a regular train service from Helsinki Central to Finlyandsky Station that took three hours and ten minutes and was, by all accounts, deeply pleasant.

There was not, in 2025, a regular train service.

There had notbeen any regular train service between the two cities since 2022, when, by an unfortunate confluence of geopolitical decisions to which Lana had not been a party, the Finnish government had closed all of its land crossings into the Russian Federation, and the Russian Federation had, from its side of the same border, closed approximately the same crossings, which had had the effect of making the eight-hundred-kilometer-long border between the two countries one of the most aggressively unpopulated borders in modern Europe.

There remained, by the ingenuity of human beings, a small number of unofficial methods of crossing it.

Sophia, in the aisle seat beside Lana, closed her paperback novel.

She said, quietly, "Reed cannot follow us in."

"I know."

"He cannot, in fact, even formally know we are going."

"I know, Sophia."

"This is a piece of work," Sophia said, "that we are going to do, in the next twenty-four hours, as four private individuals, on hostile soil, with no federal jurisdiction, with limited diplomatic recourse, and with the understanding that if any one of us is captured by Russian state authorities, the federal apparatus we have spent the last six days building will be unable, by the laws of the world we currently live in, to retrieve us."

"...I am aware."

"You are aware in the abstract, Lana. I want you to be aware in the operational sense. If you are captured, in St. Petersburg, by anyone we have not contracted directly, you will spend the next several years in a Russian penal institution. Reed will be unable to extract you. I will be unable to extract you. Declan, who has, in his career, been in two Russian penal institutions, will tell you, at length, that they are not pleasant. The honest version of the next twenty-four hours is one in which the four of us go in, get the work done, and come out, and the Russian Federation does not, until well after we are gone, become aware that we were ever there."

"...I understand."

"Do you want to step out at Helsinki."

Lana, in the window seat, looked at her sister.

Sophia was, again, offering the exit.

Lana thought about this for half a second.

She said, "Sophia."

"What."

"You really need to stop asking me that."

Sophia, after a moment, allowed a very small, dry smile.

"...you are right. I do."

"...I am also," Lana said, in the tone of a younger sister who had, in the previous six days, been doing increasing amounts of homework, "going to need to start checking your work, Sophia. Because you have, in the last forty minutes, told me about the Russian penal system, the Finnish border closures, and the limits of federal jurisdiction, and you have not, at any point, told me how we are getting from Helsinki to St. Petersburg."

Sophia, after a moment, said, "Margit is, even now, having that conversation with someone."

"...of course."

"I would like to be surprised, also."

* * *

Helsinki-Vantaa Airport, at six in the evening local time, was the and slightly cool place a Finnish airport always was in late spring. The sun, at this latitude, in this season, would not, until midnight, give up trying to be the sun. The terminal was clean and pale and smelled faintly of pine. Lucas, who had not previously been to Helsinki, looked around the long arrivals hall with the wide-eyed appreciation of a man who had recently developed a strong personal preference for places that were not, in any way, a Russian penal institution.

Their contact at the airport was a woman in her early sixties, with short steel-grey hair and a navy raincoat, who held up, with a quiet smile, a small handwritten card that read SOLANGE BRIAND in the unhurried block letters of a person who had used that particular alias before.

The woman's name, when she introduced herself, was Aino.

Aino was, by Sophia's brief whisper as they walked toward the parking garage, one of the few people in Northern Europe Margit trusted with this kind of work. Aino had been, in her previous life, a senior Finnish customs officer. She had retired in 2018. She had, in her retirement, become, for reasons she had not, in Margit's hearing, ever fully articulated, the person Margit called when something needed to cross the Gulf of Finland in a way that did not, in any official record, cross.

Aino's car was a battered grey Volvo XC90 with the kind of mileage that, on European cars, told you the car had outlived its original owner. She drove them, with Finnish precision, down a coastal road for approximately ninety minutes, past small fishing villages and patches of dark pine forest and the occasional summer cottage with a single light on in its window.

She stopped, eventually, at a small stone-walled marina in a town called Loviisa, about a hundred kilometers east of Helsinki. The marina had perhaps thirty boats in its slips, most of them small recreational sailboats, a few of them working fishing boats, and one of them a battered forty-foot wooden hull that, by the look of its stern, had seen, in its time, several oceans.

The forty-foot boat was called *Anneli.*

Standing on her deck, in a yellow oilskin jacket and a black wool watch cap, was a man in his fifties whom Aino introduced, with a small dry inflection, as *Aino's brother, Toivo.*

Toivo did not, by any visible sign, look Aino's brother. Toivo was, Lana noticed, a man whose face had been weathered by a different latitude. He looked like a Lithuanian.

Sophia, climbing down into the boat, said, "Toivo."

Toivo, in a voice with no detectable Finnish in it, said, "Sophia. I was not, when Margit called me, prepared for it to be your face. I was prepared for it to be Helena's face. I have not, in two and a half decades, gotten over Helena's face. Please tell your sister that I will not, on this voyage, stare. I am only, at this moment, briefly, processing."

Lana, climbing down behind her sister, said, "Take your time, Toivo."

Toivo, gently, smiled.

"Your mother," he said, "once kept me out of a Latvian prison, on a Tuesday in 1997, by an act of professional kindness for which I have not, in twenty-eight years, found a way to repay. I have, in the interim, found a small dignity in keeping the lights on, just in case her daughters should, one day, need to be ferried across a body of water without anyone asking us inconvenient questions. This, I see, is the day."

He cast off the lines.

The *Anneli* slid, slowly, out of the slip and into the dim glow of the long Nordic dusk, and Loviisa, behind them, retreated into the deepening violet of the eastern sky.

The crossing was four and a half hours long.

For the first hour, the sea was calm and the sky was, as late-spring evenings at sixty degrees north, the kind of pale, lingering blue that did not, properly, become night. The *Anneli's* engines were a steady low diesel mutter under the deck. Toivo, at the wheel, did not, except to occasionally adjust their bearing, speak. Aino, who had stayed in Loviisa, was already, by Sophia's report, halfway home.

In the cabin below the wheelhouse, the team checked their gear.

Lana, with the laptop on her knees, had, by the end of that first hour, mapped a complete real-time picture of the security disposition around 17 Petrograd Embankment, the address Henrik had given them as Markov's office, into a layered intelligence brief that Sophia could load on her tablet in the field.

The building was, in many ways, exactly what Lana had expected. Six stories of pale neoclassical limestone on the embankment of the Bolshaya Nevka River, three blocks from the Trinity Bridge, with a private parking garage in the basement, two sets of elevators on the publicly accessible side, one private elevator in a service shaft that connected the parking garage directly to the boardroom on the fifth floor, and a security desk on the ground floor staffed, twenty-four hours a day, by men whose backgrounds, Lana had determined on the previous afternoon, were, with one exception, all Russian Federal Security Service alumni who had retired into private security over the past decade.

The exception was a young man named Pavel, twenty-six years old, who had, by the data Lana had pulled out of his publicly available LinkedIn profile, joined the firm only two months earlier, who had not previously worked in security, and who was, by his own apparently un-vetted public-facing biography, a former hospitality manager at a hotel chain in Sochi.

Pavel, by his shift schedule, was on overnight tonight.

Lana had, in the previous hour, also identified that the building's HVAC system was managed by a third-party Russian contractor whose remote diagnostic credentials were, by the standards of such things, dispiriting.

She had, after some consideration, declined, for the moment, to take advantage of this.

Sophia, beside her in the cabin, looked at the brief.

Sophia, after a long moment, said, "...the boardroom is on the fifth floor."

"Yes."

"The private elevator runs from the basement."

"Yes. The basement is restricted at the elevator level. The full Council membership rolls down the elevator from the parking garage. They never appear in the lobby. They never appear on any building security log. Markov has, by my estimation, designed this exact piece of operational discretion as the central feature of his real estate."

"Which means they will, all of them, be in one room, on the fifth floor, for the duration of the meeting."

"For the duration of the meeting. Which is, by Henrik's last input, scheduled for ninety minutes."

"...and they will not, during that ninety minutes, leave the room."

"They will not, during that ninety minutes, leave the room. The elevator, when the meeting is in session, is locked off at both ends. The door of the boardroom is, by the firmware specification I have just retrieved from the lock vendor's website, electromechanically sealed during the meeting and is keyed to disengage only on the manual command of the room's occupants."

Sophia closed her eyes for a moment.

She opened them.

She said, "...Lana."

"Yes."

"You are telling me that, for ninety minutes tomorrow, between fifteen hundred and sixteen-thirty Moscow time, the entire active leadership of the Council is going to be in one fifth-floor room, sealed in by their own firmware, with no working elevator to the basement, and no working stairwell access from the lobby, and only one door, which they have to, themselves, manually disengage to leave."

"Yes."

"That is," Sophia said, very quietly, "the cleanest piece of operational stupidity I have encountered in fifteen years."

Declan, in the corner of the cabin, who had been cleaning the rifle, looked up.

He said, "It is not stupidity, Sophia. It is hubris."

"...there is a difference?"

"In Markov's case," Declan said, "yes. He has been doing this for thirty-six years and he has, in those thirty-six years, never been seriously challenged. He believes that the door of his own boardroom is, by design, an asset. He believes that nobody in the world has the access to use it as a vulnerability. He has, until you and your sister, been correct. The protocol he has built is one he believes is operating in a world that will never, in fact, look closely at it. He has not, in his career, ever needed to consider what that protocol would look like in the hands of a person who had already, three days earlier, gotten a tier-two credential, a complete set of building schematics, and a federal cyber forensics tap on his vendor's data line."

He set the rifle down.

He looked at Sophia.

"It is the same," he said, "as Marcus and his self-destruct panel. Marcus believed that his self-destruct panel was, by virtue of its self-destruct function, a protective feature. Marcus was wrong. He was wrong because Marcus had, for twenty-two years, been operating without serious adversaries. We have, in the last six days, presented Marcus and Markov with serious adversaries for, in both their cases, the first and last time. Hubris, Sophia, is the failure mode of a man who has been, for too long, surrounded by lesser people. Both of these men have been surrounded by lesser people for thirty years. They are, in their ways, profoundly unprepared for the morning we are going to give them."

The *Anneli* rocked, gently, in the small evening swell of the Gulf of Finland.

Sophia, after a moment, said, "Declan."

"Yeah."

"That was, frankly, the most coherent sentence I have ever heard you speak."

Declan, with a small dry curl of his mouth, said, "I have, Sophia, been saving it."

* * *

They came in sight of the Russian coast at midnight.

The coastline, on Toivo's chart, was a small inlet on the Karelian Isthmus, about ninety kilometers northwest of the city, in a stretch of pine forest and rocky shore that had, between official border crossings, been, for decades, one of the gray-market coast routes in and out of the Russian Federation.

Toivo brought the *Anneli* into a small hidden cove without lights.

A second boat was waiting in the cove, at anchor, twenty meters from the rocky shore. The second boat was a small fast inflatable, of the kind used by Russian customs in some decades and Russian smugglers in others, with a single man at its motor.

The man was wearing a dark fishermen's sweater and a black wool cap. He was, by the look of his face in the dim moonlight, somewhere in his forties.

His name, he indicated by a single small lifted hand, was Mikhail.

Mikhail spoke no English. Mikhail, by Toivo's quiet briefing, did not need to. Mikhail's job was to drive the inflatable for forty minutes, at no lights, into a private marina on the outskirts of the city of Vyborg, where a contact of Margit's had pre-positioned a black Mercedes Sprinter van with Russian plates and a full tank of fuel, and to drive away again, in the same inflatable, with the eight thousand euros that Sophia, on Toivo's quiet nod, was now handing him.

He took the eight thousand euros without counting them.

He made a small, polite, lifted-hand gesture, by which he indicated to Sophia that he had, on his side, also taken the small precaution of bringing a sealed envelope of his own.

He held it out.

Sophia took it.

The envelope was thin. The envelope had, in a careful hand on its front, in Cyrillic, a single word: *СЕСТРА.*

Sophia, who read Russian at a fluency that, Lana now realized, she had not previously had occasion to display in front of her sister, breathed out very slowly through her nose.

Lana said, "What does it say."

"It says," Sophia said, "sister."

She did not, by any visible sign, indicate that she was either pleased or surprised by this. She tucked the envelope, without opening it, into the inside pocket of her jacket.

She gave Mikhail a small unhurried salute.

He returned the salute, with the shadow of a smile, and pulled, in his small inflatable, the throttle, and the inflatable, with a quiet diesel buzz, drew away from them across the dark inlet.

Five minutes later, the team transferred from the *Anneli* into a slightly smaller third boat, Toivo's working dinghy, and Toivo rowed them to shore in five minutes of careful work that did not, by any sound, alert the seven-acre-radius of pine forest around them to the existence of any human activity whatsoever.

He set them onto the rocky beach.

He gave Sophia, before she stepped off, a very long look, and then he said, in his quiet not-Finnish accent, "Sophia. If I am, in this lifetime, ever the man who can do something for the daughters of Helena Harper that involves them coming back to Finland, I will, on that day, weep."

Sophia, softly, said, "Toivo. We will come back."

He nodded, once.

He pushed off from the shore, and the dinghy, by his quiet rowing, slid back out across the dark cove toward the *Anneli,* and within four minutes the *Anneli* itself, by Toivo's quiet seamanship, had slid out of the cove and back into the wider gulf, and was gone.

The team was, on the rocky beach of the Karelian Isthmus, on hostile soil, with no plane, no boat, no federal cover, and one black Mercedes Sprinter van, which they could now, faintly through the trees, see parked at the end of a forest service road approximately three hundred meters inland.

Lana said, quietly, "Sophia."

"What."

"What did the envelope say. Inside it. Tell me."

Sophia, in the dark, by the thin moonlight on the Gulf of Finland, took the envelope out of her jacket. She slit it with the thin blade she kept on the inside of her wrist. She unfolded the single sheet of paper.

She read it.

She did not, for several seconds, speak.

Then she handed the page to Lana.

Lana, who did not, by any reasonable metric, read Russian, read it anyway, by the lamplight of her tablet.

The note was, in elegant Cyrillic handwriting, four lines long.

Sophia, at her elbow, translated.

"Dear Sophia. Welcome to my country. I have arranged a clean route for you. The men who would, in any other case, intercept you have been, by my arrangement, redirected to other matters tonight. You will encounter nothing on the road to your safe house, and I will not, until you arrive at the Petrograd embankment, send anyone to meet you. I have been waiting to meet you, in person, for sixteen years. I would like, in the small mercy of fellow students of an old man, to give you tonight to rest, and to tell your sister whatever you have not yet told her, and to make the call to your father you should make. You will, in the morning, be the woman I meet at the end of a corridor. I owe you this evening, and I am giving it. I look forward, very greatly, to meeting you. Yours, Wren."

The forest, around them, was very quiet.

Lana, after a long moment, said, "...Sophia."

"Don't," Sophia said.

"Sophia."

"Lana, I am, at this moment, processing several things, and I would prefer not to discuss them on a Russian beach in the middle of the night."

"Okay."

"...thank you."

They walked, in the dark, through the pine forest to the van.

* * *

The drive to St. Petersburg, on the M-10 federal highway, was three hours and twenty minutes long, and was, by the prediction of the woman called Wren, entirely without incident.

They were not stopped. They were not followed. The few cars they passed on the highway, at this hour, were ordinary Russian late-night cars, driven by ordinary Russian late-night drivers, none of whom registered, in any observable way, the existence of a black Mercedes Sprinter van with two American women, one Irish-Belgian mercenary, one panicked accountant from Connecticut, and a tactical kit of a sort that, if the van had been searched at any point in the next three hours, would have ended the team's career on the spot.

The van was not searched.

The van rolled, unmolested, into the outskirts of St. Petersburg at three forty-five in the morning, and into a small, anonymous, courtyarded apartment building in a quiet residential neighborhood called Petrogradsky District at four-twelve, where Margit's contact, a woman named Yekaterina who did not, in their entire brief encounter, give any other name, met them at the courtyard gate, handed Sophia a single small key, and disappeared back into the building before any of them, including Lucas, had quite worked out which apartment door she had come from.

The key opened a third-floor apartment of approximately ninety square meters, with three bedrooms, a small windowless central living room with a heavy wooden table, a working kitchen with a kettle, a working bathroom with hot water, and, in a sealed cardboard box on the table, the second tactical kit Yekaterina had pre-positioned for them.

The kit was, by Sophia's quick inventory, complete.

It contained, in addition to a small redundant stock of weapons and comms gear and breaching tools and one set of uniform coveralls in the colors of the Russian utility company that had, eight months earlier, been contracted to do routine HVAC work on a building at 17 Petrograd Embankment, a single small additional item that Yekaterina had not, on the briefing, been asked to provide.

The item was a hand-painted ceramic cat, about the size of a fist, in the style of the Northern European folk-art tradition that had been popular in the late twentieth century.

The cat had, on its underside, in pencil, in Margit's slightly cramped handwriting, the single word *bring it home.*

Sophia, looking at the cat, did, for a small private moment, the thing she did when nobody was watching, which Lana had now seen her sister do exactly six times in the previous eight days.

She closed her eyes for a half second longer than the closing took.

Then she said, "Sleep. All of you. Lana. Six hours. Lucas. Six hours. Declan. Four, then take watch. We will be at the embankment at thirteen hundred Moscow. We will have, until fifteen hundred, two hours to be in position. We will move on the building from approximately fourteen-fifty. The board meeting will commence at fifteen hundred sharp. Markov, by his protocols, will not, until we are there, be aware that we are in the building. We will, before they finish their first agenda item, be in his office."

Lucas, who had, on the highway, fallen asleep against the window of the van, said, "...I am okay with all of this in the abstract."

"Sleep, Lucas."

"Yeah."

He went, in something like ninety seconds, to sleep on the small couch.

Declan, with a small nod, took up a position by the apartment's only window with his rifle and a thermos of coffee Yekaterina had also, by some miracle of advance planning, left on the kitchen counter.

Lana, who had, in her own small way, been planning to follow Sophia's order, did not, at first, go to sleep.

She sat, instead, at the heavy wooden table in the central living room, with the ceramic cat in front of her, with her tablet in her lap, with the fluorescent lamp above the table casting its long, slightly green-tinged industrial light over the room, and she did, for thirty minutes, the careful work of finishing the technical preparations for the morning.

She wrote the deployment scripts.

She tested the federal coordination feed she had built with Reed's people in Vienna.

She set up the secure channel by which, at fourteen hundred Moscow, she would, on Sophia's signal, transmit the contents of the Stillman Asset Management server stack, in a single coordinated cascade, to the Reuters Moscow bureau, the BBC Moscow bureau, the Süddeutsche Zeitung, the U.S. Department of Justice's public information office, and a small cluster of independent investigative journalists Margit had, in the previous eight hours, identified as the people most likely to publish a leaked Russian financial corruption story without first asking too many questions about its provenance.

The cascade would, at fourteen hundred Moscow tomorrow, hit the global news cycle approximately ten minutes before the Council's board meeting was scheduled to begin.

Markov would, by the time he sat down at his table, already be the leading story on every major newsroom on the planet.

He would have approximately thirty-five minutes of professional life remaining when he sat down.

Lana, in the green-fluorescent kitchen light of an anonymous Petrogradsky apartment, looked at the deployment script for the cascade, and she made, with a small dry smile that had no observers, a single small edit to the timestamp.

She had a sense of theater that, as her sister had recently identified, came from her mother.

She moved the cascade publication time from fourteen hundred Moscow to fifteen hundred *and one* Moscow.

It was not, in any operational sense, a meaningful change.

It was, in the way of artistic decisions, the funniest thing Lana could think of doing under the circumstances.

She closed the laptop.

She got up.

She went, very quietly, into the small back bedroom Sophia had taken, and she found her sister, fully dressed, on top of the covers, with her eyes open, looking at the ceiling.

Lana stood in the doorway.

After a moment, Sophia, without looking over, said, "Lana."

"Yes."

"There is, in my jacket pocket, a sealed envelope. The envelope is twenty-three years old. It was given to me by Mom in 2002, in a basement in Wilmette, in a fireproof briefcase. The envelope, on its front, says, *Lana, when she is twenty-five.*"

Lana, in the doorway, did not, for a moment, say anything.

Sophia, after a beat, said, "I have, in the last fifteen years, considered, several times, opening it on your behalf. I have, every time, decided it was not mine. I have, in particular, considered, in the last forty-eight hours, that there is a non-zero chance that one or both of us will not come out of tomorrow morning in the condition we go in. I have decided, in the last hour, that the letter is yours. That it has been yours for twenty-three years. That it has, in particular, become yours in the last six days, in a way that I had not, when I was holding it in 2002, fully understood. I have decided, in the last three minutes, that I am not, in any moral universe, going to be the woman who keeps that letter in a safe-deposit box in Zurich one more night. I would like, Lana, to give you the letter. Now."

Lana, in the doorway, with her hands at her sides, said, very softly, "...you brought it."

"I brought it. I have been, for the last twenty-three years, an extremely cautious woman. I retrieved it, with Margit, before we left Innsbruck. It has, since then, been on my person."

"...Sophia."

"Lana."

Lana, after a long moment, walked into the room.

Sophia, on the bed, sat up. She reached into the inside pocket of her jacket. She drew out, very carefully, a small flat envelope, its paper yellowed by twenty-three years inside a fireproof case, sealed with a single line of silver-grey tape that had been, in 2002, the kind of tape an intelligence officer used when she did not want a seal to be broken without her knowing.

The envelope, on its front, in Helena Harper's hand, read, *Lana, when she is twenty-five.*

Sophia held it out.

Lana, with hands that did not, by any visible sign, shake, took it.

She sat down, slowly, on the edge of the bed, beside her sister.

She said, quietly, "Will you stay."

"...I will stay."

Lana opened the envelope.

She did not, immediately, read it.

She held it, for a long moment, and looked at the handwriting of a woman she had not, in her conscious memory, ever seen write a sentence. The handwriting was a little angular, a little hurried, the way the handwriting of an intelligence officer in a basement under time pressure would be. The handwriting was also, in its small steady way, the handwriting of a mother.

The letter was ten pages long.

Lana read the first line out loud.

The first line, in Helena's hurried, careful, twenty-three-year-old hand, read:

"Sweet pea, I know that this is, when you read it, going to be late. I am sorry. I have been doing the math, and I cannot find a way to be on time. So I am going to start by telling you, before everything else, that I love you, and that no matter what has happened in the time between this letter and this morning, none of it is your fault."

Lana stopped reading aloud.

She read the rest in silence, in the dim green light of the back bedroom of an apartment in Petrogradsky district, with her sister's shoulder warm and steady against her own, and the small ceramic cat, in the next room on a heavy wooden table, watching, patiently, over the small, full, twenty-three-year-old shape of a silence that had finally, in the last hour before the most dangerous morning of her life, been allowed to speak.

She did not, when she finished, cry.

She had, in the last eight days, run out of new ways to cry.

She folded the letter, very carefully, back into its envelope. She tucked the envelope, very carefully, into the inside pocket of her own jacket, where it sat, warm, just under her heart.

She turned to her sister.

She said, "Sophia."

"Yes."

"...thank you."

Sophia, softly, said, "I love you, Lana."

"I love you too, Sophia."

They sat, on the edge of the bed, in the dim green light, for a long, quiet moment.

In the next room, the clock above the kitchen sink read four forty-eight.

In nine hours and twelve minutes, Victor Markov's board meeting would begin.

In nine hours and four minutes, the team would be at the elevator.

In ten hours and forty-two minutes, somebody, by the mathematics of Helena Harper's daughters, would die.

Chapter 14: The Boardroom

The white Mercedes Sprinter van that pulled up to the side entrance of 17 Petrograd Embankment at thirteen forty-eight Moscow time bore the cyrillic livery of a regional HVAC contractor named *Северный Климат-Сервис,* which translated approximately to *Northern Climate-Service,* and which had, according to the building maintenance records Lana had spent the previous two hours building convincing forgeries of, been the firm responsible for the Markov building's commercial chiller maintenance for the previous fourteen months.

The van was, Lana had noted with appreciation, the kind of vehicle nobody ever looked at twice in any city in the world. Battered. Slightly dirty. Two ladders strapped to the roof rack. A small dent in the rear panel from some long-ago encounter with a low concrete bollard. The kind of vehicle that, if it pulled up at any service entrance in Russia and produced any halfway plausible work order, would generally be waved through without comment.

Sophia, in the driver's seat, in the navy coveralls of a Severny Klimat-Service technician, with a clipboard and a tool belt, presented the work order to the security guard at the side gate.

The work order, by the contributions of everyone on the team, was perfect.

The guard, in his small kiosk, read it for the better part of forty seconds. He looked up at Sophia. He looked at the van. He looked at Declan, in the passenger seat, also in coveralls, also with a clipboard.

He said, in flat businesslike Russian, "You are not on my schedule for today."

Sophia, in the driver's seat, in equally flat Russian that had, in its inflection, exactly the right northwestern industrial-suburb accent for a working contractor, said, "It is, indeed, not on your schedule. We received an emergency callout this morning at zero seven hundred. The building's western chiller bank has been running approximately twelve degrees above target since approximately oh-five hundred. It is not yet at risk of shutdown but it is operating outside of vendor specification. We are required, by the service contract, to attend within six hours of any reported anomaly. I assure you, sir, none of us would prefer to be here this afternoon. My wife and I have, this evening, theatre tickets."

The guard considered her for a long moment.

He said, "What kind of theatre."

Sophia, without missing a beat, said, "The Maly. We have been on the wait list for these tickets since November. If your shift, sir, has by any chance ended by twenty hundred this evening, and you should find yourself wanting a ticket, my number is on the work order. I would be grateful to a man who, by helping me through this gate, becomes the man I owe."

The guard, at the kiosk, allowed himself, for the first time in the conversation, a very small smile.

He stamped the work order. He waved the van through. He said, "Good luck with the chiller, friend."

The van rolled into the building's small interior service yard.

Sophia, very softly, in English, said, "...the Maly was a piece of cover Margit prepared for me approximately twelve years ago. I have, over the years, used it three times. She would, on hearing this, take a personal day."

In the back of the van, Lana, in her own pair of navy coveralls, with the deployment laptop balanced on her thighs, said, "Sophia. The Maly tickets are, by Margit's documentation, currently at sixty-two thousand rubles per pair, which she has, since 2013, charged me, at fifteen percent annual interest, against a notional account she pretends she is keeping. I will be, on this trip's completion, formally bankrupted by my own sister's stage mother."

"...it is the price we pay," Sophia said.

"It is *literally* the price."

The van pulled into the assigned maintenance bay.

The team, with the practiced calm of four contractors who had done this kind of routine inspection many times before, exited the vehicle.

Lucas, in the passenger seat of a second vehicle three blocks away, a slightly newer Sprinter van of the same livery that Yekaterina had, by an additional small miracle of advance work, also pre-positioned, settled into his comms station with his thermos and the small, slightly weathered confidence of a man who had, over the past nine days, become a person.

In Lana's ear: "Comm check. All channels live. Building cameras are mine. Lobby coverage is mine. Fifth floor coverage is mine. Basement coverage is mine. The HVAC vendor's diagnostic feed, also mine. The local cellular cell, also mine. We are, on this op, the building's own nervous system."

"Copy, Lucas."

"Pavel?" Sophia, into her own collar mic.

"Pavel," Lucas confirmed, "is at the lobby desk. He has been at the lobby desk since oh-five hundred. He is on hour eight of a twelve-hour shift. He looks, by the camera, tired. He has, in the last two hours, eaten a small bag of sunflower seeds and read approximately fourteen pages of a paperback novel that I cannot, from this angle, identify. He is, by every visible indicator, a young man who would prefer to be somewhere else."

"Good," Sophia said. "Lana. You're up."

Lana, with the careful precision that the previous nine days had made habit, picked up the small leather portfolio Margit had also, by some other previously unmentioned act of preparation, included in their Yekaterina kit, and walked, with Sophia and Declan, to the back staircase that connected the maintenance bay to the building's ground floor.

She had, in her ear, the live feed of Pavel's lobby camera. She had, on her tablet, his full personnel file. She had, in her chest, a very particular and slightly mean piece of curiosity about what kind of paperback a twenty-six-year-old former hotel hospitality manager on hour eight of a twelve-hour shift in a private corporate lobby in St. Petersburg in May of 2025 was reading.

The paperback, when Lana, in coveralls and a clipboard, pushed through the staircase door into the lobby and walked up to the security desk, was, on closer inspection, a small dog-eared Russian translation of a deeply unauthorized 2008 Donna Tartt novel that she had, when she had been seventeen, also read.

Lana, leaning in slightly across the security desk, in her best contractor-Russian, said, "...you're on chapter twenty-two."

Pavel, who had been mid-sip of cold tea, looked up.

He took her in for a long second.

"...you have read it."

"I have read it," Lana said. "I read it, in English, at seventeen. It is a book that, if you are reading it on hour eight of a long shift, you are probably reading because you wish to be elsewhere. I have, in my own life, on long bad afternoons, used it the same way. The thing I will tell you is that the next chapter is the one where everything starts going wrong. So you may, in the next forty minutes, want to be ready for that."

Pavel, with a flicker of something almost human across his tired face, said, "...I am, perhaps, ready for things to start going wrong."

"Pavel," Lana said, "that is, why I am here."

He looked at her.

He looked at Sophia and Declan, who had, by now, come up to the desk behind her in their navy coveralls.

He looked at Lana again.

She placed, very carefully, on the security desk in front of him, a single sheet of printed paper, in Russian, on a letterhead that had been forged forty minutes earlier from a federal seal Lana had pulled from a Russian Ministry of Justice public records database.

The letter, in three brief paragraphs, indicated to one Pavel Glukhov, twenty-six, of Vasilevsky Island, that the Russian Federation's Anti-Corruption Operative Directorate had, on the preceding morning, opened a sealed case file on the activities of Mr. Victor Ilyich Markov, currently of this address; that Mr. Glukhov was, by virtue of the previous twenty-six months of his security clearance application, a known commodity to Russian state authorities; that he was, as of the moment he read this letter, formally invited to assist in the operation by maintaining exactly his standard professional disposition over the course of the next ninety minutes; that he would, in compensation, receive an immediate one-time emolument of ten million rubles, deposited to a clean account he could nominate within twenty-four hours; and that his cooperation, by signing the letter, would be considered, by the Directorate, as constitutive of his complete personal indemnity.

Pavel read the letter in roughly twenty seconds.

He read it, again, more slowly.

He looked up at Lana.

He said, very quietly, "...this letter is forged. Is it not."

Lana, very calmly, said, "Pavel. It is."

He did not, by any visible sign, react.

He looked, instead, with the tired honesty of a man who had, over the previous several months, begun to reach a private and unwelcome understanding of where he had taken his career, at the lobby of the building he had, until two months earlier, never been inside.

He said, "...the ten million rubles."

"The ten million rubles," Lana said, "will, by an entirely separate and entirely unforged process, be in any account you nominate within forty-eight hours, regardless of whether or not you sign this letter. The letter is, in operational terms, theatre. The compensation is, by my honest disclosure, real. I am, as you may have suspected, nota Russian federal officer. I am, more precisely, a person who has, in the previous nine days, very thoroughly disrupted the financial architecture of the man whose lobby you are sitting in. I am, in the next ninety minutes, going to take from him approximately everything that he has not yet fully understood he has lost. I am, in the spirit of efficient operations, asking you whether you would like to receive ten million rubles for sitting at this desk and reading the next forty pages of your novel without, in any way, picking up the phone."

Pavel, after a long moment, said, "...what is your name."

Lana, gently, said, "Pavel. That is, I am sorry, the question I cannot answer."

He, slowly, smiled.

He said, "In your country's idiom, ma'am, what you are asking me is whether I would like to *call in sick*."

"That is the idiom."

"...I would. Yes. I would very much."

He closed the paperback novel. He set it, page-down, open, on the security desk. He picked up his cold tea. He took, with the great and complete dignity of a young man who had, in the last forty seconds, just decided to be a different man, a long, slow, deeply unbothered sip.

Sophia, behind Lana, said, softly, "...that is one of the cleanest pieces of social engineering I have seen in fifteen years."

Lana, with the dry tone of a woman who had been, in the previous nine days, learning, said, "I had a feeling, Sophia, about Pavel."

* * *

The team took the public elevator to the fourth floor.

The fourth floor, on the building's official map, was the executive marketing department of *Markov Holding,* the publicly traded face of Victor Markov's private corporate empire, which had been, by the careful work of its parent organization, kept entirely, immaculately legitimate for the previous thirty years.

The fourth floor was, at fourteen hundred Moscow on a Wednesday, a quiet open-plan office of approximately forty marketing professionals doing the small earnest work of marketing, none of whom, in any meaningful way, knew what the rest of their own building was for.

The fourth floor also had, in its eastern wall, a service door labeled *МАСТЕРСКАЯ, Workshop,* beyond which lay a small unmarked utility closet, and beyond the utility closet, behind a panel that did not, by any of the building's official blueprints, exist, lay the back of the private elevator shaft that ran, unmarked, from the basement parking garage to the boardroom on the fifth floor.

Sophia, in the workshop closet, with her hand on the panel, paused.

She turned to her sister.

She said, "Lana."

Lana, who had, in the previous nine days, stopped flinching at the look her sister was now giving her, said, "...yeah."

Sophia, after a moment, did the thing that, in Sophia, was a substitute for many other, larger things.

She set her hand, briefly, on the side of Lana's face.

She said, "I will see you in eleven minutes."

Lana said, "You will."

Sophia removed her hand.

She removed the panel.

She and Declan, with practiced silence, stepped into the small dim space at the back of the elevator shaft, where a service ladder ran the full six-story interior height of the building, and where Sophia, by the unhurried agility that had been her ordinary and Declan, with somewhat more grunting, would now climb the four floors up to the service hatch on the back of the boardroom-level elevator car, in order to be in position when Lana, at fourteen fifty-eight, opened the elevator's primary door from the fifth-floor lobby with Markov's own diverted access credential.

Lana, in the workshop closet, watched her sister climb out of sight.

She closed the panel.

She walked, in her navy coveralls, with her clipboard, with the tactical laptop in the leather portfolio over her shoulder, back through the marketing department, into the elevator vestibule, and pressed the button for the fifth floor.

The fifth floor, on the building's official map, was an executive conference and dining suite. In the careful actual fact of the building, the fifth floor was the only floor on which the public elevators stopped that was, to anyone not on the meeting list, entirely inaccessible. The doors of the public elevator did, on the fifth floor, open. The vestibule on the fifth floor, beyond the doors, was, however, a small wood-paneled antechamber with a single security desk, manned, on the day of a Council meeting, by a single internal personal asset of Mr. Markov, who would, on Lana's emergence from the elevator at fourteen fifty-six, be slightly surprised by the sight of an unscheduled HVAC technician.

The personal asset was, on Lana's read of his profile, a mid-fifties former Russian special forces operator named Gennady, who had been, since 2009, Markov's daytime personal security lead.

Lana, in the rising elevator, in the small bright steel of the public elevator's interior, said into her collar mic, "Lucas."

"Yeah."

"Are we good."

"Gennady is, by the camera, on his phone. The phone, by the cellular feed, is, in fact, the call I placed forty seconds ago from a forged Russian Ministry of Internal Affairs caller ID, advising him that there is, on the building's east face, a small unauthorized civilian protest gathering that may, in the next ten minutes, attempt to disrupt the meeting upstairs. He is, on hearing this, about to leave his post for approximately ninety seconds in order to investigate the east face."

"...what unauthorized civilian protest gathering, Lucas."

"Three of Margit's contacts, with handmade signs, who are, even now, gathering on the embankment about a hundred meters north of the building. They are, by their cover identity, anti-corruption activists. They will, when Russian internal security arrives, very quickly disperse. They will not, in any way, be detained."

"...you area competent guy in the chair, Lucas."

"I have been working at it, Lana."

The elevator, with a very small chime, reached the fifth floor.

The doors opened.

The vestibule was, as Lucas had promised, empty.

Lana, with the walk of a contractor who had every reason to be on this floor, stepped out of the elevator. She crossed the small wood-paneled vestibule. She went up to the security desk. She set her clipboard down. She, with one hand, in the manner of someone touching a piece of decorative furniture, lifted the small enameled pen-holder cup off the desk.

Underneath the pen-holder cup, on the desk surface, was a single small magnetic card key.

The card key was Gennady's.

Gennady carried, by his protocol, his card key in the front pocket of his uniform shirt. He had, on receiving the call from the forged Ministry caller ID, removed it from the pocket and placed it under the pen-holder cup, in order to leave it for the colleague who was, by the same call, going to relieve him during his absence.

The relieving colleague, also by Lucas's quiet arrangement, had been, in the previous ninety seconds, briefly delayed by a separate small false alarm on the second floor.

Lana picked up the card key.

She walked, with the same unhurried clipboard-carrying air, across the vestibule to the heavy walnut double doors at its far end, with the brass plaque that read SOVET in elegant Cyrillic.

She held the card key to the reader.

The reader, with a small green chirp, accepted the card.

The lock disengaged.

The door, with the soft pneumatic hiss of a heavy, well-balanced door, swung open three inches.

Lana looked at her watch.

The time was, exactly, fourteen fifty-nine and twelve seconds.

She pushed the door, fully, open.

She stepped into the boardroom of the Council.

* * *

The boardroom was a long, stately, panelled chamber with a single immense oval table of polished black walnut, fourteen leather chairs, a wall of tall windows on the river side that looked out over the Bolshaya Nevka and the old Peter and Paul Fortress beyond it, and, on the opposite wall, a recessed bank of six flat-screen monitors that were, at this exact moment, displaying the muted live feeds of four different international news channels and two financial market tickers.

Eight of the fourteen leather chairs were occupied.

The man at the head of the table was, as Lana had spent the previous eight days expecting him to be, Victor Markov.

He was a small, neatly built man in his middle sixties, with close-cropped silver hair, a charcoal three-piece suit with a small enameled lapel pin she could not, from this distance, identify, and the mildly amused face of a man who had been, for the previous thirty-six years, entirely confident in the way the rooms he sat in tended to behave.

He was holding a small porcelain cup of tea.

He was, at the moment Lana stepped into his boardroom in navy contractor coveralls, looking at her with great interest, the way a man on a long Sunday afternoon looked at a small unfamiliar bird that had landed on his windowsill.

He said, in his beautiful, unaccented English, "...Lana Harper."

Lana, in the doorway, with the door closing behind her with the heavy sound of a well-balanced lock disengaging on the inside, said, "Mr. Markov."

The other seven Council members, around the table, all of whom had turned, at the sound of the door, to look at her, did, in turn, the various small involuntary motions of people whose afternoon meeting had just been interrupted in a way that was, on its face, deeply implausible. One reached, by reflex, for the inside of his suit jacket. The man two seats from him, an older woman with a steel-grey bob and a small aquamarine ring, put her hand, very softly, on the first man's wrist, and shook her head, and the first man, after a half-second, withdrew his hand.

Markov, at the head of the table, with the same interest, said, "Please, sit down. Will you have a tea."

Lana, calmly, said, "...I will not, thank you."

"As you wish."

She walked, in her contractor coveralls, the length of the long room, between the row of leather chairs and the wall of monitors, until she was standing approximately three feet from Markov's left shoulder. She did not, at any point, draw a weapon. She had brought no weapon other than the tactical laptop in the leather portfolio over her shoulder, the small ceramic cat from Margit in the inside pocket of her coveralls, and the sealed letter from her mother that lay, against her sternum, just under the heart.

She set the leather portfolio on the table beside Markov's tea.

She opened it.

She turned the laptop, with its already-glowing screen, gently around, so that the screen faced the table, which faced, also, the bank of monitors on the far wall.

She said, "Mr. Markov. Ladies and gentlemen of the Council. I would like, for the next ninety seconds, your collective attention."

The wall of monitors, by the work Lana had done, in the green-fluorescent kitchen of an apartment in Petrogradsky district eleven hours earlier, simultaneously cut from their respective international news feeds to a single coordinated image, transmitted via the building's own signal system from her laptop on the table.

The image was a still photograph.

The photograph was Helena Harper, age thirty-seven, in a kitchen in Wilmette, Illinois, in 2002, sitting at a Formica table, with two small girls on either side of her, eating, in the small, hurried, ordinary way of a Sunday morning, scrambled eggs.

Helena was wearing a pale-blue cardigan.

The smaller girl, on her right, with a small lopsided ponytail, was Lana.

The taller girl, on her left, with her hair in a serious dark-blonde braid, was Sophia.

The photograph stayed on the wall for two full seconds.

The Council members, around the table, looked at it with the various small horrors of people whose colleagues had, individually and severally, in the course of their respective careers, all heard, several times, the name of the woman in the photograph.

Then the photograph cut, in a coordinated transition Lana had timed personally, to the live feed of the Reuters Moscow bureau homepage.

The Reuters Moscow bureau homepage was, at fifteen hundred Moscow and forty-eight seconds, displaying a single breaking news banner, which read, in twenty-point font, in both Russian and English:

EXCLUSIVE: VICTOR I. MARKOV, RUSSIAN FINANCIER, NAMED BY U.S. FEDERAL INDICTMENT AS LEADER OF MULTINATIONAL CRIMINAL CONSPIRACY DATING TO 1989.

Beneath the banner, in smaller font, were the names of all eight Council members in the room.

Beneath those names, in still smaller font, was a small photograph of each of them.

Beneath each photograph was a small live ticker of the current frozen status of the principal financial assets, by jurisdiction, of the named individual.

The tickers, on the monitors, were, in real time, updating.

The tickers were, in real time, going to zero.

The Council members, around the table, did not, immediately, speak.

Markov, at the head of the table, with his small porcelain cup of tea still in his hand, looked at the bank of monitors for a long, slow, unhurried second.

Then he looked at Lana.

He said, in his beautiful, unaccented English, "Ah. There she is."

He set his tea down.

He smiled.

It was a very small, very tired smile.

He said, "...your mother used to look at me exactly like that."

* * *

The Wren came up the back stairs with a small, unhurried, professional patience that suggested a woman who had rehearsed, in the privacy of her own head, exactly the cadence with which she intended, today, to walk.

She was wearing dark fitted tactical clothing that was, on first observation, almost identical to Sophia's. Her hair was pulled into a tight knot at the back of her head. Her face, in the dim light of the back stairwell, had been, for the first time since the print shop in Bridgeport, exposed: a sharp, narrow face with high cheekbones, dark hooded eyes, and a small thin scar that ran from the corner of her left eyebrow back into her hairline.

She had, on her hip, two curved knives in a leather double-sheath of a design that Sophia had not, since 2009, seen except on the wall of Janos Mariakos's storage room in Hungary.

The knives, of course, were Mariakos's.

He had, by his will, left them to whoever, of his students, was the last one standing in the Council's eventual reckoning. He had, in his careful old way, expected this reckoning to involve Sophia. He had not, by what Sophia could now read in the way Wren wore the sheath, anticipated that, in the careful unfolding of his own affairs, those knives might end up belonging to the wrong student.

Sophia, at the top of the back stairwell, where the corridor that ran the length of the fifth floor met the small unmarked back service hallway, stood in the dim light, with her own back to the doorway through which, in approximately seven minutes, Lana would, by the operation of the cascade and the protocols of Markov's own boardroom, be forced to retreat.

Sophia had, before she had taken up her position, removed her own coveralls. She was wearing a black tank top and dark tactical pants. She had her own knives at her own hip, which were nothing in particular, by any meaningful provenance. They were, in fact, two well-balanced commercial blades from a Swiss manufacturer who had, in 2018, given Sophia an extremely friendly bulk price.

The knives were not, by any standard, equal to Mariakos's.

The hands, however, that held them, were.

Wren reached the top of the stairwell.

She stopped at a polite three-meter distance.

She did not, by any visible sign, draw.

She said, in flawless, unaccented English, "...hello, Sophia."

Sophia, softly, said, "Hello, Wren."

"You came."

"I came."

"I am so glad."

"Are you."

"I have been," Wren said, "alone with this for a very long time. The old man, in his way, gave me you. He did not, in his way, give you me. I have been, since I was nineteen, the only one of us who knew there was an *us*. I was, when I learned of you, deeply uncertain about how I felt. I have, in the years since, settled the question. I am pleased, today, to meet you. I am sorry, today, that we are meeting in this corridor, in this circumstance, in service of these particular men."

Sophia, very calmly, said, "You are not in service of these particular men, Wren. You are, by your contract, in service of one of them in particular."

"...yes."

"You could," Sophia said, "set the knives down."

Wren, very gently, said, "Sophia. You know that I cannot."

"I know."

"He has, in the boardroom, by my arrangement, twenty-eight seconds of warning before your sister enters. He has had, by my arrangement, seven days of preparation for this morning. He will, by his own protocols, be able to fight your sister in his own way, with what he has at his disposal. I will, by my own contract, be unable to interfere. I am, however, also unable, by the loyalty of a person who took an old man's money to learn a particular discipline, to come up these stairs and to *not* meet you in this corridor. The discipline, Sophia, is older than the contract. We were both taught, by the same teacher, that the discipline comes first. The discipline says: when you find the other student, you finish the lesson."

"I know."

"You may, of course, kill me."

"I do not, in any meaningful way, want to kill you, Wren."

"I know," Wren said. "But you may. And I, by the same discipline, may kill you. I am contracted to. We have, in this corridor, a window of approximately eleven minutes before the building's response teams reach the floor. We have, in that window, the only conversation our teacher's discipline obligates us to have. After that conversation is over, one of us walks away."

Sophia, in the dim light of the back corridor, said, "...the woman in Vienna."

Wren paused.

For the first time in the conversation, her face did, very faintly, something.

She said, "...you know about the woman in Vienna."

"Rourke."

"...ah."

"She is, by Rourke's account, the only person you have, in your career, refused to kill."

"That," Wren said, very softly, "is correct."

"Why."

"Because she was reading, in a small café off the Stephansplatz, a paperback novel I had read when I was eighteen, and she was reading it on the same page I had been reading it on, when, in 1996, in a different city, the woman who had given it to me was killed by people who had been, at the time, my uncles. I had not, in the eighteen years between those two readings, ever met another person reading that book on that page. I made, on the spot, a decision. I have, since then, been very disciplined about decisions."

She paused.

She said, "You should know, before we begin, that the discipline does not, in my understanding of it, require that we both leave this corridor alive. The discipline only requires that we *meet.* We have, now, met. The discipline is, in that small sense, satisfied. What follows, over the next several minutes, is our private business. We have, between us, choices. I am, in my way, going to make mine."

She drew, in a single, unhurried, beautifully-trained motion, both of Mariakos's knives.

Sophia drew, a half-second later, her own.

The corridor, dim and narrow and lined with the closed doors of office-suite doors that none of the building's occupants had, in the past eleven minutes, opened, became very quiet.

Wren said, gently, "...begin."

She moved.

* * *

The fight, when later, in clinical conversation, Sophia would attempt to describe it, she would describe in a series of short clean sentences that would, in their cleanness, fail to communicate the actual experience of being inside it.

She would say: *Wren is faster than I am.*

She would say: *Wren is, in particular, faster from the wrist. The hands of a person who has trained on Mariakos's sand-bag drill for two years are, by the unfair physics of muscle memory, faster than the hands of a person who has trained on the same drill for nine. We are, in our discipline, the kind of practitioners who come into our true speed at year four. After year four, the speed plateaus. Wren, however, hit her year four in 2013, when she was twenty-three. I hit my year four in 2007, when I was seventeen, and have, since 2007, been, as practitioners, slightly slower, every year, than I was the year before. She is, in this corridor, by approximately eight percent, the better hand.*

She would say: *Eight percent is, in this corridor, the entire difference between living and dying.*

She would say, also, after a long pause: *Eight percent is, however, not the entire difference between* winning *and dying.*

The fight, in its actual physical unfolding, began with a feint.

Wren's left hand, holding the smaller knife, came up at Sophia's throat in a clean diagonal that was, on first read, the strike.

Wren's right hand, holding the larger knife, was, on first read, in a defensive low position covering her own midline.

It was a feint.

The strike was the right hand. The right hand came in low and fast, under Sophia's elbow, in a kidney-strike that, if it landed, would put Sophia on the floor in twelve seconds and dead in forty.

Sophia, in the half-second she had, did the only thing the half-second permitted.

She did not parry the right hand.

She moved her body away from the right hand, by a quarter-step backward and a quarter-step sideways, and she used the half-second she had bought herself to put her own left-hand knife into the soft tissue of Wren's leading thigh, six inches above the knee.

The knife went in, by the fortunate physics of an off-balance lunge, eight inches deep.

It went into Wren's quadriceps.

It cut, by the dispassionate arithmetic of human anatomy, the rectus femoris muscle.

Wren, in the half-second after the knife went in, did the small thing a person did when their leading leg suddenly stopped being a leading leg.

She did not, however, stop fighting.

She rotated, with her bad leg as the pivot, and brought her right-hand knife around in a continuation of the kidney-strike's motion that put the blade not into Sophia's kidney but into Sophia's left forearm, six inches above the wrist, in a slash that opened the forearm to a depth of approximately three-quarters of an inch and, in the precise way

Mariakos had taught both of them, severed the tendon that controlled the function of Sophia's left ring finger.

Sophia's left hand, by the loss of the tendon, went, for the rest of the fight, partially numb.

She lost her grip on the knife in her left hand.

The knife clattered to the floor.

Wren, in the same motion, brought her left-hand knife back up and stabbed Sophia in the right side, just under the ribs, in a thrust that, by the further fortunate physics of Sophia's quarter-step backward at the start of the engagement, did not penetrate to a depth that would, in the next ten minutes, render Sophia non-functional.

It was, however, deep enough to bleed.

It was, moreover, deep enough to, by the medical realities of perforated abdominal-wall musculature, render Sophia, in the next half-hour, profoundly less effective than she would otherwise be.

Sophia, on her remaining knife, did the calculation.

She had approximately ninety seconds of full operational capacity left in her body, before blood loss began to make her stupid.

Wren, with one immobilized leg, had approximately the same.

She had, for the first time in her career, met an opponent whose mathematical envelope, in the immediate moment, was the same as her own.

The fight, after the first exchange, became, in the way fights at this level became when both opponents had committed to it past the point of either survival being likely, the kind of slow, terrible, exquisitely careful waltz that Mariakos had used to call, in his accented English, *the conversation between two old friends who have, finally, run out of things to say.*

It lasted, on the security feed Lucas would, in eleven minutes, be carefully not watching, a total of three minutes and four seconds.

In those three minutes and four seconds, Sophia took two more cuts: one across the back of her right shoulder, and one along her left jawline, that, in another inch, would have opened her left carotid.

In those three minutes and four seconds, Wren took: a deep cut across the inside of her right wrist that severed the small extensor tendons of her right hand and rendered her primary knife arm, by the same small physics, partially nonfunctional; a stab wound to her abdomen on the same side as Sophia's, but two inches deeper; and, at three minutes and one second, a cracked ribcage on her right side from a strike Sophia made with the steel pommel of her remaining knife.

At three minutes and four seconds, Wren, by the fair calculus of cumulative damage, had, in her body, less remaining capacity than Sophia did.

Wren, kneeling on her bad leg, with her bad arm at her side, facing Sophia at a distance of approximately four feet, with her remaining knife still in her left hand, did the thing the discipline, in its one and only ambiguity, allowed her to do.

She did not lift the knife.

She held the knife, point down, on the floor in front of her, in the small unhurried gesture that was, in Mariakos's lineage, the gesture by which a student acknowledged that the master, in his lifetime, would have called the bout.

Sophia, watching, saw the gesture, and recognized it, and did, in turn, the gesture that the lineage required of her in response.

She lowered her own knife.

Sophia, quietly, said, "...Wren."

Wren, very quietly, said, "Sophia."

"...you broke."

"I broke, Sophia. The discipline says the bout is over. I am, by my contract, obligated to come back, on a day of my choosing, to the conversation we have not yet finished. I will, however, today, withdraw."

"You will not, then, take Lana."

"I will not, today, take Lana."

"...thank you, Wren."

"Sophia. Will you, in turn, allow me, by the discipline, to leave this corridor."

Sophia, after a long moment, with the lower part of her tank top heavy with her own blood and her left hand, by the severed tendon, hanging mostly limp at her side, said, "...go."

Wren, slowly, with the assistance of the wall, rose to standing.

Her bad leg, by the destruction of the rectus femoris, was not, in any meaningful sense, going to support her weight for very long. She was, however, by the inconvenient discipline of an extremely well-trained operative, going to walk, by sheer professional will, the seven meters back to the back stairwell, and she was going to descend, by the same will, the four flights of stairs to the parking garage, and she was, by the rest of the small operational protocols she had, in advance, prepared, going to disappear, quietly, into the streets of St. Petersburg.

She would not, over the next several years, be heard from.

Sophia, watching her go, said one more thing.

She said, in the quiet tone of a younger sister, "Wren."

Wren, in the back doorway of the corridor, paused, with one hand on the doorframe.

She did not turn around.

Sophia said, "...the woman in Vienna."

"...yes."

"Tell her, when you next see her, that I am glad you let her live."

Wren, after a long moment, said, "I will, Sophia. Thank you."

She closed the door behind her.

The corridor, in the dim afternoon Petersburg light coming in from the small frosted window at the far end of the hall, was, again, very quiet.

Sophia, very slowly, sat down against the wall.

She put pressure on the wound at her side.

She said, into her collar mic, in a voice that had, by the various small inconveniences of cumulative blood loss, gone slightly hoarse, "Lucas."

Lucas, in his ear, with the terrible focus of a man who had been forcing himself, for the past three minutes, not to look at his secondary corridor camera, said, "Sophia."

"...I will need a medic."

"Reed has one in the second van. Two minutes out."

"...tell him to bring the second medic."

"...copy."

Sophia closed her eyes for ten seconds.

Then she opened them.

She said, into her mic, "Lana."

Lana, in the boardroom, with Markov's tea cooling on the table beside her, with the wall of monitors behind her, said, "...yes, Sophia."

"Finish."

* * *

The boardroom of Victor Markov, by the time Sophia's voice came over Lana's earpiece at fifteen-oh-six and twenty-three seconds, had become the kind of room that, with care of rooms in distress, knows it is a room in distress.

Three of the seven other Council members had, in the previous five minutes, attempted to use their phones. The phones were, by Lucas's continuing work, on a complete cellular blackout for the entire building. They had then attempted the boardroom's hardline. The hardline, by Lana's continuing work, had been, since fifteen-oh-one, configured to reach exactly one number, which was the publicly listed press desk of the Russian Federation's Anti-Corruption Operative Directorate, and which, on each call, was answered, within two rings, by a woman who said, in a calm voice, "This is the press desk of the Anti-Corruption Operative Directorate. Please state your name and your business." The woman was, a real woman at the real press desk. Lana had not, in any way, falsified the receiving end. The hardline had been routed there, exactly as designed.

The Council members had, on each call, panicked, and hung up.

The Council members had then attempted, by the boardroom's electromechanical exit lock, to leave.

The exit lock, by the precise firmware specification Lana had, two days earlier, found on the lock vendor's public-facing documentation portal, had been, since fifteen-oh-three, in the *meeting in session* state. In the *meeting in session* state, the lock would, by the published spec, only disengage on the manual command of a sitting board member, entered through the boardroom's central control panel, with the required two-factor authentication of a card key and a six-digit PIN.

The card key for the lock, by Markov's protocol, was carried by Markov himself.

The PIN for the lock, by Markov's protocol, was known by Markov himself.

The other seven Council members, in the boardroom, did not, by the protocols Markov had personally designed, have the ability to leave the room without his cooperation.

This had been, until fifteen-oh-three, considered a feature.

It was, beginning at fifteen-oh-three, considered, by the seven Council members not named Markov, increasingly less of a feature.

Markov, in his chair at the head of the table, had not, in the entire seven minutes since the cascade had hit the wall of monitors, moved.

He had finished his tea.

He had set the cup down, gently, on the saucer.

He had, with the calm of a man whose entire civilization was, in the next ten minutes, going to end, kept his hands folded on the table.

He was looking at Lana.

He had been looking at Lana for the entire seven minutes.

Lana, in her contractor coveralls, in her position three feet from his left elbow, with the laptop on the table between them and the wall of monitors continuing, in its quiet relentless way, to broadcast the ongoing dismantlement of his life behind her, said, finally, "Mr. Markov."

He said, "Lana."

"...what would you like to do."

He smiled.

It was, again, a very small, very tired smile.

He said, "You are asking me a question I have been asking myself, in different rooms, for thirty-six years. The answer, today, has changed."

"...how."

"Today, for the first time, I do not know."

The other Council members, around the table, had, by this point, all stopped trying things and had subsided into the terrible quiet of seven extremely powerful adults whose various futures were, in real time, being decided, on the wall behind them, by mechanisms they did not, anymore, control.

Markov, looking at Lana, said, "I had your mother killed, Lana. I want to be clear with you, in this room, that I had her killed."

Lana, calmly, said, "...I know, Mr. Markov."

"I want to be clear, also, that Henrik told you the truth that I regretted it. I do regret it. I have regretted it, in the unhelpful way of men in my position, for twenty-three years. The regret is, I will not pretend otherwise, professional rather than moral. Your mother was, by any measure available to me at the time, the most competent intelligence officer of her generation, and I have, in the years since her death, been unable to recruit, anywhere in the field, an analyst who could replace her. I have been forced, in her absence, to operate on a slightly more limited information envelope than I would, in another life, have preferred. The regret is real. The regret is also, by any moral standard you and I both, in different ways, hold, irrelevant. I had your mother killed, Lana. I had her killed because she was about to expose me. I would, in identical circumstances, have her killed again. I am, by the careful honesty of a man whose protocols have stopped working, telling you this because I would prefer, at the end of my career, to be at least the kind of man who does not lie about the women he had killed."

Lana, in the boardroom, did not, by any visible sign, react.

She said, "...thank you, Mr. Markov."

He inclined his head.

He said, "What would you like, Lana."

She thought about it.

She thought about it, in the way she had been taught, by a woman she could not remember, on a porch in Wilmette, while feeding applesauce to a stuffed bear.

She said, "I would like, Mr. Markov, for you to disengage the door of this boardroom. I would like, after that, for you to walk, with me, alone, to the public elevator on the other side of the vestibule. I would like, after that, for the seven other people in this room to remain in this building, by the unhurried agency of the Russian Anti-Corruption Operative Directorate's tactical detachment, who are, by my agreement with their director ninety minutes ago, in the lobby of this building as of fifteen-oh-eight Moscow time, accepting the formal seven-person referral package that I have, by the federal apparatus of the United States and the ongoing assistance of Agent Reed, transmitted to them at fifteen-oh-six."

She paused.

"I would like, after that," she said, "to walk you out of this building, on Russian soil, in Russian custody, into the protocols of a Russian Federation that has, over the previous nine days, had a number of opportunities to consider whether it would prefer to be, in the small available economy of the international news cycle, the country that protected you, or the country that did not. I would like, Mr.

Markov, in summary, to allow your country to decide what to do with you. I do not, on consideration, particularly want to be the woman who decides."

Markov, in his chair, looked at her for a long, long moment.

Then he said, softly, "...that is exactly what your mother would have done."

Lana, gently, said, "...I know, Mr. Markov."

He stood up.

He smoothed, with the careful gesture of a man whose habits were the only things he had left, his suit jacket.

He walked, alone, with Lana three feet behind him, to the boardroom's central control panel. He produced, from the inside pocket of his suit jacket, the small magnetic card key. He held it to the reader. He entered, on the small panel keypad, the six-digit PIN.

The boardroom door, with the soft pneumatic hiss of a heavy, well-balanced lock, disengaged.

He held it open for her.

He said, in his beautiful unaccented English, with the ironic gesture of a man whose courtesies had, in his lifetime, never not been performances, "After you, Lana."

She walked out of the boardroom of the Council, ahead of the man who had, twenty-three years earlier, killed her mother.

In the wood-paneled vestibule beyond, four men in plain dark suits, with very small earpieces and the professional quiet of operatives who had been, in the previous ten minutes, briefed in great detail, were standing.

The man in front, a small, bald man with the deep-set tired eyes of a Russian career investigator, looked at Markov, and looked at Lana, and inclined his head, very slightly, to Lana.

He said, in heavily accented English, "Madam. We will, from here, take Mr. Markov."

Lana, very softly, said, "Thank you, Director Belov."

He took Mr. Markov by the elbow, with the gentleness of an extremely powerful man making a decision he had been considering for some weeks. The other three operatives, in their plain dark suits, fell in around the four of them. Markov, with the ironic smile still on his face, allowed himself, in the small quiet way the situation now required, to be led.

He looked, at the elevator, back at Lana.

He said, "Will I see you again, Lana."

Lana, in her contractor coveralls, with the ceramic cat in her inner pocket and her mother's letter against her sternum, said, "...no, Mr. Markov."

He nodded, once.

He stepped into the elevator with his escorts.

The doors closed.

Lana, in the wood-paneled vestibule, stood for a long, slow moment in the silence.

Then she walked, very calmly, to the public elevator on the opposite side of the vestibule, and pressed the button for the basement, and rode the elevator down.

* * *

In the parking garage, four minutes later, by the pre-arranged plan, she found, beside their second white Sprinter van, her sister, sitting on a small folding stool that one of Reed's medics had unfolded onto the concrete floor.

Sophia was, by the terrible visible accounting of a person who had been bleeding for eleven minutes, paler than Lana had ever seen her.

A medic in a Reed-affiliated black plain jacket was, with the unhurried efficiency of a very experienced trauma practitioner, packing the wound at Sophia's right side.

Declan, beside her, with a wad of gauze pressed to his own forearm where, in the climb up the back of the elevator shaft, he had, by the unkind physics of a slipping handhold, opened a six-inch gash, was watching Sophia with the terrible quiet of a man whose long career had, until that exact moment, never required him to watch a particular person's wound be packed.

Sophia, on the stool, looked up at Lana.

Lana, walking up to her, did not, at first, say anything.

Sophia, softly, in the dim concrete-echoing space, said, "...Markov."

Lana said, "He's in custody. He walked out with Belov. He is, by Belov's protocol, in a holding facility on the outskirts of the city as of approximately three minutes ago. He will, by the ongoing sequence of bureaucratic steps that began this morning at oh-eight hundred and which are now, by the international news cycle, irreversible, be in front of a Russian magistrate by tomorrow afternoon."

"...you didn't kill him."

"I didn't, Sophia."

"...why not."

Lana, after a long moment, with one hand resting, gently, on her sister's hair in a gesture so unselfconscious that, on later reflection, she would barely remember having made it, said, "Because you, Sophia, in 2002, were the older one, and so I had not, until today, ever been the older one, and the older one is the one who decides what kind of family we are going to be on the other side of all of this. And I have decided, today, that we are going to be the kind of family that, by the accumulated arithmetic of the women we are descended from, lets the world deal with them. We have done our part, Sophia. We have set the stage. We have, in a single morning, set the stage to a degree that is, frankly, going to keep the international press busy for approximately the next nine months. The world is, as of now, fully informed. It is, as of now, the world's job. We have, in our way, finished Mom's case."

Sophia, on the stool, with the medic finishing the packing of her wound, did not, at first, say anything.

Then she said, very softly, "...I love you, Lana."

"I love you, Sophia."

"...you did run rings around all of us."

Lana, in the quiet smile of a younger sister whose mother had, on a porch in Wilmette twenty-three years earlier, predicted exactly this, said, "Mom said I would, Sophia."

Sophia, after a long moment, said, "Mom did say that."

The medic finished his work.

Declan, with the quiet care of an old friend, helped Sophia to her feet.

The team, in the small concrete echo of the parking garage, walked, slowly, to the second van.

Lucas, who had, by Lana's careful arrangement with Belov, been, in the previous twenty minutes, allowed by Russian state authorities to drive the second van directly into the building's parking garage with no questions asked, was at the wheel, with the engine running.

He said, as Lana climbed into the back, "...we're going home."

"We're going home, Lucas."

"...where, technically, is home."

Sophia, with the medic helping her into the back of the van, with her left hand, by the severed tendon, useless at her side, with her tank top dark with her own blood, with the smile of a woman who had, by the unfair small arithmetic of the previous nine days, finally outlived a piece of work she had been carrying since she was twelve, said, "...London."

Declan, climbing in after her, said, "London?"

"Margit," Sophia said, "has, in London, a townhouse. It is registered to a shell. The shell is registered to a shell. The shell is registered to a small charitable trust that has, since 2003, been, on paper, paying its rates. The townhouse has four bedrooms, a back garden, a working fireplace, and, by Margit's last email, a very large, very judgmental grey shorthair cat who Margit's contact in Chicago, three days ago, retrieved from a one-bedroom apartment over a Thai restaurant, and who is, by Margit's report, currently presiding over the second-floor library."

The van, in the quiet of the parking garage, paused.

Lana, softly, said, "...Pixel."

Sophia, with the ironic look that was, by the previous nine days, the one expression Lana was beginning to consistently recognize, said, "Pixel."

Lucas, at the wheel, said, "...how long has *that* plan been in motion."

"Since approximately," Sophia said, "the night of the chandelier."

Lana, in the back of the van, with her sister's good hand in hers, with her father, somewhere on a different continent, alive, with her mother's letter against her sternum, with a small ceramic cat in her pocket, with the unfamiliar warm shape of a future, in her chest, finally, finally, beginning to take its actual form, smiled.

She said, "Drive, Lucas."

He drove.

The van pulled, slowly, out of the parking garage of 17 Petrograd Embankment, into the late spring afternoon of the city of St. Petersburg, and onto the long road back into the rest of the team's lives.

Epilogue: Shadows in the Light

Six weeks later, in a small whitewashed room on the second floor of a working farmhouse in a part of the world that did not, on any of the world's maps, currently contain anyone of professional interest to any sitting government, a woman with a long pink scar in the inside of her right wrist, a slight permanent limp in her right leg, and the quiet face of a woman who had, for the previous six weeks, been doing nothing but reading, sat in a wicker chair by an open window with a small unfamiliar paperback in her hands and a cup of tea on the sill beside her.

The paperback, on its cover, in elegant English lettering, said *The Goldfinch.*

The woman had finished *The Secret History* the previous week.

The woman, who had not, over the past six weeks, given anyone, including the elderly couple who owned the farmhouse, a name, was teaching herself, in the way of women in her line of work who had decided, at thirty-five, to take a sabbatical, the rest of Donna Tartt's bibliography. She would, as her decisions, be ready to be a working operative again in approximately ten months.

The window, beyond her, looked out over a green valley in which nothing of any concern was, at this moment, happening.

A grey shorthair cat, apparently the property of the elderly farming couple, jumped up onto the windowsill, considered her, and decided, after a moment, to lie down in the sun beside her tea.

She turned a page.

She read.

* * *

The London townhouse was on a quiet white-stuccoed crescent in a part of South Kensington that had, in 1881, been laid out by a Victorian architect with a strong personal preference for symmetry, and which had, in the hundred and forty-four years since, been, by the careful work of every successive owner, gently maintained.

The townhouse had four floors, a small back garden with a single ancient cherry tree, a working fireplace in the sitting room, a small library on the second floor whose previous owner had left, by the private agreement of the sale, all of his books, and a kitchen that, by the renovations Margit had quietly authorized eight years earlier, contained, at this moment, a Lavazza espresso machine that Lana, in the previous three weeks, had begun to take, in her small new way, deeply seriously.

In the sitting room, on a Tuesday afternoon in late June, Declan was at the small writing desk by the window, with the Times crossword and a cup of black coffee, with a fresh white cast on his right forearm under his rolled-up shirt sleeve, working on a clue that involved the word *quaternion.*

In the library, on the second floor, Lucas was at a bank of three new monitors, with a small brass plaque on the shelf above them that read PROPERTY OF THE LAMP WARRIOR, with the lamp base it referred to displayed in a place of honor between a lava lamp Margit had, on hearing about it, sent him as a housewarming gift, and a small framed certificate from the United States Department of Justice acknowledging his cooperation in *the largest single financial intelligence operation in the history of the federal apparatus.* The certificate, by Lucas's own preference, was hung slightly crooked, because, in his words, *the wonky angle is more in keeping with the spirit of the actual operation.*

In the small office at the back of the second floor, with the window open onto the garden, Max King, in a worn cardigan and reading glasses, was drafting the eleventh article of what would, in the coming year, become the Pulitzer-winning investigative series that would, by the unfair calculus of the modern news cycle, finally make Helena Harper's case famous on the only stage that had, in 2002, been unable to receive it.

In the kitchen, on a small espresso saucer beside a copy of the morning's *Financial Times* with the headline VANEK ESTATE FROZEN PENDING SECONDARY PROBE, Pixel was sitting in his most regal possible posture, with his tail wrapped around his paws, glaring, with great patience, at the espresso machine, which he had, in the previous three weeks, decided was the central rival for his household's attention, and which he was determined, in his small ongoing way, to outlast.

He had, by the photograph Lana had taken the previous evening, gained an additional half a kilo since his arrival in Britain.

Lana, on the small balcony outside the kitchen, with her own espresso, in the unhurried late-morning sun, was reading, on her phone, a text from her father.

The text contained a photograph.

The photograph, taken in the front yard of a small lime-green-painted cottage on a quiet street in the Notting Hill area of London approximately one and a half miles from where Lana was, at this moment, sitting, showed a man in his sixties in a flannel shirt, holding, with apparent helpless affection, a small white terrier puppy, in front of a hand-lettered sign tied to the cottage's wrought-iron front gate that read, in Lana's father's handwriting, in the Sharpie of a man who had decided, at sixty-eight, to start a very small new chapter:

THE NEW HARPER PLACE.

The sign was, with great pride, half-covered by a Union Jack tea towel.

The text under the photograph read:

Kiddo. The puppy's name is Helena. Don't yell. I asked your sister first. She approved the name. The pup likes the cherry pie at the corner shop. So do I. Come over for tea this evening at six. Tell your sister to bring her cat. The puppy wants to make friends. Love, Dad.

Lana, on the balcony, in the long quiet sun of a late June morning in London, with the ceramic cat from Margit on the table beside her espresso, with the lopsided smile that the previous six weeks had been, very gradually, teaching her how to make, did not, for several minutes, type a reply.

She put a hand, briefly, against the inside breast pocket of her cardigan.

The pocket contained, as it had contained every day since the night of the apartment in Petrogradsky district, a small flat envelope of yellowed paper.

The envelope, on its front, in her mother's hurried, careful, twenty-three-year-old hand, said, *Lana, when she is twenty-five.*

The seal of the envelope had, six weeks ago, been broken by Lana's own thumb, in a back bedroom in St. Petersburg, with her sister's shoulder warm and steady against her own.

The contents of the envelope had, six weeks ago, been read.

The contents of the envelope had not, since, been read again.

The contents of the envelope were, with care that letters from mothers to daughters could be, in the rest of Lana's life, going to live in a private place inside her where her mother, in the various small ways the previous six weeks had been teaching her, had begun, finally, to live.

She did not, on this Tuesday, take the letter out.

She did not need to. She knew, by heart, what it said.

She put her hand back on her espresso.

She typed, with her thumb, *We will be over at six. Tell Helena that Pixel is, frankly, a difficult cat, and she should not, on first meeting, take it personally.*

She put the phone down.

She picked up the espresso.

Sophia, behind her, in the kitchen doorway, in a soft grey cashmere sweater whose left sleeve was, by the quiet honesty of her wardrobe in the previous weeks, rolled up over the long pink line of the scar on her left forearm, said, "Tea at Dad's at six?"

"Tea at Dad's at six."

"...the puppy is named Helena."

"The puppy is named Helena."

"Pixel is going to lose his mind."

"Pixel is going to lose his mind. Yes."

Sophia, behind her, in the kitchen, made the small dry sound that, in Sophia, was as close as Sophia got, in any room, to laughter.

In the library upstairs, Lucas's voice, on the small intercom Margit had insisted on installing because, in her words, *families need intercoms,* came down to the kitchen.

"Ladies. Reuters is reporting that a sealed Russian magistrate's order, this morning, formally indicted a Mr. Victor Markov on twenty-three counts of organized criminal activity, fourteen counts of state corruption, and one count of, quote, *complicity in the wrongful death of a foreign intelligence officer in 2002, identified by the U.S. Department of Justice as Helena Sara Harper.* The indictment is, quote, *the longest formally filed under the Anti-Corruption Code of the Russian Federation since the act's 2010 amendment.* The trial, by the article, is expected to last several years."

Sophia, in the kitchen, picked up her own espresso.

She walked, in her cashmere sweater, with her left sleeve rolled up and her left ring finger sitting, by the permanent inconvenience of a severed tendon, slightly higher than the others, out onto the balcony beside Lana.

She set her cup down on the wrought-iron table.

She looked, for a long, long moment, at her sister.

Then she said, very softly, "Helena Sara."

Lana, with her hand back on her cardigan pocket where her mother's letter rested, very quietly, said, "Helena Sara."

The two of them, in the clean morning light of a small white-stuccoed house in a quiet Kensington crescent, raised their espresso cups, in a single, unrehearsed, twenty-three-years-late toast, to a woman in a pale-blue cardigan, in a kitchen in Wilmette, on a Sunday morning in 2002, who had, in her short life, by the patient unfairness of competent women, set, in motion, exactly the people who had, in the end, finally, finished her work.

They drank.

In the library upstairs, Lucas put on, by his own small private call, an old Cat Stevens record.

In the back garden, the cherry tree moved, gently, in the small late-June breeze.

In the kitchen, by the espresso machine, Pixel, the deposed monarch of an apartment over a Thai restaurant in a city he was no longer in, prepared, in his small ongoing way, to outlive everyone in the household, including, in fairness, the espresso machine.

Somewhere, in a quiet whitewashed farmhouse in a part of the world that nobody had, that morning, been looking for, a woman with a long pink scar on the inside of her right wrist turned another page of *The Goldfinch,* and the small grey shorthair cat on the windowsill, beside her, did not, by any visible sign, mind.

Somewhere, in a building in Moscow that the small new ongoing weight of an international news cycle was, slowly, going to unmake, a man in a charcoal three-piece suit, who had been, until six weeks earlier, the most patient predator of his generation, sat in a small unfurnished holding cell with no porcelain cup, and waited, with the composed dignity that was the only thing he had left, for his next interrogation.

Somewhere, in a kitchen in Wilmette, Illinois, that no longer existed, a woman in a pale-blue cardigan, in a memory that had finally, after twenty-three years, been allowed back into the daylight, was, on a Sunday morning, scrambling eggs.

The two girls at her elbows were, in that memory, six and twelve.

They were, in the memory, laughing.

The memory was, in the patient way of Helena's daughters, finally home.

ABOUT THE AUTHOR

Ken Konet (M.Ed., MBA) writes across psychological thrillers, literary fiction, dark fantasy, self-help, philosophy, memoir, and the occasional middle-grade adventure. His catalog is held together less by genre than by a single recurring obsession: the quiet, stubborn dignity of people who have decided, often against their better judgment, to keep going anyway.

By day, Ken is a corporate instructional designer who has spent over two decades teaching adults that *learning* is not the same as *being talked at slowly,* a distinction he wishes more graduate programs would internalize.

He lives in Florida with his wife, Isabella, who is patient with him in approximately the way a small lighthouse is patient with the weather. He spends his off-hours on motorcycles, on hiking trails, around campfires, and (under Isabella's expert tutoring) at the controls of a video game character who is, by Isabella's report, "trying his best."

He is a frequent collaborator with author Ibrahim Roble and a few other new authors.

Accidental Assassin is the first book in **The Harper Sisters** series.

Find him at humbolton.com, or wherever capable women like his wife are quietly running the world.

www.ingramcontent.com/pod-product-compliance
Lightning Source LLC
LaVergne TN
LVHW020659110826
845149LV00012B/2058

* 9 7 8 1 9 6 6 7 0 3 3 4 1 *